KU-246-379

The Sunken Land Begins to Rise Again

Also by M. John Harrison:

The Committed Men
The Centauri Device
The Ice Monkey
Viriconium
Climbers
The Luck in the Head (with Ian Miller)
The Course of the Heart
Signs of Life
Travel Arrangements
Light
Nova Swing
Empty Space

The Sunken Land Begins to Rise Again

M. John Harrison

GOLLANCZ

LONDON

First published in Great Britain in 2020 by Gollancz
an imprint of The Orion Publishing Group Ltd
Carmelite House, 50 Victoria Embankment
London EC4Y 0DZ

An Hachette UK Company

3 5 7 9 10 8 6 4 2

Copyright © M. John Harrison 2020

The moral right of M. John Harrison to be identified as
the author of this work has been asserted in accordance
with the Copyright, Designs and Patents Act of 1988.

All rights reserved. No part of this publication may be
reproduced, stored in a retrieval system, or transmitted
in any form or by any means, electronic, mechanical,
photocopying, recording, or otherwise, without the
prior permission of both the copyright owner and the
above publisher of this book.

All the characters in this book are fictitious, and any resemblance
to actual persons, living or dead, is purely coincidental.

A CIP catalogue record for this book is
available from the British Library.

ISBN (Hardback) 978 0 575 09635 6
ISBN (Trade Paperback) 978 1 473 23215 0
ISBN (eBook) 978 0 575 09637 0

Typeset by Deltatype Ltd, Birkenhead, Merseyside

Printed in Great Britain by Clays Ltd, Elcograf S.p.A

www.gollancz.co.uk

For Deborah Chadbourn

Gradually the sunken land begins to rise again,
and falls perhaps again, and rises again after that.

Charles Kingsley, *Thoughts in a Gravel Pit*

... some things are drawn to water and behave
differently when they are near it.

Olivia Laing, *To the River*

Behold, I shew you a mystery; we shall not all sleep,
but we shall all be changed.

1 Corinthians 15:51

One

I

Spending All Day with the Dead

During his fifties Shaw went through a rough patch. That was how he put it to himself. His adult life had been, until then, perfectly normal. He had been determined on normality. Perhaps that had been the problem. Anyway, his life lost shape and five years were expended on nothing very much. They slid into themselves like the parts of a trick box and wouldn't open again. He would wake up to himself with utter clarity in – say – a crowded first-floor noodle bar at night, talking to people he didn't know while he looked down into a street full of brand-new motorcycles. Then everything would slip away again, to be lived at one remove for a week or two.

A woman he met – one of several who instinctively discarded him during that period – came closest to defining what had happened to him. Her name was Victoria, and on greeting someone new her habit was to announce that she worked in a morgue. 'Oh, I don't mind,' she would say vaguely, however you responded to that, 'but then I'm someone who saw her first corpse when she was fourteen.'

It was an effective line, especially in a Hackney pub on a wet Monday evening. A doctor's daughter already in her forties, Victoria had bleak red hair, an eroded look and the studiedly flat humour of the high-functioning romantic. She was one of those people only partly aware of their own nervousness; half detecting that agitation, she would project it onto you, and say, 'You haven't really got time for me now, have you? I can tell from your voice.' Shaw found it confusing at first. Some discipline was required, or you would be caught up and, becoming nervous in turn, start fulfilling the prophecy by looking at your watch. The night they were introduced she was drinking heavily, obsessed with something her father had once told her about a subspecies of people born looking like fish.

'Truly,' she said. 'Fish.' She opened her eyes quite wide. 'Don't you think that's amazing?'

Shaw didn't know what to make of her.

'I've never heard anything like it,' he answered truthfully. He was more interested in the morgue. 'How weird is that,' he suggested. 'Spending all day with the dead.' To this she replied, with an inexplicable bitterness and as if referring to some pivotal event in her own life:

'Well, at least they never answer you back.'

Victoria, whose surname was either Norman or Nyman, at that point Shaw wasn't sure which, wanted to be talked into something, but that left him only the fish people to work with. Her father had described them as living in South America or somewhere similar. Most of them were born male, though it was women who carried the gene. They could live normally, do everything a human being could do. Isolated in deep estuarine valleys west of the Andes – perhaps stronger, certainly more intelligent than the ordinary tribes which had cast them out – they formed communities of their own, which, though small, survived and even thrived.

'If that's so,' Shaw said, 'why aren't there more of them? Why haven't I ever seen one?'

Victoria laughed the way laughter is reproduced on the

internet: hahahaha. 'Because this isn't South America,' she reminded him. 'It's Columbia Road. Anyway, it was just a joke of his on a little girl.' She tapped her empty glass encouragingly, and when he got back from the bar added, 'Perhaps you *have* seen one. Perhaps we're all fish-people. Of one sort or another.'

They met a couple more times, went to bed, argued back and forth in the way people do when they're just slightly more than attracted to one another; but when, one night at the Spurstowe Arms, Shaw tried to put things on a more permanent basis, she shivered. 'You seem like a decent man,' she said, holding his hand briefly across a table littered with empty glasses and the remains of potato ravioli with wild mushrooms, 'but you've forgotten what everything's about.' He wondered if he had. If he had, how would he know? What would be the epistemology of that? The rain was coming down outside the pub. People were running in and out with coats over their heads, laughing. Shaw had lost his nerve, Victoria went on to say, and she didn't think she could handle someone else's anxieties in addition to her own. 'To be honest, I've never met anyone in such a panic.' At the time this assessment seemed less hurtful than meaningless. Later he would have more than one chance to appreciate the clarity of it. Meanwhile life drew itself closed as suddenly as cheap curtains and they saw less of each other.

Shaw's problem wasn't a breakdown. It was too late to be a midlife crisis. It wasn't any of the predictable things. Perhaps, he thought, these periods of retraction happen in a life; perhaps you can't be on all the time. The moment he felt free of it, he redirected himself like a parcel, as far from Hackney as seemed humanly possible; fetching up south and west of Hammersmith Bridge in a quiet suburban badlands between East Sheen and the Thames, bounded by Little Chelsea on one side and Sheen Lane on the other. There he rented a room in a Georgian house that smelled of dogs and fried food.

2

Washed Up

There was no wharf on Wharf Terrace and no evidence there had ever been one. Authentic Georgian frontage remained for about half the length of the street, but the houses behind it had been subdivided long ago into warrens of small low-ceilinged rooms. Shaw's room at number 17, which he took furnished, was at the very top of the house. Almost filled by a single bed and a stunted-looking wardrobe, it smelled like a charity shop. He thought that in better days it had been a passage or landing of some sort, which had served the more spacious room next door. From the window he could see between buildings to the Thames, where squalls of rain hung across the tideway in the mornings. There was a garden at the rear, full of dusty buddleia.

Number 17 stood too far back to catch the river's fogs; nevertheless it always seemed damp. Everyone there seemed to be someone else's subtenant. Most of them were as suspended in their lives as Shaw himself. They came and went on a weekly basis. A smaller, more permanent core had the beginnings of careers over in Hammersmith or Fulham: though they would stay longer, places like this would be, in the end, less of a way of life for them. When the time was right they would move not on but up, to nicer rentals, to homes of their own, to the provinces. Meanwhile they had taken on some of the smell of the house itself. Above that they wore a layer of soap, anti-perspirant and something Shaw couldn't identify at all except as the smell of success. The men wore irreproachable Paul Smith suits and Ted Baker shirts from Covent Garden; the women were in middle management at Marks & Spencer – it was pretty full-on, you'd hear them say, but worth it for the security. Six in the morning, they left for their daily 7k in Richmond Park, each one gait-perfect, Pilates-balanced, thin as a ceramic knife in their BAM base layer and compression tights; at the weekends it was swim and spin.

The women, particularly, presented Shaw to himself as a paradox: on one hand he didn't seem to exist for them; on the other, his retro bowling shirts, teenage jeans and used-looking skate shoes were clearly an irritant. When he crossed them on the landings in the evening, talking in their twos and threes, his ready smile went unacknowledged and conversation wasn't resumed until he had moved off. He didn't expect more.

From the start he was aware of something odd going on in the room next to his. The first afternoon it was open-throat singing, which he associated vaguely with Radio 4; a thud that shook his floorboards; and a voice saying, distinctly, 'Damned!', followed by silence as loud as a sound. Then open-throat again, or perhaps sobs. Shaw smiled and carried on unpacking. By now he was used to partition walls and the noises you heard through them.

Unpacking didn't take long. He was used to that, too. He'd salvaged a few bruised cardboard boxes, contents undecided, from whatever discredited life he'd lived before his crisis; otherwise only clothes, which, folded loosely, still failed to fill an eighty-litre tarpaulin bag. Among the IT-sloganised T-shirts and washed-out Muji underwear were interleaved layers of paperwork – tax forms, receipts, severance notices from this or that HR department. He also found a travel clock, a second-generation smartphone the battery of which wouldn't hold a charge, and two or three unread 'modern classic' novels including *Pincher Martin*.

As soon as he had retrieved and rehabilitated what he could, Shaw went next door to introduce himself. No response: though when he knocked he thought he saw the door shiver briefly in its frame, as though the occupant had pulled at it from inside then suffered a change of mind. The landing was cold. A little river-light filtered in through its small barred window. Commuter traffic could be heard building up on Mortlake Road. Shaw put his ear to the door. 'Hello?' he called. Just above the skirting board, he saw, the plaster was bruised and dented as if, on some bored afternoon long ago, someone had kicked their way methodically around the landing walls. Feeling exhausted by the emotional investment this project must have required, he retreated to his own room, where he imagined next door a figure in shirt and underpants sitting hunched on the edge of a bed in the gloom. Someone like himself, trying to decide whether to open a door.

For a week or two, that was how things went.

He knocked again. He Blu-Tacked a piece of paper to the door – *Hi, I recently moved in next to you* – and took to waiting just inside his own room until he heard movement on the landing, at which he would pull open his door. On springing this ambush, all he ever caught was a glimpse of a retreating back. Meanwhile there was coming and going on the stairs, especially at night. Voices were raised. Two in the morning, someone dropped a heavy object on the landing, while downstairs someone else leaned on the bell-push or shouted indistinctly from the street. Next door's sash window, its frame warped by years of river fog, slid up with a long grunting sound. Next day Shaw might glimpse a figure making its way quickly across the landing to the communal bathroom, which it occupied for longer than a normal person; afterwards there was a smell in there. All of this seemed curiously old-fashioned. It seemed like behaviour from the fifties and sixties of the previous century, when the occupants of bedsitters across London, from Acton to Tufnell Park, were forced by a rigid if deteriorating public morality to pursue, in a kind of furtive dream, lives which would now seem perfectly normal.

South-west London was convenient for Shaw. His mother already lived there, in dementia care the other side of Twickenham on the A316.

The first time he visited after his move, he found her standing in the downstairs common room as if she had just turned away from someone else, a tall angular woman in a heather-coloured wool skirt and cashmere twinset, bent a little at the waist, staring out of the window into the empty garden. She was repeating, 'The days pass so quickly. The days just pass so quickly,' and her shoulders were rigid with something between anxiety and anger. He convinced her to go upstairs with him to her room, where he held her hand until she seemed to relax. Even then she didn't acknowledge him, only stood in the middle of the floor and whispered: 'It's better out there now. I'm going to do some gardening.'

'Come and sit down first,' Shaw tried to persuade her.

'Don't be such a fool,' his mother shouted. 'I don't want to sit down. I'm going to do some gardening, but first I must find my boots.'

'Come and sit down, and I'll see if they can make us some tea.'

She turned her head and shoulders away from him and shrugged. 'When I was younger I wouldn't have been seen dead in clothes like these,' she said distantly.

'I can believe that,' Shaw said.

'They won't make tea. We can't expect them to make tea at this hour.'

'Let's try anyway. Let's see what we can do.'

'Oh where are my boots?' she asked herself, in the voice of a four-year-old. She picked distastefully at the hem of her skirt. 'Where are my good boots?'

Nothing was easier than tea, it turned out.

'You see?' Shaw said. 'Nothing easier.'

'People can be very helpful when it suits them.'

They drank their tea in silence. It was often hard to get her to talk, always hard to know what to talk about. He felt that she expected him to share memories, but when he brought them up she laughed bitterly and looked at the wall. 'That time I had diarrhoea on the way home from school — do you remember? You were so angry about that!' The things he expected to say would not, in the end, emerge. Their absence only filled the room further with rage. Shaw felt he should bring her news, but wasn't clear, in the end, what news might be: how it might be constituted. He heard nothing from the family, for instance; neither, he suspected, did she. Family was a concept fraught with complexity for them both. To repeat the national news didn't seem appropriate. In the end he defaulted to his own; most of the time, he knew, she wasn't listening anyway.

'This new place,' he said, 'I'm enjoying it—'

'My mother was a real Christian,' she said suddenly. 'But never to us. Never to us.' As soon as she had his attention, she put her cup down carefully and turned to the window. 'It will snow soon.'

Shaw put his cup down too. The tea had a metallic taste, as if it was dissolving a spoon.

'It's May,' he reminded her.

'I love the snow. When we were young it fell as big as pennies on the sea.' And then, in a voice not quite her own: 'I fell out of love with my parents quite soon. They humiliated me before I was five years old. I was a small, friendly girl, but nervous. Always nervous. I liked the beach. I liked fishing. I liked being up early and late.' She laughed dismissively. 'Too anxious on my own, too anxious in company. I was happiest with one other person. I was frightened of my father and very frightened of my grandfather. My grandfather gave me an old sea-fishing rod he had finished with, but I preferred to go fishing with my uncle.' A huge smile transformed her face. 'Snow on the sea!'

'It's summer,' he said. 'It won't snow now.'

She stared out of the window, smiling quietly.

Shaw tried again. 'I'm enjoying this new place,' he said, 'but it's not very clean.' He already avoided the bathroom, which was windowless, bigger than the dimensions of the landing seemed to permit, and lit by a forty-watt energy-saving bulb that filled it with an even yellowish-brown gloom. Centrally placed on the eroded chessboard lino stood an old-fashioned cast-iron tub, with chipped enamel, hard-water minerals concreted around the taps and a permanent chemical-looking tidemark. There was a separate shower stall. A fungal smell came up from the drains whenever you ran the hot water. 'The first time I went to the lavatory I thought I saw something in the bowl! I didn't feel as if I could use it until I'd cleaned it out.' He had tried to clean the bath, too, prior to washing some of his underwear in it one Friday night when the house seemed empty. The stain remained, cupric, slimy, recording some mysterious high-water event.

'How old are you?' his mother said. 'Grow up.'

Shaw shrugged.

'Don't muck about,' she warned him. 'Don't wait for your life to start. I was always waiting for my life to start. Everything that happened seemed like a good beginning, but it turned out to be the thing itself.'

'Everyone feels like that about their lives,' Shaw said.

'Do they? That's what they all feel, is it?'

Neither of them spoke for a moment. She watched something in the garden. Shaw watched her. 'Everything that should have happened in my twenties,' she went on, 'was stretched out over a lifetime. I get to seventy-five and I've just about collected enough tokens to begin.' Then she sat down, filled her mouth with tea, bent over the table and – making eye contact with him like a toddler – allowed it to dribble out over the tablecloth. 'What have I got left?' she said. 'Tell me that.' He hated her moments of clarity, but they never lasted long.

By the time he got up to leave, she was looking out of the window again. She let him pull the door half closed before she said in a surprised voice, 'John! John! Don't just go like that!' but as soon as he turned to go back in began repeating, 'The days pass so quickly,' again until he shrugged and let the door swing shut behind him.

'I'm not John, Mum,' he said. 'Try again.'

Policy at the home was that the staff address their charges by forename; but they always called his mother 'Mrs Shaw'.

He found a landline in his room and had it reconnected. A few days later, the phone rang and a voice said, 'Is that Chris?'

'No one called Chris lives here,' Shaw said.

'Not there? Chris?'

'You must have the wrong number.'

The voice recited a number, which Shaw half caught.

'No one called Chris here,' he said. 'Are you the engineer?' There was no answer. 'You've got a wrong number, I think.' As he closed the connection, he heard the voice say, 'I must have a wrong number then.' Immediately he began to worry that, mishearing the name Chris and failing to recognise someone he knew, he had missed his first call. He picked the phone up again and dialled 1471, in case he could identify the number he'd been called from. He went through his things in search of an address book he thought he might have kept, but that turned out to be a ten-year-old diary, the 1 January entry in which read, 'Be more outgoing.'

3

The Fish Talisman

The same day, he called Victoria Nyman.

'Hello, stranger,' she said. 'What happened to you?'

'What happened to *you*?'

'Not much.' She thought for a moment. 'I bought a car. That's exciting, isn't it? I always meant to.'

And then after a pause, 'Are you OK?'

Shaw said he was fine. He had to admit that the place he lived now had its drawbacks – he felt bound to mention the toilet bowl, the noises from the room next door – but the river was close by and he was getting into the psychogeography of that. He was walking a lot, he told her, making his way dérive by dérive up the Brent River from the boatyards at its confluence with the Thames, past Wharncliffe Viaduct and the zoo, towards the A40 at Greenford. It was all hospitals and sports parks, mud and child murder up there. 'But some surprisingly nice pubs, too.' Victoria received this report in silence; then suggested that, to her at least, he seemed a bit low. Was he doing anything tonight? Because she could easily drive over after work – perhaps bring a house-warming present? Shaw said no, it was too far out of her way, she shouldn't bother, he was fine really.

'Really, I'm fine.'

'Exactly what way of mine,' Victoria asked, 'would that be out of?' She added: 'Trust me, you sound like shit.'

'Thanks.'

'Don't thank me until you've seen the present.'

'At first I thought you said "house-warning",' Shaw said.

'Expect me at seven, or if the traffic's bad, midnight.'

Suddenly anxious, he suggested, 'Let's not meet here. Let's meet somewhere else.' So they met at a pub on King Street, Hammersmith, then ate tandoori trout at one of the mid-market Indians just up from the Premier Inn. Victoria seemed nervous.

'How do you like my hair?' she said.

Thinned out in some way, centre-parted, chopped off with a kind of calculated incompetence a little above the jawline, it clung lankly to the sides of her face and head, curling out tiredly at the ends. 'Neo-bluestocking,' she said. 'Very effective from certain angles, though I can see you don't think so.'

Over the evening she drank a bottle of house red – 'Nothing to see here. No change here' – and talked about her car. Shaw said he would stick to beer. When he said he wasn't much of a driver, she looked down at the charred tails and dyed red flesh of the remains of their meal, the filmy bones like the fossil imprint of a leaf, and said, 'Who is? It's not really about driving. I go to the coast a lot now.' She laughed and made confused steering-wheel motions. 'Up and down. Hastings and Roedean. Very slowly. Dungeness, of course.' Then: 'I think I've grown out of London.' And finally: 'I love the little spines of these fishes, don't you?'

'All I see,' said Shaw, who felt better, 'is my dinner.'

He then admitted: 'I was in a bit of a state when we last met.'

'You aren't all that much improved.' She laughed at his expression. 'Come on! I should talk! I don't believe I've been entirely sane since I was thirteen ...'

Shaw filled her glass again.

'Is that when you saw the corpse?' he said, hopefully.

'. . . although I did have a moment of clarity in a sauna in about 2005.' She stared around the restaurant as if expecting to see someone she knew. 'Eventually you take what you can get where clarity's concerned. You have to feel you're steadying down.'

'There's some value to that,' Shaw agreed, though he had no idea what she was talking about. She didn't seem to hear him anyway.

'Actually, I'm not even sure it should be called clarity,' she said, adding: 'To speak of which, how is your mother?' And then, without giving Shaw time to answer, 'I know, I know, you don't want to deal with it. Who would? Mine went completely off the rails the day my father died. To be honest, I didn't see her much after that. I was down here, she was still up in the Midlands somewhere. I felt as if I had my own life.'

He had thought about this precise thing, Shaw said, and he believed that while some families cling together, others have a more ballistic tradition. The latter soon can't stand the sight of each other or forgive anything. Unable to manage conflict, the individual members fly apart, start new lives. But even those lives don't hold.

'They lose the ability,' he said, 'to contribute to any myth but their own.'

Victoria stared at him as if he had become briefly unknown and interesting to her. Then she said, 'They're both dead now.'

She was too drunk to drive. They left the car where she had parked it in Hammersmith and walked back to 17 Wharf Terrace along the river. There, she poked around his room as if she was out for a bargain in used furniture. 'The bed's a bit small,' she said, looking at him brightly. Picking through his books, she found a John Fowles; made a face. 'You can't like any of his stuff. Not really.' Then: 'And is this the famous shared wall!' She tapped with one knuckle, as if sounding the ancient plaster for its weaknesses. She put her ear to it. 'He seems quite quiet now, your unknown neighbour.'

Shaw found something else they could drink – the end of a litre of Absolut so old the shoulders of the bottle were sticky with all the condensed, gritty airs of London – and, sitting on the edge of the bed, unwrapped the house-warming present. 'Look at that!' she said, as if their roles were reversed and he had given it to her. It was made of silver, with an articulated body five or six inches long and hinged side fins. 'It's Peruvian,' she said. 'It's a fish. It's quite old, 1860.'

Shaw weighed the fish in his hand, moved one of the fins cautiously. Its scales were tarnished and cold. 'Hi, fish,' he said.

'See,' Victoria said. 'You like it. You like it already.'

'I do like it,' he said.

'Come here and thank me properly then.'

Later, returning from one of her frequent trips across the landing, she paused, hands braced against the doorway, leaning in – lit as harshly as a woodcut, rib and collarbone picked out like hardening ripples on damp sand – to study with amused disgust the bed, the beaten old chair and scattered clothes, the uncurtained window.

'What?' Shaw said.

'Oh, I don't know.'

'No, go on,' he said: 'What.'

'Nothing happening next door. No show. I'm disappointed. I think you've lured me here for purposes of your own, you lonely man.' Then: 'Jesus, that bathroom. Why do we all live like this?'

'Who's we? Last I knew, you had a nice mortgage in Dalston.'

'You know what I mean.'

Shaw agreed that he did. 'Come back to bed,' he suggested.

Instead she went over to the window and gazed out across Wharf Terrace, where a light night rain was wafting up the street and the thin but definite smell of the InBev brewery hung about the upper storeys of the buildings on the other side. 'Aren't you ever dissatisfied? Don't you want something more?' She raised the sash, propped it open with the John Fowles and extended her hand into the rain, palm up. 'I thought of moving,' she said. 'Out of Dalston, out of London entirely. I don't suppose I will. I don't know.' An ambulance hee-hawed into the distance on the Chiswick shore, moving away obliquely for what seemed a long time. She listened until it had gone then got back into bed and, before he could defend himself, rubbed her cold wet hand across his stomach.

'You wriggle like a girl,' she observed. 'How cute.'

Sex only seemed to make her more restless. She woke intermittently, called out in her sleep and was gone before morning to collect the car. Shaw searched his room as if he might still find her there. She had left a note, weighted down by the Peruvian fish. 'It was so nice to talk to you again! I'll email you when I know what I'm doing! Your friend Victoria!' The fish goggled at him from eyes of turquoise glass inset above its archaic, fat-lipped mouth. *We were here before you arrived*, it seemed to be warning him silently: *We'll be here after you've gone.* At some point while he slept, Victoria had read a few pages of *Pincher Martin* and abandoned it face down on the floor. 'You don't seem settled yet,' a postscript said, 'but I'm sure you will be. I'm sure you will be. I mean I hope you will, really. I hope you will.'

★

19

In fact he was reasonably content. It was a relief not to have a life. He read. He visited his mother in the care home. He looked for a new IT gig, and when he couldn't find one, he wandered the banks of the Thames, sometimes downstream to Putney, where he ate ice cream in Bishops Park, but mostly upriver via Chiswick to the Brent confluence and beyond. At 10 a.m. the Thames pubs – old-fashioned, ramshackle and ramified, driven to complex use of space by virtue of being crammed between road and river – had a strange, welcoming calm. There was no one in them. Water light illuminated their greyish floorboards and shabby tables. Shaw drank half a pint in the Bull's Head, Strand-on-the-Green; later ate tomato sandwiches at the Fox near Hanwell Bridge. In the evening, as the bars filled up inexorably with commuters, he fought his way back from snug to snug along one side of the river or the other, often via the graveyards distributed between the houses: Mortlake Old Cemetery, Fulham New; the tiny, secretive St Mary Magdalen, blessed with Isabel Burton's tragicomic tented memorial to the great orientalist; Barnes Old Cemetery, abandoned in 1966 among thick woods, a prime cruising destination not far from the site of the scabrous Elm Guest House on Rocks Lane. In this way, almost home one night, he came across a man kneeling in the ground ivy at the base of a wall in a forgotten half-acre of headstones off South Worple Way.

Shaw stopped and watched.

'Are you OK,' he said.

The man said he was fine. At first sight he seemed to be searching for something in the casual graveyard litter; but this layer – predominantly discarded condoms and wrappers – was soon scraped away to reveal a fibrous black mousse, and in that a shallow impression the shape of a footprint, with an elusive glint of water where you would expect the front sole to be. This he proceeded to deepen, pushing his knuckles forcefully into it, deftly pulling up roots and throwing them aside until he had a hole containing perhaps two inches of muddy water. Into this – employing a quick, furtive gesture that seemed to confirm the nature of all his other efforts – he dipped a small ribbed-glass Victorian medicine bottle. 'This'll interest you,' he promised. 'It's a bit like netting for pond life when you're a kid.' He sealed the phial with his thumb, shook it briefly and held it up to the distant street light.

'See? See?'

Shaw said he didn't see anything at all.

'Nothing? Oh dear. You're sure? Oh well. Let's go and get a drink.'

He looked down at his fingers, black with graveyard tilth. 'My name's Tim,' he said. 'I won't shake hands. Although there's a natural antidepressant in soil.'

And when Shaw only stared at him: '*Mycobacterium vaccae?*'

'Ah,' Shaw said.

'It's absorbed through the skin.'

Five minutes later they sat in the warmth and loud music of a pub called the Earl of March, surrounded by very much younger people. Tim was tall, fiftyish, a little curved in the upper spine, as if he spent his work day standing hunched over something. He wore Clarks desert boots, jeans and a white shirt, in a way which would have been elegant when he was young. You could see that he had been slim then, but now he had run to fat around his shoulders and high on his stomach just under the ribs. You would say that he had run to fat over an essential boyishness; and that this reflected the unmended divisions in his personality. Tim would be generous with himself, Shaw thought, if you could get him to focus on what you needed; the rest of the time he would look both hapless and driven. He already seemed to feel he had let Shaw down.

'Sometimes they're easier to see,' he apologised.

'What actually were you looking for?'

'You know about this blog everyone's reading? *The Water House*? Some people are saying it's spot on about everything.'

Shaw, who had no idea what he was talking about, cast around for something to say, then admitted:

'I'm not on the internet much. It's too like work.'

They bought each other a couple of drinks then said good-bye.

There was a lot of noise at 17 Wharf Terrace later that night, a lot of coming and going on the stairs and in the room next door. Drifting from one unconsoling dream of Victoria to the next, Shaw heard a voice call, 'Can't you bloody shut it? Can't you just bloody shut up for once?' only to realise in confusion that it was his own. He banged on the wall, then went back to sleep. Next morning, he met Tim again, this time wandering vaguely across Church Road, Barnes, with some dry-cleaning. There was a swelling of the soft tissue surrounding his left eye that Shaw hadn't noticed the night before. 'No one knows how to carry dry-cleaning,' Tim said. 'It's one of the basic puzzles of being human.' He had his folded over both forearms and clutched to his chest, as if it was a lot more substantial than a cotton jacket and a pair of chinos; a lot heavier.

'I wondered if you wanted a job?' he said.

He kept an office on a houseboat a hundred yards down-stream of the Brent confluence. Originally it had been a Thames lighter, rusty, broad, thuggish in the bow. Every kind of mooring line attached it to the shore – ropes, cables and chains hanging in weighty curves, the slack wire railings of the gangplank – as if Tim was afraid it might drift away from him, or with him. But the tide never seemed to lift it much, and it sat down on the sloping mud in a way that made you think it wouldn't move again. A rectangular wooden site shed took up most of the deck.

'What do you think?' he asked, the first time they went there.

Shaw looked the lighter up and down. He knew nothing about boats. 'Impressive,' he said. He had liked it immediately he saw it, though he couldn't have said why.

Inside, the site shed was painted off-white, with a couple of desks pushed together under a map of the world in which the oceans and the land had been coloured so that they reversed out, the continents looking like seas, the seas looking like continents. Two large windows, equipped with slatted metal blinds, gave views of river and towpath. 'It's not much of a job,' Tim said. It would just be some filing, and answering the phone. 'I won't be here all the time. You'd be in charge of yourself.' Shaw said that suited him. He could work on his own. He'd worked on his own before. 'There might be some travel,' Tim warned him. It would be a kind of sales work. Shaw said that suited him too, though he had to be clear he had no experience in that line. They agreed a wage, and also that the job wouldn't go on anyone's books. They agreed that he would begin work on the following Monday. A pause followed, during which Shaw tried to locate the toilet; there was another door, but it was padlocked.

'I keep the key for that,' Tim said. 'It doesn't go anywhere.'

This reminded Shaw of a dream he sometimes had, in which he entered a room piled with bloodlessly amputated legs, all a threatening bluish-white colour and somewhat larger than life-size. Once the door of this room had swung to behind him, there seemed to be no way out. But then another door would be flung wide, or an entire wall would fall away, and another room became accessible from that, and another, in endless series. Anxiety drove him on. Walls kept on falling, doors kept on opening, like walls and doors in an advertisement for mobile internet. Each subsequent room was filled with so many discarded legs that Shaw felt sick. They wore socks in the colours of the Euro nations and were often cut cleanly along a vanished pelvic crease. Behind this stacking of limbs lay not so much an act of meaning as *the entire possibility of meaning*, contained in a single event. Something was implied. It could not fail to be revealed. It was both immanent and imminent. Shaw understood he had run foul of the dream language, in which structure and content are reliably the same thing. Still he longed to wake up; and eventually, each time elated to escape his own separation from some absent body, did.

'So Monday's the next time we meet, then,' he promised Tim, as they made their awkward goodbyes on the sunny post-modern apron of Soaphouse Creek; only to be proved wrong a few hours later.

7.30 p.m.: the beginning of an ordinary Friday evening at 17 Wharf Terrace. The suits were returning reluctantly in ones and twos from their offices in Hammersmith Broadway. Someone had just showered. The air smelled strongly of coconut shampoo. A lavatory flushed on the floor below. Music started up, something springy yet thoughtful driven by a walking bass. Gold light, dimly luxurious, penetrated the dusty landing window. Shaw – on his way out, dressed to visit his mother at the care home – was startled to encounter a figure at the door of the room next to his. It was bending to the lock, struggling to insert the key. It was Tim. Unable to take this in, Shaw registered for a second two separate but superimposed figures: someone he knew and someone he didn't. So disturbed that he could only address the latter, he heard himself say:

'Oh hi! These doors are rubbish, aren't they?'

Tim gave him a weak open-mouthed smile and began fiddling with the lock again. The key engaged, the door sprang open: Tim went inside.

'Have you always been here?' Shaw called after him.

The door closed. A moment or two later it opened again, just a few inches, allowing Tim's head to appear in the gap, a little lower than you would have expected to see it if he'd been standing fully upright. 'I think it best we don't talk about this,' he said. In the gold light, the bruised eye looked like an embedded prune; the other seemed to look away. Behind him could be seen the vague shadow, the sketchy appearance, of a room.

'I couldn't believe it,' Shaw told his mother. 'We'd been living next door to one another all along! The weird thing is that I didn't even want the job. Not really.'

'Everyone wants a job,' his mother said.

For a moment he thought she had actually listened to him, but as soon as the novelty of the response had caught his attention she began staring into the corner of the room as usual and calling him by a Christian name that didn't belong to him. She had an inexhaustible supply of these names. They coded for the deep strata of her life, now buckled, chaotic, discontinuous.

'It's Alex, Mum,' he said, to test her. 'I'm Alex.'

She stared at him with contempt.

'I don't know why you can't get things right,' she said, 'or learn to live with them when you haven't. That's what life is.'

Shaw shrugged. 'I did my best,' he said.

As far as he could make out, Shaw had several half-brothers and -sisters from previous marriages and affairs of his mother's. From the age of twenty, she had left a different man every five years or so and started a new family somewhere else. All the partial siblings hated her because they felt she had short-changed them; they hated each other because they had been forced to share her. The majority of them had gone off to live in Canada, South Africa, Australia. It was hard to tell who was who, because she had offered conflicting stories even before dementia set in.

'There's less to everyone than meets the eye,' she told Shaw as he left. 'You were always a cunt, William.'

'No I wasn't.'

4

Anabasis

Shaw's favourite song was 'Janitor of Lunacy' by Nico. His favourite film – played and replayed on a thirteen-inch MacBook, the rubbery base of which had deformed in some overheating event so that it displayed the colour, texture and surface contours of a bracket fungus growing out of a tree – was the 1975 Arthur Penn neo-noir *Night Moves*. This he preferred to watch with someone else, excitedly identifying for them those points at which Gene Hackman's detective reaches – without understanding that he's reached – the limits of his emotional intelligence. On his own, he tended to play it late at night, the sound dialled down until he had to strain to follow the dialogue, observing with a kind of forensic intensity Hackman's growing unease and unconscious embrace of his inevitable fate.

Since his crisis it was true of all Shaw's own encounters with people that he lagged behind the leading edge. Events seemed to happen too fast and too completely for him – either that, or nothing seemed to be happening to him at all. Before it he had been a normal human being. Now he saw himself as only partially connected to the stream of events. His first task for Tim was to pick up some used-looking cardboard boxes from the office then accompany him by train to another town.

They left so early in the morning it still seemed dark. The train – formed of nine coaches and carefully air-conditioned to be too warm in the winter, too cool in the summer – was curiously mute and decorous as it rushed along. It was empty. Once they had secured the boxes in the luggage rack, Tim asked Shaw if he had a seating preference, adding immediately that he usually took the window.

'We could sit anywhere,' Shaw pointed out.

After a while Tim produced an off-brand notepad, connected it to the website called *The Water House*, and began to scroll through the most recent entries there. Soon he was nodding and chuckling at some comment below the line, turning to smile complicitly as if he would be happy to share. Shaw eyed the notepad screen covertly – 'Uptake of Denisovan genes', he read, and then: 'Un couple préhistorique enlacé découvert en Grèce' – then busied himself instead with the landscape swinging past the windows on the opposite side of the carriage at a hundred miles an hour. He walked down to the buffet car and bought a cheese and tomato sandwich, which he ate in his seat, staring out across the violent yellow fields of rape and chewing the damp bread slowly. The train stopped at every station. Every time it started again the PA whispered, 'Welcome to this Virgin train.'

Not far from their destination Tim shut down the notepad and said: 'When we get to Smart World, we'll be talking to Helen. Helen's no one, although she'll act as if she's someone. I don't want you to look surprised at anything she says.'

Shaw had no idea how to answer that.

He sat silent for a minute or two, then he said, 'Smart World!' and laughed. He looked out of the window. 'I can never get used to the speed of a train.'

'I'm telling you what to do when we get there,' Tim said.

Shaw ate the last piece of his sandwich. It was one of the corners, with no cheese or tomato in it. He hated to be left with the taste of margarine.

'I see that,' he said. Then he added:

'You should never talk about women as if they're no one.'

'That's not the point,' Tim said. 'It's not the point that Helen is a woman.'

'Welcome to this Virgin train,' the piped voice said again. The train was less virgin than greasy. The seats were greasy. The miserly little seat-back trays were greasy. The grease got on your hands and on your personal objects so that thereafter they adhered very slightly to one another. Your fingertips came away from everything with an inaudible but somehow perceptible little noise.

'You never feel them stick,' Shaw told Tim, 'but you always feel them unstick.'

Tim didn't answer. Rain spattered diagonally across the window.

When they arrived, things weren't much better. It was some abject light-engineering town – forty-five thousand souls somewhere in the Potteries – a hundred miles from anywhere. The clouds were down not far above the buildings. The wind drove across the deserted cattle market and the Midland Hotel, drew ragged smoke from the chimney of the cement factory. Tim wouldn't get a taxi, so they walked a mile to the pedestrianised centre in the rain, carrying three cardboard boxes each, while the place woke up around them. Behind the central maze of new-build units, down the side of a Marks & Spencer the size of a suburb, chilly meaningless ramps and steps descended to a forgotten region of shopfronts from the late nineties, signs obscured, plate glass a palimpsest of ancient posters and faded closure notices.

Now that it had become just another underexploited retail opportunity, what Smart World had sold in its heyday was unclear. Snowy packing beads lay in drifts against the skirtings of an expansive laminate floor. Askew fitments and loose bundles of dusty electrical cable hung from the bruised walls. The bulky white counter opposite the entrance, misaligned and temporary-looking, proved to be a glass-fronted chiller cabinet, its sloping shelves piled with collectibles, especially books and magazines in yellowing plastic sleeves. Helen lounged behind it, arms folded, an irritable woman about forty years old, half visible in the dull, chalky light, dressed in a royal-blue business suit and fending off the approach of some familiar boredom. She looked exhausted and yet ready to trade. She looked like someone's mother, Shaw thought; though not his own. She didn't seem pleased to see Tim, who enquired with no pre-amble:

'Is he here?'

'You know he's never here on a Wednesday.'

Tim looked over her shoulder when she spoke. Any engagement between them, this look said, could only ever be temporary. It could only ever be a substitute for something more rewarding. There was a silence, at the end of which she shrugged and concluded:

'He won't want them. You should have phoned first.'

'He'll want what I've got here.'

'I'll have to phone him, you know I will. His idea is we need a change of pace.'

Tim began stripping parcel tape off one of the boxes. He worked rapidly, as if against a deadline. 'He'll want these,' he said. 'Don't you worry.'

This was received with a faint, scornful shrug, but Helen showed no sign of phoning anyone; and, after a brief sight of the contents, even agreed to let him leave the stuff in the stockroom. 'But I don't want you opening those,' she warned him, 'then saying we can't return them.'

The stockroom, a narrow passage accessed from the door behind the chiller cabinet, was blocked halfway down its length by a plastic-wrapped static bicycle and some paint-splattered ladders. Its overheated air smelled of dry-cleaning fluids, there was barely room to turn round, and all its contents would have seemed more comfortable somewhere else. Alone in there, Shaw quickly felt he had been forgotten. A kind of calm went over him. He took the opportunity to undo one of the boxes and look inside. Rows of ribbed Victorian medicine bottles met his eye, full of cloudy water and shrink-wrapped by the dozen onto warped cardboard trays. He folded the flaps of the box together, stacked it with the others beneath a blue and lilac poster celebrating some long-forgotten fantasy novel, and backed carefully out into the shop. There he found Tim and Helen leaning across the chiller cabinet, heads close, conversing in low, intent voices. The woman looked sleepily up at Shaw, then away again with a little impatient shake of the head – as if, after all, there had been nothing there to see. She blinked.

'That's that done, anyway,' Shaw said. He dusted his hands: a gesture sufficient to release them from their mutual hypnosis.

'He'll only make you come back for them,' Helen told Tim brusquely. 'Annie doesn't want him to take any more of it'; while Tim gave Helen an odd, feral-looking smile and asked: 'What's Annie got to do with it?' Some of the parcel tape had wrapped itself round his hand. He pulled at it savagely, then, finding it stuck to his fingers, grabbed Shaw by the elbow and pushed him out of the shop. 'Just what the fuck business is it of Annie's?' he called over his shoulder.

'Come on,' he said. They walked back hunched up through the rain, past the cattle market, to the railway station.

'I hate places like that,' Shaw said. 'Who's Annie?'

Throughout this encounter, Shaw felt later, Helen had given him the benefit of the doubt. But she had acknowledged him only once, when she caught him looking at the miserable piles of shrink-wrapped books in the chiller cabinet, and then only to say: 'We're a wholesaler, really. We sell on in bulk.' The extraordinary self-deception of this was Shaw's introduction to the business; or to that side of it.

From then on he would make two or three trips a week to similar premises – bookstores, crystal shops, candle parlours, short-let niche operations selling a mix of pop-cultural memorabilia and truther merchandise from two or three generations ago – which had flourished along the abandoned high streets of the post-2007 austerity, run by a network of shabby voters hoping to take advantage of tumbling rents. Their real obsession lay in the idea of commerce as a kind of politics, expression of a fundamental theology. They had bought the rhetoric without having the talent or the backing. The internet was killing them. The speed of things was killing them. They were like old-fashioned commercial travellers, fading away in bars and single rooms, exchanging order books on windy corners as if it was still 1981 – denizens of futures that failed to take, whole worlds that never got past the economic turbulence and out into clear air, men and women in cheap business clothes washed up on rail platforms, weak-eyed with the brief energy of the defeated, exchanging obsolete tradecraft like Thatcherite spies.

Shaw spent more time in this faded psychic landscape than he expected. He caught the early train out and the late train home. He watched the fields change colour from spring to early summer. Evenings in late June, the pedestrianised precincts of Peterborough, Lichfield and Birmingham took on a brassy inner glow, as if they could actually satisfy the complex yearnings people brought to tattoo parlour and discount sports outlet. His own yearnings proved difficult to articulate. Meanwhile, though it never seemed to sell anything, Smart World turned out to be one of his more dependable sales calls – if that was what they were. He got to know Helen, the woman behind the counter – so well, indeed, that towards the end of July he found himself on the floor of the stockroom with her, wedged between the stationary bicycle and a bale of local freesheets dating from October the previous year. Her skirt was up around her waist. It was at that point, or shortly after, she admitted that the business belonged to her. Any other impression he might have gained, she said, was a fiction.

'Some reps won't take no for an answer. Not from a woman. So it's convenient for me to pretend I'm the help.'

'It didn't work with Tim,' Shaw pointed out.

A faint irritability crept into her expression.

'You'd hardly call *him* a rep,' she said. She shrugged. 'Anyway, it works with all the others. I think we'd better get up now.' In the circumstances it seemed odd to be talking about Tim, but apart from the stockroom floor he was all they had in common. Tim's problem, Helen believed, was that he couldn't see how wrong – how basically out of date – his ideas were: 'That's Annie's opinion.'

'I've never understood the business with Annie,' Shaw offered, as if he had any idea who Annie was. 'What's the story there?'

Helen laughed.

'I could tell you stories about Annie and Tim,' she said, 'if that's what you want.' Then: 'Who knows? But we all know which of them's the power behind the throne.'

In addition to her MBA, Helen had a Level 3 Special Populations Health and Exercise qualification. 'I'm not ashamed to say I enjoy my life,' she said. She drove an Audi R6, and owned a house near Kinver on the outskirts of Birmingham. This four-bed new-build, tacked onto an older site under the cave-raddled lip of the sandstone edge near Holy Austin Rock, featured two acres of sloping shrubbery (out of which had struggled sometime in the 1920s a couple of gnarled brachial-looking Scots pine) and a long rectangular garden pond, both of which pre-dated the building by a hundred years or more. There, although she claimed to live alone, she insisted they had sex in an unheated spare room, on a John Lewis divan bed from which she stripped the sheets immediately upon rising the next morning.

Sex with Helen was disconcerting. Her flesh had a kind of white puffiness; it felt, Shaw told himself, white to the touch. She talked in a low voice throughout, often about personal finance, often in detail. Her main regret seemed to be that she had failed to sell half the garden to a property developer in 2006, just before the crash. One night Shaw woke up and heard her whispering fiercely, 'I don't know why people aren't a lot more disgusted with themselves than they are.' He couldn't find her in the bed, but he could hear her with peculiar clarity, as if her lips were an inch from his ear. She had positioned her-self to one side of the window, facing into the room, palms of the hands flat against the wall, neck turned awkwardly to look down into the garden, where a strong, slanting rain roared in the shrubbery and splashed off the eroded stone surround of the pond. 'You stiff a lot of other people over their mortgages, pensions and insurance, and because you have good hair, and what you do is always right for you, oh no, you can't go wrong. *You* aren't doing anything wrong.'

'Are you on the phone?' Shaw said. She wasn't.

'It was 3 a.m.,' he told her the next day, 'and you weren't even awake. You were talking in your sleep.'

'I don't like someone watching me at night.'

'I just woke up,' Shaw said, sounding more apologetic than he felt. 'The rain woke me. It was pouring down out there.'

Like everyone else in the country they were doing their best to co-operate and failing. The affair, if it could be described as that, ended not long after, amid the usual recriminations; and the next time Shaw called, Smart World had closed. He tapped at the dirty glass door a few times, then walked back to the station. 'Even the chiller cabinet was gone,' he said in his report to Tim, who looked puzzled for a moment, then shrugged.

5

Passing Water

Between trips like this, Shaw worked at the office. He had the key to the site hut, so he could start as early as he liked, often crossing the Thames by Barnes Bridge at six o'clock in the morning and walking to Chiswick, where he bought and ate an almond croissant. It wasn't the most demanding employment. He kept the client list, and answered most queries by saying, 'I'll pass that on to Tim, then, shall I?'; he sold the occasional copy of a print-on-demand book entitled *Journeys of Our Genes*. Lunchtimes he ate a sandwich from the local Pret, usually chicken and avocado; or went to the Earl of March for sausage and mash with onion gravy. If the weather remained good he would drag the typing chair outside and sit on the towpath staring up and down the river in the glassy afternoon light, Oliver's Island in one direction, and in the other the deserted residential quays of the Brent confluence.

The office soon became familiar. It was furnished with old things. The floor creaked and gave with every tide. A steel filing cabinet yawned away from the wall when you walked past it. Open the desk drawers – the dense, not unpleasant smell of ancient pencil shavings rose up – and they proved to be full out-of-date office supplies: ink-stained rulers, tubs of mapping pins and perished elastic bands, headed stationery for another business altogether, something which had called itself Utility Solutions Ltd until at the front end of the eighties it had slipped without a whimper beneath the briny, agitated surface of the Thatcherian economy.

Shaw put some of these items on the desk – a desiccated stamp-pad in a colourful tin box; a block of yellow Post-it notes beginning to curl up, on one of which he found scrawled the words 'Dendrogramma', 'thickened jelly-like layer', then what looked like 'the deep continental slope'; and an IKEA lamp that, while it resembled neither a lay figure nor a wooden model of a gallows, appealed to design elements of both. To personalise the arrangement he added the copy of the *London Review of Books* he had been leafing his way through for a month. If he wanted coffee, there was an electric kettle with a worn cloth flex.

He felt well served, even redefined a little, by this stuff; though, like the pornographic magazines printed in grainy black and white on curiously glossy paper that he found in the one unlocked drawer of the filing cabinet, it seemed like the shyly offered produce of a vanished age. His only problem was the lack of a toilet. Apart from rattling the padlock occasionally, he had given up on the site hut's second door: clearly, whatever lay behind it wasn't a lavatory anyway. But he couldn't be bothered to walk to the Earl of March every time he needed to pee, so he began going in the thick undergrowth that had established itself on an abandoned barge a few yards upriver.

It was no chore, indeed he rather enjoyed the sensation. There was something voluptuous about the enclosing, dusty smells, the glitter of the water seen through leaves indistinguishable from the glint of broken glass at the shallowly bedded roots of the buddleia and willowherb, the quiet movements of a disturbed bird, the mild thrill of being both on the water and on fixed earth. Wet days, he stayed inside, listening to the rain on the river. He watched Netflix, or studied through narrowed eyes the curious map of the world Blu-Tacked above the desk, its coastlines pierced in rust-stained clusters by vanished pins. Or he scrolled through his emails, among which he would often find one from Victoria Nyman.

Victoria had made good her threat to leave London. 'Well, it's done,' she wrote. 'Goodbye, Dalston. I took only what I could get into the little car. Everything else went into storage. As you can imagine, it was goodbye to the priceless antique carpets and family silver.' Or, sent from her phone: 'Help! Lost in the Midlands again!' She approached the whole business as obliquely as the rest of her life. But she was making friends, she said: she was enjoying herself at last. She was cleaning two old chairs with white spirit and 'linseed oil the colour of Lagavulin'. It was a running commentary. Shaw looked forward to each new instalment, but always felt he had missed a pivotal message. Where had she actually gone? What was she doing now?

'Anyway,' she wrote, 'like all the other losers, I cashed out for the provinces. Lots of love. Hope you are enjoying your fish, and that, just as importantly, the fish is enjoying you.'

In fact, he had decided to give it to his mother.

The reasons for this he would have found difficult to explain. If you picked the fish up and encouraged the street light to angle off its hand-etched scales, it seemed more deco than Peru, more 1930s than nineteenth century; to confuse matters further, the hallmarks were Spanish. A tiny bashed pentagram indicated, so Google advised him, silver of .915 purity. These failures of alignment between the facts of the fish and Victoria's narrative of it only seemed to echo a deeper cultural disconnect. There was a curious, halting feel to its aesthetic – as if the artist, in the attempt to kitschify the ethnic product of one culture, had stumbled on evidence of a completely different culture hidden inside it. Under the lamplight the movements of its cleverly articulated body fell just short of sinuous.

It was too like a fish. Its rubbery lips and accusing blue eyes dismayed him, especially when he woke in the night, disoriented by the noise from the room next door. There, arguments continued to break out in the early hours. A door would slam, down in the body of the house. Someone would stumble on the lower landing, then recover and move on. There was music or something like it, sometimes accompanied just before dawn by vocal sounds less identifiable. Knowing who lived there made no difference except that, Tim now being his employer, Shaw felt he could no longer complain. When they ran into one another in the course of things, on the stairs or by the bakery shelves in the Sainsbury's Local at the Mortlake end of Wharf Terrace, Tim seemed as distracted as ever. He was a man in search of motives – never finding them yet acting anyway, lost among the structures we all inherit and manage to make use of. Shaw opened the bathroom door one morning to find him kneeling on the pitted lino in front of the lavatory. He had taken off his summer jacket and bundled it up in a corner. The left sleeve of his shirt was rolled past the elbow. He had turned his head to one side as if he didn't want to look at the lavatory bowl down which his arm was so firmly thrust.

'Ah,' he said.

'You should always lock this door,' Shaw recommended, as if reminding a child of one of the social duties that would hence-forth complicate its life. He was off to catch the Twickenham train to the care facility, and already felt as if the day was going wrong. 'Because anyone could walk in off the stairs.'

39

Then he said he would leave Tim to it, adding only: 'That floor's quite wet.'

'I expect you wonder what I'm doing,' Tim called after him.

In her day, Shaw's mother had been much admired. Consequently she could now be found staring out, as vague and stormy as an empty seascape, from several albums of photographs. She seemed fascinated by these relics – misundertaken marriages, embarrassing births, funerals at which no one seemed to know the deceased – but left unsupervised would suffer inexplicable rages and try to tear them up. Even of the most recent prints – taken a month before on Shaw's phone – she would sometimes say: 'Don't be ridiculous. Don't be so ridiculous. This is no more me than fly in the air.' Perhaps she was right: they showed an old woman, generic, collapsed-looking yet somehow still impenitent, sitting in a care-home common room, a reproduction of Arnold Böcklin's spectacularly odd 1887 oil painting *Sea Idyll* clearly visible on the wall behind her.

That was where he found her now.

'You needn't think I want that bloody thing in here,' she said, as soon as she saw the parcel that contained the fish.

'I've got to laugh,' Shaw replied, 'because you don't even know what it is.'

'It's not something I want.'

'You don't know what it is. Look, it's a present, it's a gift. At least unwrap it.'

Instead she sat stiff with rejection for half an hour in one of the curiously upright wingback chairs arranged beneath the Böcklin. Every so often she glanced quickly at the parcel then away again. 'I don't know what you want, Peter,' she said eventually, as if they had been arguing to and fro all morning. She sighed. 'I honestly don't know what you want.' The accompanying vulnerable flourish of her shoulders – not quite a shrug, too complex to unpack, always a means of covering the weakness of her position – he remembered distinctly from being ten years old.

'My name isn't Peter,' he said.

'Darling, aren't we having the photographs today? I *so* love them.'

Shaw was prepared for this. 'When you've unwrapped your present,' he promised, 'we can. We can have the photographs and a cup of tea.'

She leaned forward suddenly and took his hands in hers.

'But you're cold!' she said. 'Is it cold in here?' Then, as if she'd thought of a new way to amuse him: 'Let's have the photographs first!'

Recognising this as her best offer, he fetched the albums. On the beach at Hastings, fifteen years old, with a bell of dark hair, a shift dress and sharp 1960s cheekbones, she looked like Myra Hindley, less hungry than unassuaged. You could see that nothing she did satisfied her even then, half a decade before she invented her primary method for dealing with life. Posed subsequently at the side of one husband or another, temporarily central to one family group or the next, she had made her life a history of the medium: tiny Kodak 127 prints, warped by their own glaze into subtle curves which reflected light away from their subject, gave way to 35mm transparencies the colour values of which had shifted dangerously to the red; then Polaroids with the muddy and furtive background tones of the late 1970s.

Before the care-home staff locked them away, she had begun and ended every day poring over these images. What she now made of them, what internal operations they still served, couldn't be imagined. 'Which do you like best?' she asked him. Shaw chose one which showed her with one of his various fathers – he thought the surname might be Carson, or Carlson – on a beach in Pembroke. Behind them an Italian greyhound was awkwardly defecating on a bank of shingle, its body curled into a vibrant hoop; the sea lay at the horizon and the weather seemed cold.

'Look,' he said. 'Here's Aunty Nancy and her little dog.'

His mother stared at him with contempt. 'When will you ever grow up?'

'What *did* they call the dog?' Shaw said. 'I know that lot always called you Aunty Nancy.' He went out into the corridor and walked up and down rapidly with his hands in his pockets and his shoulders hunched. When he got back in the room, she had already torn up the print – she was sitting at the table by the window, carefully stirring the shiny pieces as if they were a warm fluid. When he took them away, as gently as he could, she only smiled out at the garden and said, 'Aunty Naughty. Aren't things just like a puzzle?'

'Now will you look at what I brought you?' he asked.

'Yes!' she said childishly. 'I will. I want to!'

But as soon as the Peruvian fish was unwrapped she began to weep, and say that she had been right all along; and the next time he visited, the staff asked him to take it away. 'It seems to upset her.'

Old hotels reeking of grease. No-star dumps in Birmingham or Leicester. Corridor floors of black boards dipping and creaking as you walked. A night man who wouldn't let you back in at the end of the evening until you had paid up all over again. Then home the next morning, with Tim always angry about refunds, being cheated over refunds or returns by some operation calling itself Golden Strangers or They Came as Waves.

He had curious reciprocal arrangements with many of them. Shaw would be given charge of a cheap framed print or a small broken item of furniture, sometimes to be left at a shop, sometimes at a house in an apparently deserted suburb two or three miles out of the city centre. He would receive in return a carrier bag full of late-seventies spoken-word tape cassettes with hand-made labels. Where the profit lay in the exchange rarely became clear. Even when money was involved, Shaw had the sense that the transaction was closed in some other medium.

The rest of the time he delivered the usual cardboard boxes. 'I'm trusting you with these,' Tim would say. When one of them came apart like a damp cheese sandwich, and inside Shaw found only half a dozen copies of *Journeys of Our Genes*, he suggested:

'This is quite an expensive way to deliver stock.'

Tim only smiled. 'People like to know who we are,' he said.

'They keep saying they don't want it.'

'They like a familiar face.'

In the end, perhaps, all of this had been an elaborate way of assessing him, because suddenly the journeys stopped – although not before Shaw found himself on perhaps the oddest errand of all.

'I want you to attend a trial,' Tim said.

'Can people just do that?'

Tim shrugged. 'Court cases are public events,' he said. 'Anyone can go.'

'But still,' Shaw said. '"Attend".'

'The defendant's name is Patrick Reed. Try and remember what he says. Write it down if you have to.'

Noisy shuddering little commuter trains, debatable links: Shaw spent half a day joining one cross-country service to another; hard enough work just to arrive mid-afternoon on the brown edge of Wales. The town, with its undecodable medieval topography and commanding position above the River Severn, had done well out of sheep; then out of brewing; and finally out of coal. Now, like most of those old places, post-colonial, post-industrial and – in the sense that its past had now become its present – fully post-historical, it was curating a collection of original burgage plots, timber-framed heritage structures and quaintly squalid street names. It had been pleased with itself for 700 years.

He found the crown court a little way out of the centre, situated awkwardly on a ring road between major traffic islands, surrounded by local colleges, a police station and two other courts. It was one of those public buildings which though purpose-built still seem unfit for purpose. You couldn't describe the architecture, except by its resemblance to a Travelodge. The lifts were out of order. There were handwritten notices in the corridors, scanned and printed hastily from every desk in the building to keep up with the day's rule changes.

No one seemed sure why the defendant found himself there. A retired civil engineer, tall, perhaps seventy years old – well kept, with a quiet voice, white hair, frail-looking prominent cheekbones and a way of standing which seemed slightly off-centre with itself – he regarded the judge with puzzled relief, as if their relationship was all he had to hang on to, as if it saved him from an existence the rules of which he didn't understand. 'I'm grateful to your honour,' he kept saying. Every time he said it he wiped his mouth.

The judge was equally tentative. 'It's my fault, I'm sure,' he said at one point, 'but could you speak up? And if you could address yourself to the jury?' Pleas like this made him seem hardly less lost, if in a different way.

What was Patrick Reed's actual crime? The charge sheet mentioned 'violent disorder', but all he seemed to have done, really, was draw attention to himself by shouting repeatedly at the busy end of the pedestrianised high street on a wet Saturday towards the end of the previous year: an impulse Shaw felt he could appreciate. No evidence had yet been presented. Instead there were endless delays. Submissions were made that no one understood. There were exchanges of papers. No witnesses were called. 'I believe my friend has agreed to this,' counsel congratulated one another: but they never told the jury what. All that seemed certain was this: the accused believed that one evening shortly after his seventieth birthday he had looked into a toilet bowl in the Black Horse on Camp Lane and realised that there was 'something alive in the water'.

That was as far as things went the first day. On the second, for reasons that never became clear, the judge closed early. Shaw ate an artisanal sandwich at the Jouissance Bistro & Well-Being Centre. Later he became lost in a system of alleys between Grope (previously Grope Counte) Lane and Dogpole Yard, where the sagging old upper storeys – apparently held together only by rectangular-section drainpipes like thick leather straps – sheltered both Jobcentre Plus and upscale underwear boutique; debouching suddenly into the long grounds of Old St Martin's, where he sat on a bench in the warm sunshine reading heritage brochures. For 1000 years, he learned, one sacred building or another had occupied the site – until 1788, when the church had collapsed mysteriously into its own crypt to leave only the melted-looking old red sandstone of the polygonal Chapter House at which he now stared. He went back to his hotel and reported, 'Nothing much going on.'

The next morning, pressed to elaborate, Patrick Reed described what he'd seen in the toilet as 'a pale greenish flake no more than a few millimetres long', which had seemed to move in an energetic, random way until he accidentally urinated on it, whereupon it grew into a 'green child' which possessed the qualities of both a foetus and a fully formed organism, and which he flushed in absolute disgust. At that time it was still growing. 'I felt,' Reed told the judge apologetically, 'that I had seen something no one should ever see.'

Could he explain what he meant by that?

He couldn't. He could only shrug. 'It was still developing,' he offered. 'Quite rapidly.'

In response to this, the judge made encouraging gestures — to the defendant, counsel and court officers — as if he hoped someone, indeed anyone, would speak.

'I think the jury might hear a little more?' he suggested finally.

'That's the heart of it, I'm afraid,' admitted Reed.

After that, he had begun seeing the things wherever he urinated. 'Passed water' was his term for it. An ambivalent usage, Shaw thought. But that was the heart of it. Everywhere Patrick Reed passed water, green children grew. Except for their colour and their translucency, which was somewhere between that of an aphid and a boiled sweet, they seemed human. 'I mean,' he added quickly, 'they seemed to have the potential to be something like us.' They didn't, for instance, resemble netsuke. They weren't clever reproductions of anything. He observed a heartbeat. He observed the pained, gentle expression shared by all foetal mammals. Small movements. If they weren't human, they were nevertheless living. And while he was always careful to flush, he couldn't assume that everyone did. 'They grew so quickly!' he appealed. 'As far as I knew then — as far as I know now — they might be everywhere.' It was at this point he began to try and warn people. If he had overstated his case that Saturday afternoon, he said, he was sorry: 'But it seemed so important at the time.'

This went on for another two or three days. Shaw could make nothing of it. Each morning the jury received the formal warning not to talk to anyone else – or even each other – about the trial. But, really, what was there to talk about? A man who, when he spoke of the sewerage system, used the words 'deep and false waters' and who believed that it sheltered a wholly new form of life? The jury looked at one another and shrugged. The one thing they were certain of was that Patrick Reed should be receiving some other kind of help. If his life had gone awry, it was nothing to do with an appearance in court. In the end they found him not guilty of the main charge, but guilty on the lesser count of being drunk in an Alcohol Control Area, namely the pavement in front of the Market Hall.

Everyone was relieved. It's hard, as the judge himself said in his summing-up, to find a man guilty of anything when he believes that 'green people' are breeding freely in the public toilets of the United Kingdom.

When Reed thanked him, he shook his head.

'I'm not sure any of us,' he said, making a gesture intended to include the jury, 'can say we've done the right thing here. But it's clear that our only other option would have been wrong too.'

That seemed to be it for the trial.

Shaw left the court, caught three trains home and conveyed the news to Tim, who nodded thoughtfully. He gave the impression that it was a satisfactory verdict, one that offered both confirmation and closure. He remained enthusiastic about some aspects of the civil engineer's narrative – 'Aphids!' he said one night in the back bar of the Earl of March. 'The only

47

animals in the world which can photosynthesise!' And when Shaw only stared: 'It's such an extraordinary idea, isn't it? A layer of cells a few nanometres below the skin that can do everything a plant does to make energy from sunlight!' – but it was clear that he was losing interest. At the same time his anxieties seemed to diminish. The provincial errands lost their urgency, tapered off. After a week or two, he told Shaw:

'I've got a new job for you. I want you to visit a medium.'

These visits, he said, should take place once a week. The medium called herself Mrs Swann and she lived in a row of working-men's cottages on the Sheen side of Old Mortlake graveyard. 'You'll pay her a sum of money in cash,' Tim said, 'and take a record of the seance.'

'What am I looking for?'

'You're looking for anything interesting. You won't have any trouble with Annie. She's a sweetie. Take a video recorder, but don't say you come from me.'

'I could use my phone,' Shaw suggested.

Tim gave this some consideration.

'Fine,' he said.

Two

6

Victoria's House

Fate had played a strange card against the maternal side of Victoria Norman's family. Entrenched provincial estate agents, solicitors and GPs, they were lively enough as young adults but suffered immobilising anxiety and depression in the middle years, regaining in late life just enough energy to die of the first age-related disease that presented itself.

They consoled themselves that it was, if nothing else, a pattern; it was the family pattern. Her grandfather on that side spent a decade encased in an armchair smelling of cigarettes and Famous Grouse, before succumbing to thrombosis; his sisters first saw to his needs then, freed from them, toppled over one Saturday afternoon in a shoe shop as a result of matching cerebral haemorrhages. Her mother, timidified in early adolescence by these kinds of scenes, wouldn't catch a bus in case it ran up the kerb or – worse – she offered the wrong fare to the driver; aged forty, she could barely bring herself to leave the house. By the time the fog lifted, it was too late: Victoria's father, who had taken up fishing in late life, dropped dead in a secluded car park on the bank of the River Severn, leaving the mother at a loss but at the same time inexplicably relieved. Relief saw her through the menopause. It saw her relocate to a small, not very picturesque town in Shropshire, where she acquired an iPhone and went home with strange men, drunk-texting crush after crush late at night until she died of a peculiarly enlarged spleen and very high levels of the thyroid hormone T4.

That was how Victoria, a month or two after her Hammersmith date with Shaw, found herself outside the South-east for the first time in fifteen years, driving her Fiat 500 into the unknown both with and without expectation. Up the hill she went, past the ironmonger's, the greengrocer's and the old Town Hall with its tall cemented-up windows, to the top, where two or three gaunt old houses stood in a row so the wind could get at them and blow the jackdaws about all day over their complex, interconnected roofs. She was tired. She was seeking change and secretly afraid of it. She had been lost twice between there and the M42.

Eventually she was able to look up at the high narrow front of her new home and shiver suddenly with the complete certainty of having done the wrong thing.

The house resisted her. The key wouldn't turn in the lock, the lights wouldn't come on and the hall seemed to be blocked with piles of shadowy cardboard boxes. The whole downstairs smelled of stale tea bags and cheese. But the kitchen ring main worked; so Victoria could get the refrigerator running, plug in the kettle, make a cup of tea and drink it in the chemical gleam of her smartphone screen, sitting on the bottom step of the stairs with her legs tucked sideways.

Looking up nervously into the gloom of the first-floor landing, she decided to stay downstairs for now and sleep on the ghostly white sofa in the front room, where you could at least hear cars going by in the street. Someone, she found herself thinking, should always know where you are – even if you find it hard to work them out or understand what they want or make them understand what you want. So the last thing she did was to get in touch with Shaw again:

'What were we ever going to do with our lives, people like you and me? We're like a lot of hermit crabs in the same shell.'

He hadn't answered any of her other emails, so she added, 'Anyway, I'm out of lovely London now, here's my address if you want it.' Then: 'I don't know what I'll do here for work. I've got enough money to last for a while.' In addition she had retained her Dalston house, installing a tenant to keep up with the mortgage; but to tell Shaw that would be to seem timid, unable to commit. She pushed the sofa cushions about, opened the shutters and fell asleep in a wash of moonlight a curious hyacinthine colour – as if it had been stored for later release by the paintwork of the buildings across the road – to wake next morning already feeling different.

92 High Street – a product of the late eighteenth-century economic delirium, built on the profits of a small limestone quarry above the Severn Gorge – had been divided in two sometime before World War I. By daylight, Victoria's half revealed itself to be everything she had ever wanted: three storeys of tall empty rooms with floorboards as dark as the planks of old ships. Yes, it had fallen from grace. There were false ceilings, a wet cellar, plaster rotting under acres of woodchip; the kitchen had been martyred to 1970s softwood panelling. But, yes, all that would be stripped determinedly away until she found herself in possession of the wide staircase, the long windows, the original proportions. Imagining these scenes, she wandered elatedly up and down the stairs, in and out of rooms, eating cereal in cold milk and unable, when she looked into the garden or into the light pouring down the stairwell, to believe her luck.

A few surprises were in store. The first was a tall woman with a lank greying bob of hair who jumped out in front of her on the second-floor landing. This apparition – wringing its hands, its expression appalled and apologetic – turned out to be herself, reflected in a full-length mirror and already beginning to murmur, 'I'm sorry, I don't ...'; behaviour she felt to be uncharacteristic, although it made her wonder. Other surprises were less unflattering if more annoying. The back door wouldn't open. And you could reset the fuse box as often as you liked, but the moment you tried to use two kitchen appliances at the same time the ground-floor lights went off again.

She made lists, and later took herself out.

The town, compressed for 1200 years or so onto a promontory of red sandstone above the Severn, had no high-rise architecture, just some church towers and the remains of the inevitable Marcher Lord's castle poking out above the Georgian roofs. Aprons of housing and light-industrial development had recently spread north and west along two or three wooded spurs descending steeply towards the river crossings. The Severn meant everything here. Commerce had begun with it; iron and industry had got their start on its banks. Winter and summer, day and especially night, it still cooled the air like a vast heat exchanger.

Mid-morning, and the streets around Hightown were busy. Rain had set to work darkening the speckled brickwork; the sky promised thunder it wasn't, in the end, able to deliver. Victoria walked in a confused spiral until she reached the base of the medieval keep. This curious ruin – thrown up in the 1200s by Geoffrey de Lacy, one of Henry III's lesser-known Savoyards, and pulled down not much more than a hundred years later during the Despenser War – featured a single triangular corner of masonry, fifty or sixty feet high and leaning fifteen degrees off the vertical, looking less like architecture than the bow of an unfinished ship: as if its founder had seen into some future of immense sea-level rises, a world in which the hill would become an island, the castle grounds a quay. It was black with damp. The surrounding Edwardian gardens were bleak and ordered.

Determined to find something to enjoy, she took herself to the top of the Portway, the old packhorse stair that fell away down the steep side of the promontory towards the river, from a narrow slot between Costa and My Little Wedding. It was quiet down there, cool and damp between tall brick walls and layers of eroded sandstone. With each turn of the stair you lost sight of what had gone before. There was only the next ten yards, a fern growing out of the wall, deepening silence as you left the traffic behind. Halfway down, the slot turned sharply left, at the same time widening to become a kind of shallow stepped ramp. Here, the rock was poisoned with oxides, thick with cobwebs; when she looked up, Victoria could see the backs of the houses and shops on the high street – old disused doors opening onto air; windows dusty and broken; then the sky, a rinsed, shocking blue.

Suddenly, warm soapy water poured down the stairs, around her feet and away, only three inches deep but strong and turbulent, with foam on it here and there, as if someone had emptied a bath without warning. It had a smell she couldn't account for, faint and chemical, perhaps some kind of cleaning fluid. The object that washed down with it, slithering then sticking to the cobbles, then slithering again, was translucent and tinged faintly with green; otherwise it looked like a stillborn kitten.

Victoria put her hand over her mouth.

'Well, I don't know!' she heard someone shout from a window high in the backs of the buildings. 'I don't know where it's gone!'

She stared down at the thing by her feet. It had a foetal look, but at the same time it seemed finished and complete. It was beached now. It wasn't a mammal, perhaps not even a fish. It made her shiver. She wondered if it was some stage in the life of an octopus, imagined a tank bursting in some half-timbered Chinese restaurant set back from the high street. She touched it with her toe, turned immediately and looked downhill, where the water was rushing away in a thinning film.

'How horrible,' she said aloud, looking up at the sky again.

When she came back up the steps half an hour later, after a poke around on the other side of the Severn bridge, there was nothing to be seen. The water had dried up. The foetus, if that was what it was, had gone. The sandstone walls and dirty windows reared up, silent and empty-looking. She hurried back up the steps and into the shopping streets. Sainsbury's was easy to find, isolated in its acres of bright, empty car parks; Marks & Spencer, though, eluded her. Eventually she found a café called Pearl's, tucked away in a square behind the shops. It was empty apart from an old man sitting at a table slowly eating beans on toast. A woman in a pink overall stood in the middle of the floor staring out of the window with a puzzled expression, as if she had started to do something else then forgotten what it was. When she saw Victoria, she got behind the counter. The name 'Pearl' was machine-embroidered on the pocket of the overall.

'Do you have wi-fi?' Victoria asked.

'We do, but it never works.'

'But can I try?'

The old man had to stop eating to follow this exchange. His eyes were sore, the skin pulled at his fragile-looking facial bones; there were big sore joints to his fingers and wrists. Despite that, something alert in him persisted. Before he left the house that morning he had put on a 1970s wet-look nylon rally jacket and carefully combed his hair. He scraped his chair back, scraped it forward again, and once this manoeuvre had gained their attention said, 'The door's not shut properly, either.'

'I'm sorry,' Victoria said. 'That's my fault.'

'You have to bang it. Bang it hard. It's never worked in all my years.'

'"All my years",' Pearl mimicked. And then, to Victoria: 'What can I get you?'

'The cake looks nice.'

'Pearl's carrot cake,' said the old man as if to himself, with a kind of musing contempt. 'A few reckon they enjoy it, but I'm not keen.'

'Just finish your beans,' the woman behind the counter said. 'Or you'll go out.'

He stared at her, then away. 'Something's wrong with them,' he complained. 'They taste of fish.' He threw his knife and fork down on the plate.

'You'll go straight out, I mean it.'

'Your grandad was a mineworker,' he said. 'You won't know what one of those was. Every hour of every day on his knees in that flooded hole by Peckforton.' His eyes watered. 'Then, when he retired, he took the seven white ponies up out of the dark with him—'

'Out you go if you don't shut up. I mean it, you old wanker.'

'His life was over, but he chose to be clean, and gave them the fine home he promised.'

Since they couldn't do an espresso, Victoria had the carrot cake with a cup of tea. The wi-fi password came handwritten on a slip of paper. Every 2 could be read as a Z, every 5 an S; there was an upper case I which might equally have been a lower-case l or only a 1. She sat at a table by the window, methodically trying the combinations. Groups of customers came and went – women carrying toddlers or Lakeland terriers; tourists who had struggled up the hill from the crowded heritage attractions along the river. Everyone chatted. Victoria had another cup of tea.

Towards lunchtime the place filled with gangs of men from the local building sites. On holiday for an hour, they steamed up the windows and shouted with laughter at something in *The Sun*; but made themselves quiet and careful for the woman behind the counter. They had the furtiveness of children. In return Pearl teased them unmercifully. She was tall, younger than she looked, practising a blank sidelong smile that didn't quite match her body language. For them there would always be some separation between her and her surface; a performed divide. She would value it, and become clever at maintaining it. Because what else is there to do in a small town located on the exact line between Shropshire and nowhere? And if – as would become plain later – there was anything more to her than that, the men in their hi-vis and site helmets would never guess what it was.

'Pearl's a nice name,' Victoria told her when they had all gone.

'You can blame it on the old bugger over there,' she answered. 'Some days I like it, some days I don't.' She stood wiping her hands on a J-cloth. 'Is it working for you, then, the password?'

'I think so.'

Pearl considered this.

'A password works or it doesn't,' she concluded.

Victoria laughed. 'I suppose you're right.'

'No suppose about it.' There was a pause. Then, looking down and away with her sidelong smile, she said quietly:

'I knew your mother.'

Because it seemed so unlikely, so sudden, such a completely inexplicable thing to say, Victoria assumed she had misheard. She got up, closed her laptop without switching it off and put some money on the counter as if it was still attended. She was embarrassed. She could see the rain coming down outside in long static lines. The old man was staring out at it too. He had carefully scooped the remainder of his beans to one side of the plate; eaten the toast. 'You were my Pearl,' he murmured, stressing the verb as if to give this old decision force. 'I called you that because you were my Pearl.' Then: 'We looked up to your grandfather like a god.' Dull metallic light reflected off the tabletops, which his daughter, who seemed unlikely to say any more, now began to rub at with her cloth.

As Victoria went out into the street, unwilling to leave on a note of such paralysis, she called back: 'I never know where the morning's gone, do you?'

Parents and children, she thought later. What can you say?

Her mother had wandered the house just like her. Like Victoria she had half unpacked, dragging cardboard boxes into the middle of rooms where she pulled their flaps apart in the hope that her own possessions might still surprise her. The new life had swept her away before she finished, and after that it was too late. Carpets, rolled and taped, remained propped in corners. The beds had found their way to the bedrooms, but her pictures, done up by the moving service in brown paper and polypropylene string, still leaned like wrapped paving stones against the bases of the walls. She had found something more interesting to do. It was a curious form of occupation, not so much tentative as careless; a curious lot of belongings with little or no connection to the woman Victoria remembered. Unsuitable shoes. Nacre-buttoned denim shirts. An air freshener that claimed to smell of a coastal walk. Fast-food leaflets gathered in drifts on the kitchen table. Pinned to the noticeboard by the fridge were lists of local trades, including a handyman who had scribbled 'Anything At All!' across the top of his flier and whom Victoria now telephoned.

'Hello?'

Silence at the other end.

'Is that ...' she looked down at the flier, 'Chris?'

No answer.

'Well,' she said, in case she was talking to an answering service, 'I'll ring again.' At once a voice replied, 'Who's this?'

'I wanted to speak to Chris?'

'He's out in the taxi for the moment,' the voice said. 'With that lot from Kinver. I can take your details but not much more.'

'It's very Brexit up here,' she wrote later to Shaw. 'Eight pubs in a mile and deep surrounding woods. I already think of it as my Brocéliande, although the high street seems to have been deforested as early as 1307.' She was sleeping on the sofa again, she told him. 'But now I have candles and everything.'

Inside one of her mother's boxes she had found a brand-new edition of *The Water-Babies*. She amused herself by copying out passages for him. Little Tom was naughty. He threw stones. He fled across the fell, by Hartover and Lewthwaite Crag, to the river. Forty pages in and he was already a joke, perhaps dead, desperate to be a fish or a baby or both, the Victorian fantasies of metamorphosis, regression and transition told as a morality. 'You see,' she finished. 'You should read my emails. I bet your life's less exciting than little Tom's!' She knew she would never in fact sign off on this: but writing it down was enough to give the effect of being in a conversation. It was as good as two glasses of red. 'I might have to keep my mother's furniture,' she confessed. 'I sold all mine.' This made her think of the house again, and she looked around and shivered with delight.

Next day the doorbell rang before she was out of bed. When she opened the front door she found Pearl the waitress's father standing there. He was four inches shorter than her. He was whistling. His hair curled damply back over the collar of his Castrol jacket. He looked a lot livelier in the sunlight.

'I had a minute,' he said. 'So I came.'

Victoria stared at him.

'It's Chris,' he said. 'Chris. Chris from last night.'

'Do you always answer your phone as if you're someone else?'

'I'll just step inside,' he said.

They stared at one another. It seemed like an impasse. In the end he held up a plastic sports bag.

'I've got everything I'll need in here,' he said.

'If I could just explain what's wanted?'

'A cup of tea would be nice since you're putting the kettle on. Then while you're making it I'll have a look round.' He smiled and went off up the stairs as if he owned them, calling back:

'I've got everything I need. Don't you worry.'

Victoria boiled the kettle in a rage. She heard him on the first landing and then on the loose floorboards near the loo. His bag of tools rattled. He hissed and whistled to himself. He was pathetic. He tapped at this and that. A second-floor sash ground itself open, then shuddered down again. It all made Victoria feel as if she didn't belong. 'How's that tea coming on?' he called. When he came downstairs to have it, he sat and ate a biscuit too. He seemed to bring a smell into the kitchen. She couldn't quite smell it, but she knew it was there.

'I like to sit down to a biscuit,' he said.

She pushed the packet towards him. 'Help yourself.'

He smiled as if he had expected this. 'I was born Chris,' he said, 'but over at Kinver they know me as Ossie.'

He had a jauntiness you couldn't explain; at the same time he wanted your sympathy. After you had watched him for a minute or two, you saw that he held himself oddly, and walked with the suspicion of a limp; he was always wiping his eyes. 'Poor health,' he said, with a kind of satisfaction. 'A lifetime of it.' He'd had bowel cancer, which they fixed; they thought his cough was asbestosis. In addition his left wrist didn't articulate, as a result of a fall in 1999, from the town Christmas tree. 'I was setting up the lights,' he said. 'I let myself in for that.' And then: 'They didn't take the decorations down in time that year. We've all suffered as a result.' He could just about use a screwdriver. 'There's a lot of perished rubber in those lighting circuits,' he informed her, after he had eaten half a packet of chocolate digestives. 'It only needs a touch to flake off.' It would mean a rewire. She had expected as much. 'Mind you,' he concluded, 'there's plenty of good new neoprene in there too.'

'You aren't going to fall off anything while you're here, are you?' Victoria said.

He was still there at lunchtime, tugging at wires in the loft.

'I could give you baked beans,' she offered.

'I don't fancy them the way I did.'

'Well, can you look at the back door before you go?'

The back door was ill-fitting and seemed home-made: four vertical planks of slightly varying lengths, with three more banged across them horizontally; the whole covered thickly in old-fashioned pale-blue paint. Victoria loved it. An array of bolts, most of which were rusted open, provided security.

There was an ancient latch. It looked as if it had served the house for decades, and a barn before that. Damp had swollen it against the jamb. 'You'd do better with new,' the old man said. The moment he touched it, though, it opened. Light, harsh but beautiful, fell across the threshold and onto the kitchen steps. Her garden! For the moment, it seemed too bright and complete to enter, like a clearing in a wood.

The old man collected his tools, zipped up the bag and shook it next to his ear. He put his coat on in the hall. 'Never anything that can't be fixed,' he said. And, stopping with his left arm half into the sleeve: 'You'll enjoy the garden.'

'How's Pearl?' she asked as he left.

'That's a good question.' He was in the street, looking at the sky, turning up his collar. 'How's the famous Pearl? I'd say she was as convinced by herself as ever. She'll walk round a corner one day and discover things have changed.'

'I thought she was very nice,' Victoria called after him.

'I'll tell her you said so.'

She tidied up the mess he had left behind; then she went out through the back door.

In Victoria's life, gardens had always belonged to someone else. She liked them but she didn't know anything about them. This one, dilapidated enough to absorb any amount of effort, was really two gardens. The nearest, accessed from a gap between well-grown box, was longer, set a little higher, and consisted of a rectangular lawn surrounded by phlox, foxgloves and montbretia. Up against the house leaned a white clapboard shed, paint flaking and windows fallen out, and in the baking sunny corner between the two, a rose so old and leggy its best use was to prop up the exhausted driftwood-coloured trunk of an even older lavender bush. Every border was edged with Edwardian barley sugar, every path overgrown with herb robert and dandelion.

At the other end, beneath an arch thick with white pre-Raphaelite rambler roses, two or three little stone steps offered access to the lower garden. There the plantings seemed to stretch off forever, though they could only be a metre or two deep. Everything was tall, packed, dense, too entangled to walk through and quickly changing its nature from tended to untended. At the centre of this confusion the second lawn lay small and silent, like a woodland pool covered in flat green waterweed. The light fell in at steep angles between the surrounding houses. To one side a black and white cat sat next to some elegantly broken plant pots, licking its paws in the dusty resonant sunshine.

'Hello,' whispered Victoria.

A few aimless piano notes issued from the open window of a house further down the hill. The cat, after regarding her briefly, moved off.

Later, something made her stand on the kitchen steps, thoughtfully opening and closing the back door in a kind of rehearsal of its possibilities. Part of her wished that she had left it stuck, because she didn't want her garden as a gift bestowed, a favour offered, by Ossie. He had puzzled her all the time he was in the house. It was the cough. It was that she would never believe a thing he said. Even more it was his softly weathered skin, which did not resemble any material she knew and was beautiful in its way. She knew that beautiful was the right word for both father and daughter in their different ways; but it was also the wrong word, especially for the father's skin, and his voice so cocky one minute, so quiet and defeated by age the next, every so often both at once.

These kinds of thoughts went in and out of her head as she opened and shut the door. But the thought she couldn't relinquish was that Ossie had been in the house before; that he was, in fact, more familiar with it than Victoria's mother had been, than Victoria would ever be.

7

Deep Roads

Sunday morning, some days later.

As if completing an argument begun somewhere else, Victoria woke suddenly, thinking: anyway, ownership is an odd thing.

It was 5 a.m. Light filled the bedroom, rebroadcast from a very blue sky by the facades of the buildings across the road. She lay for a minute or two, listening to dogs barking at the far end of the high street and shivering with a delighted sense of all the space that now belonged to her:

The space inside the house. The space inside the street outside the house. The space inside the town around the street, the space inside the land around the town. Ownership gave her access to this vast translucent Russian doll of geography, stretching away all light and air, all new, all hers. She stopped at every landing window on the way downstairs. So what, she thought, if someone else unstuck the back door? The garden, with its ridiculous as yet unflowered hollyhocks, was hers. In the hall she found a pair of walking boots – a good brand, barely used. She put them on and went straight out.

Old paths behind the houses, tucked between hawthorn, sloe and bramble. A metal kissing gate interrupting a vanished hedgerow. Dog walkers appeared and disappeared, rarely closer than the middle distance. It was already warm. Every field, she discovered, had its pylons; every field had its pool. The pylons made a curious muted ringing clatter, like a bottling plant heard on the wind from three miles away. As for the water, some of it looked shallow, some looked deep. Some pools were graced with a pylon of their own, or with a couple of willows or cows; some featured a single moorhen stalking about. When you got close, they all had a recent quality; they were as beachless as if water had been poured into a grassy hollow the night before. They glittered in the glassy light.

A mile and a half from the town, where the land fell away abruptly into wooded north-facing slopes, she heard a man calling 'Moya!' – or it might have been 'Viya!' – into the trees. His voice was light, with some Midlands intonation unfamiliar to her. It had inviting tenor tones; it was cajoling, never peremptory, yet intrinsically demanding. He might have been addressing a woman or a dog. Perhaps not a child. For a moment, Victoria thought she saw him, not far off, moving easily away from her downslope, hands in pockets. She waved.

'Isn't it a lovely morning?'

No answer; and though she was forced to follow him, because that was the way the path went, curving first through oak, birch and holly, then ash and wych elm, she never caught up. From then on she would hear him every so often, near or far, summoning his reluctant consort from some overgrown bell pit or abandoned lime kiln. The woods were soft. Sluggish brooks dissected them at random. Beneath sphagnum and hart's tongue and crusts of dead leaves over black mud lay the contorted and paradoxical strata from which, for almost a thousand years, the local profits had been gouged. Coal for the Cistercians in their abbey; then limestone; then iron and clays for the ironmasters, with their Silicon Valley rhetoric, their promises of a future, their estates called Paradise or Heaven. Further down, above the old railway line, a thin waterfall spattered at the back of a quarry; light fluoresced electrically in the moss. There were none of the picturesque qualities you might expect. So when she heard the word 'Mira!' spoken quite close and from behind her, Victoria shivered and went home, where she ate cornflakes and fell asleep quite suddenly on the sofa.

When she woke, it was early afternoon. She had been dreaming of something, she couldn't remember what.

The first thing she heard was 'Come here!', spoken just outside the house.

She jumped up and stared into the street. Nothing. The air had turned humid; it smelled of petrol. She couldn't see anyone. She went to the back door, but that was stuck again.

'Moya?' Then a pause and, moving away: '*Voya!*'

A lot later, just before closing time, just to finish off a puzzling day, she thought she heard the voice once more, calling from directly across the road then drifting away to be absorbed into the general noise of the town nightlife. She was sorting her mother's things, a box of dolls here, there a pile of photographs in paper wallets from the 1970s, overexposed faces spilled over the front-room floor. She crossed to the window but there was nothing to see. All she could hear was the pubs emptying and refilling one last time like peristalsis up and down the street. 'Coom 'ere. Coom 'ere.' Would Viya or Moira come back to him? Who was punishing who? It was a hard one to answer. Victoria tried to imagine the dog – a Patterdale terrier, a Parsons – rough-coated, muddy and stubborn – still tireless after a day in the woods; but in the end only succeeded in visualising some hapless rural goth, basically thin but with a layer of soft fat beneath very white skin, for whom ignoring the sound of her own name called over the road from the doorway of a pub was a weekly protest against the tie that binds. Victoria shivered, closed the shutters, tidied the photographs. She emailed Shaw.

'I can feel all the distinct spaces around me. The space in the loft, the space in the cellar, the space on the first-floor landing, which is different not just in shape but in silence and resonance, and the way the air moves to the space on the third-floor landing. I love this place! I sit on the stairs and read in the sunshine. I've got so much silence here. I can't get over to you how much of a relief that is after London!'

Then she added:

'I wish they were all a bit less energetic, though.'

Victoria pushed her mother's furniture around the bedroom until the arrangement suited her. She knew she would never be able to live with the shelf units, which boasted florid lip-like frontal curves; when she pulled them down, plaster fell away from the old rawl plugs like damp talcum. She put her finger in one of the holes and felt a small electric pulse, the slightest flicker of life, as if the house was speaking to her. It spoke in other ways too. The floorboards needed attention. The fuse box continued to switch off everything but the ground-floor ring main just as it got dark. A persistent leak in the bathroom – something to do with the supply to the bidet – dripped through the floor and into the kitchen. Wood-boring beetle had colonised the joists and, further up the house, could be heard counting down at night like some old, heavily specialised kind of clock.

'Your wall plates are gone,' the carpenter explained. 'Oak this old, it's either like iron or wet sand. Still, we'll save what we can.'

The same morning, scaffolding went up for the roof work.

For a month now, the house would be full of trades. They had set up shop. Like the carpenter they were men in their fifties with outdoor faces and integrated skill sets. They came recommended – often by each other, or by Pearl's father, whose curiously used-up air they shared – and were accompanied by an occult personal baggage of religion, alcohol, noise-induced hearing loss, bad chests and a significant motorcycle accident aged thirty; a lifetime of concussion and breakages, of arteries stented just in time and knee problems the mechanics of which their GP had never quite been able to explain. They were generally garrulous but, underneath it, shy. They would always have a cup of tea, but they brought their own sandwiches or at lunchtime wandered down the street to an old-fashioned tea room called Brenda's where they sat staring about them in their bib-and-brace chainsaw trousers like aged toddlers in a buggy.

'I bet no one's used that bidet for years,' Victoria told the plumber. 'To be honest,' she was forced to admit, 'so far I've only ever cleaned my shoes in it. I mean, what use have I got for a bidet?' The plumber stared at her, and then away again, as if thinking of something suddenly.

'Oh dear,' Victoria said. 'Was that too much information?'

They didn't seem to fit properly in a house. They could build one but they didn't know what to do after that, except go and build another one. She caught them staring into a tool chest or the gap beneath the floorboards, a blank look in their watery eyes as if they'd forgotten for a second not what they were doing but who they were. The roofer was in his sixties and ready to retire. His name was Steve, he liked music, pubs and smoking. His voice was phlegmy with roll-ups and whisky; his speech reflective. His wife was a charge nurse. His forearms were deeply tanned, sleeved in tattoos so faded

Victoria couldn't tell which heavy-metal bands they had been designed to commemorate. She knew the day had begun when she heard Steve on the top stage of the scaffolding: up there you could see right across the county to Clee Hill, while the constant breeze blew dust off a litter of discarded tiles, lumps of mortar and half-empty sealant containers. It had become her habit to make him a cup of tea, clamber out of the bedroom window with it, then carry it carefully up the final ladder to the roof. She was proud of this accomplishment, and liked to think Steve respected her for it.

In return, he told her about his van, which was off the road just now because it needed a vital but quite ordinary part. This item had to come direct from Japan. You were seven weeks on the waiting list, he said; then it was seven hundred quid straight out of your pocket. 'They assemble them in Spain, but the supply chain's so tightly managed they can't take a part off the production line. They have to ship it to you separate, from Japan.'

'Seven hundred pounds?' Victoria said.

'Seven. Hundred. Fucking. Quid,' he agreed, more in wonder than anger.

After a while he indicated the roof, as if all along it had been a subset of their conversation. 'Don't you worry, though. You'll not need to do this again. This'll outlast both of us now. In my case that won't be hard.'

He placed the palm of his hand flat on the tiles. 'Quick to warm up,' he said, 'slow to cool down. And if it's like it was yesterday today, that'll be just perfect for me. Just perfect.' He pronounced the first syllable 'purr', leaving a noticeable pause between that and the second. 'I'll be able to finish up.' Then, looking across the rooftops towards Birmingham: 'Of course, as a country we used to do our own engineering.'

71

The day he left, she climbed the ladder to give him his tea and his money and found that he had already cleared the top stage. All the rubbish was gone. On one side you saw the lines of neatly relaid tiles. On the other, the town fell away — shining, busy and cheerful — towards the Severn. That morning everything struck her as so *ordered*, as if Steve had calmly repaired not just the roof but the rest of the world too. Now he sat on a tool bag in the sunshine turning the pages of a paperback book; which he closed and offered to her.

'Ever read this?' he said. 'A lot are, now. A lot are reading it.'

It was a gesture Victoria couldn't understand, one which she would think of later as having somehow broken the bond between them. What she wanted was for him to take his tea and congratulate her, as he always did: 'Purr-fect! Not a drop spilled!' She didn't want a book, especially not *The Water-Babies*, so she stood there offering it back to him, unsure what to say next but finally managing: 'I've already got this, thanks. It was my mother's.'

'Keep it anyway, pet,' the roofer said. 'You never know.'

Nothing could be made of the tone in which he had spoken. Later, when she looked for her mother's copy, she couldn't remember where she'd put it.

Victoria found a less depressing way down into the Gorge, then followed the Severn round the heel of the town into the maze of the sixteenth-century religious quarter. From there she made her way steeply back up through Friars and St Mary Gate to Pearl's café. It was a Wednesday and everything else was closed. Early afternoon had fixed the old man and his daughter in their places like figures in a symbolic painting, the one hunched eternally over his meal, the debris of which had spread to the table around the plate; the other behind the counter, with her damp cloth, her still life of cupcakes under glass and her long-distance stare. Everything had a rare clarity, but also a sense of being hardened in time.

'Hello!' Victoria said, slamming the door shut. 'Cake and a cup of tea, please!' She felt that a responsibility had been placed on her to wake them from their daze, set them in motion. 'I came up from the river. It's such good exercise! I went out behind Peckforton Hall and along by Pale Meadows. Don't you think that's a wonderful name?'

They turned slowly to look at her.

'For a lane?' she said. 'Pale Meadows?'

'You want to be careful at night down there,' said the old man.

'I'll just find a seat,' said Victoria, as if most of them were taken.

Whatever the day was doing elsewhere, a curious kind of light – in which several colours were represented but only faintly – came and went the other side of the steamy windows of the café. When the glass cleared after the lunchtime rush, you found yourself looking out onto a car park, a pay-and-display machine and a yellow gritting bin like a plastic toy, the last two items of which had the air of being ineptly photoshopped onto a previous landscape. Sometimes the old man would park his car out there, a bleached mid-range Toyota with taxi markings on the side. He would leave it in the rain for days, go out in it suddenly after receiving a phone call, then return to eat three sausages and mashed potato with onion gravy and complain about the things people wanted him to do. His eyes – red-rimmed, wary, wet in the corner, lids as soft and worn as an old wallet – made him appear vague and indifferent. He was always blowing his nose.

'I hope I've closed the door properly for you,' Victoria told him.

He watched her closely for a moment, then, instead of answering, slid his plate to one side, turned his upper body away from her at the waist, and faced the wall. He began to eat as if he was famished, bending low over the table and shovelling the food up into his mouth with both knife and fork.

'Pay him no attention,' Pearl advised.

'I came out to get away from the builders,' Victoria said. 'They're all quite odd.'

Pearl smiled down at the counter. 'The seven dwarves of trades, that lot. Steve, Dozy, Beaky, Mick and Titch.'

'You know them then?'

'What you've to ask yourself,' Pearl said, 'is who don't I know.'

The old man dropped his knife and fork onto his plate. 'You don't know how to count,' he said. 'I can say that without fear of contradiction.'

She came out from behind the counter, snatched the plate away and began to wipe up the food he had spilled. 'He doesn't want you to call him *Chris*,' she said over her shoulder to Victoria, as if they were alone in the café having another conversation entirely. '*Chris* isn't the name he *wants*. He wants you to call him what that lot at Kinver call him. What do they call you, Dad? What is it they call you, when you're out driving them all the hours God sends?' He made a sudden frightful face at her, and she laughed. 'Is it Wee Ossie? Is that what they call you?'

'Anyway, I think Pale Meadows is a wonderful name for a street,' Victoria said.

'But do you know what it means?' Pearl said. She gave the table an angry final wipe, then moved away before Victoria could answer.

'You want to be careful down Pale Meadows at night,' the old man repeated.

His eyes were the oldest, most used-up part of him. Yet back in the blue of the iris something still glittered patiently, and you wondered if it was in the thin bone of the orbits too. On a rainy afternoon the café seemed to talk to itself via eighties and nineties music set at a thoughtful volume, and his daughter stared out of the windows whispering, 'It's been non-stop all week in here.'

The weather held. Victoria took longer walks. The house evolved behind her: every time she returned, something had changed. The stairwell, replastered and painted in Easy Neutrals, sang with light. Warm air topped up the garden in the evenings, while she stood quietly barefoot on the lawn – wondering what changes to make, listening idly to the drinkers in the streets, the dogs barking at the edges of the town – and watched the flowers fade like chalky neons into the dark. One by one, the trades left. The central-heating engineer, who kept himself to himself and would start only when all the others had finished, was the last to go. The scaffolding had already come down, across a morning, pole after pole ringing on the bed of the waiting lorry like the parts of an experimental xylophone. Feeling a little lonely, she crossed the road and snapped pictures on her phone. Because I'm determined to enjoy my life, she thought, perhaps for the first time ever.

The facade, done in pale grey with a lime-white trim, shone in the lunchtime light – a lively effect, though it threw into contrast the seared-looking Midlands brick of number 91, the other half of the original structure. Victoria wasn't yet convinced by her choices. They were correct rather than bold: the only risk was that these colours would live together happily – or happily enough – ever after, but all that time look as if they yearned quietly for one of the nicer streets around Clapham Common.

Still, she thought: It's my house. Perfect!

At this, the door of number 91 banged open abruptly and Pearl the waitress emerged. She was wearing a white T-shirt and stonewashed boyfriend jeans; a dry-cleaner's bag containing her work overall was folded in the crook of one arm. She waved, turned to lock the front door behind her, then, after unlocking it again to call inside, 'Don't forget to bring them over later then, else he'll have a fit!', came and stood next to Victoria; who was too surprised to speak.

'So it looks nice now,' she offered.

'Do you think so?' said Victoria. And then, shyly: 'The front door's "London Clay".'

'Is that what they'd call it down there.'

'I didn't know you lived next to me. You didn't once let on.'

'We don't,' Pearl said. The house, she explained, had belonged to Ossie's father, who had been known as Old Ossie, and who ran it as a pub. The whole building had been a pub until he died and his son split it back in two again. 'Then it was used as storage until Ossie sold your mother the other half.' She smiled at Victoria's expression. 'Oh yes, I knew your mum all right. We were close enough at one time, me and her. We swam. We swam a lot. Mostly at the indoor pool, but sometimes I could get her to go outdoors too.'

Victoria stared. 'My God,' she said.

'She was a strong swimmer, that one.'

'I can't imagine it.'

'Well she was,' said the waitress. 'She turned out all right, your mum.'

76

After this inexplicable judgement, there didn't seem to be anything for Victoria to contribute. All she could do was shade her eyes and study the front of number 91, where slack grey curves of net curtain transected the ground-floor windows at odd angles and a faint but definite darkening a foot or two below the gutters gave the effect of a high-water mark forty feet in the air, as if the street had been flooded at a time when it was much lower than the top of the hill. Quick white clouds had appeared in the sky above the dipped roofline; against them stalks of willowherb could be seen, silhouetted, flourishing, vigorous. Eventually Victoria shook her head. The only substance in which she could imagine her mother swimming was gin and tonic.

'I had no idea,' she said.

'Not much to look at it, is it? Everywhere down this street has been a pub at one time or another. We were in here until I was ten, but when Old Ossie died we went to live with that lot down in the Gorge.' She gestured vaguely north, to where the high street pivoted into Woolpit Road then toppled swiftly away between new-build and sparse woods towards the Severn. 'That was originally a pub too. Publicanism – always the preferred trade in that family,' she announced, as if she wasn't a member of it. 'A lot of good it's done us,' she decided.

The wind rose a little, bringing smells of fried food and the faint sound of jackdaws keeping watch from the ruins of Geoffrey de Lacy's keep. To get some idea of its own strength, perhaps, it rustled about in the dry-cleaner's bag on Pearl's arm. She looked down absently and then away again. 'You know what we should do?' she went on. '*We* should get out and swim! You and me!'

Victoria shivered.

'I don't think so,' she said. 'I hate water.'

Ashamed by her own vehemence, she was forced to add, 'I'm sorry, I didn't mean that to sound so abrupt!'

Pearl only looked away down the high street, smiling quietly to herself. She waved and called, 'Orright then?' to someone Victoria couldn't see. Then she advised: 'You want to take things more as you find them. I've often said as much to your mum.'

'This weekend I was thinking of buying roses for the garden,' Victoria said, then, before she could think, added: 'Would you like to come?'

They got in the Fiat at ten the next Saturday morning so that Victoria could drive it briskly along the lanes north-east of the town, somewhere in the maze of which they expected to find Childe Beckwith, a sixteenth-century manor house rebuilt in the early 1830s to have Greek revival stylings. They arrived closer to noon than eleven, and the car park was already crowded. Bright sunshine glittered off the chrome of last year's SUVs, spraying up into dark surrounding growths of yew. Among the trees silent, determined children ran about in bands of three or four, attracted by any kind of stream or bog. It was the pure heritage experience. You paid, you bought the guide, you extracted yourself from the gift shop in the old stableyard and were instantly steeped in someone else's idea of history – ninety hectares of parkland featuring two artificial lakes, extensive woods and a garden temple with Ionic columns. Long lawns dropped away around the ancient cedars; the formal paths became mossy and quiet underfoot, leading only into thoughtful copses; while behind the main building the sandstone steps and flags took on a hollow sound as you walked by.

'It's lovely to get out,' Pearl said, 'but I'm not sure about all these urns.'

Though the present-day Beckwiths had long since ceased to regard the estate as an asset – looking instead towards their interests in Hong Kong, Palo Alto and Dubai – they maintained out of nostalgia the family's traditional business, still contained in two acres of walled garden patrolled famously by 'the Childe peacocks'. There, as a foil to the constant drama – the uncontrolled, essentially tragic abundance – of the roses, they had opted for a radiant formalism. Each scrupulously tended bed resembled a supermarket aisle for blooms, accessed via arches at either end and confined by long, low, fiercely geometrical box hedges. Along one radial the colours stepped ingeniously from white to yellow; halfway down the next you were surprised by how the faintest blush of pink, spurting without warning into blood hues, exhausted itself so quickly to purple. At the centre a long slim rectangular pool lay in its warm limestone surround, watched over by matching stone benches. There was, day by day, 'a riot of colour' – musk hybrids looking like something loosely folded out of faded paper; banked masses of species rose, dainty and frail. The Beckwiths, at ease with the possibilities of a fully mapped *Rosa* genome, anticipated new forms of cultivation – engineered colours, novel scents, expanded markets. In the meantime, everywhere you went in the garden you pushed your way past swags of a determined old off-white rambler (named Vivienne Dulac in 1852 but known to family insiders since 1979 as 'the Iron Lady').

It was quite as much a show as the brochure claimed: yet Victoria felt less excited than subdued. Finding so many of her favourites in one place seemed to overpower then depress her. Crammed into the invisible cages of the planting, they had the look of captive animals – territorially stressed but at the same time compelled to lean up against one another for comfort and support.

'It's a zoo,' she said.

Then, reading from the brochure: '"Shropshire Lass, a fitting consort for our popular rambler, Shropshire Lad. New for this year."' She stared around helplessly. 'I haven't a clue what to get.'

'Lunch. Let's get lunch.'

'People like this always kept a private zoo.'

The tea room served a scone and local cheese – with wild garlic pickle made to the estate's own seventeenth-century recipe – on the terrace, where a whippet the colour of latte wandered disconsolately between spindly Italianate iron tables. It wasn't easy to find somewhere to sit. Later, thundery light swung in, flat to the flagstones, to which it lent a sullen gloss; and off in the south the low hills slumped on an overheated skyline under architectural-looking cloud. By then Pearl was growing bored. Eating her lunch like a burger, she had spilled pickle on her bleached denim dungarees. She had worked hard to interest the whippet in the remains of the scone, but managed only to make it nervous. It stared at her as if she had tried to undermine one of its most carefully internalised moral imperatives, then mooched off and was sick near someone's feet.

'He doesn't like the heat, poor thing!' she called over to them; and aside to Victoria: 'They'll be off now. That's the way to clear a table. Dog sick. I'm just the same with the smell of sweet peas.'

'I'll go and pay,' Victoria suggested.

'We've already paid, pet. You go and pick your roses while I have a wander about.'

'Are you sure?'

'If you miss me I'll be at your little car. Or down by the lakes.'

But they missed one another in the car park, and at both lakes. For half an hour Victoria hiked about in the woodland. Every hill or valley looked like an idea of itself developed from some barely disguised digital model. The footpaths draped themselves along the contours in a perfect imitation of three dimensions, from the Ionic temple to the Chinese bridge and thence to the Orangery. There was no sign of Pearl in any of these places. Neither was she to be found in the Elizabeth Berrington Gallery, lost in thought among the collections of silver toilet services, woodcuts of rolling winter plough and lively contemporary bronzes of hares with exaggerated ears.

When Victoria did track her down, it was to the centre of the rose garden. She was lounging beside the rectangular pool with her shoes off, her feet wet and her legs stretched out in front of her, smiling ambiguously at a wall covered in creamy pink centifolias. Behind her, a diminishing perspective of standard roses blazed like lamps; while a man in a tweed coat bent down to pat a box hedge as if congratulating it. 'This is solid!' he called to someone they couldn't see. 'This'll have been here a few years!' From two gardens away, one of the Childe peacocks screamed in glee. Some kind of exotic clematis, white with a purple stripe, had woven itself into the centifolias.

Pearl shaded her eyes and blinked up at Victoria. 'It reminds me of being seven,' she said, 'when the whole world looked like this.' She sat up and dipped her feet in the water. Glittering eddies whirled off across the surface. 'Don't you remember when everything looked like this?'

Victoria shrugged. 'People always think that.' She could see her own face in the pool, of course; and beneath that something overgrown.

'Tell me you haven't been wading about in here,' she said.

There was some idea that they should spend the evening at one of the pubs down by the Severn, but by the end of the afternoon all of this had left her tired and in some way anxious. So she dropped the waitress off in town and went home to eat baked beans on toast and write an email to Shaw.

'You never saw so many roses in one place!

'As for Pearl, I'm not sure you'd get her. She's her own woman, Rosie the Riveter meets Jacqueline Kennedy and they talk about everything in the world but men. I quite like that. Then again she's a bit of a mystery, I don't know who she is.' Admitting this to herself made her consider for a moment before going on: 'My latest discovery? Her whole family used to live next door! I suppose I don't know who any of them are, really. But they knew my mum – or so they say. And here I am, alone in a new town, so what am I supposed to do but make a friend?

'Anyway,' she finished, 'in the end I didn't buy anything. I couldn't make up my mind.'

Then she pressed delete and went to sleep.

8

'Nothing's Ever Good Enough for Our Pearl'

People talked in loud voices all day outside the house.

They bustled out of their cars, slammed the doors, greeted each other in unison an octave apart: 'Orright?' The subsequent exchange often took place under the auspices of saying goodbye. Over before it began, it nevertheless seemed difficult to complete. No one was anxious to let anyone go.

'Well, cheers, love, see you Saturday. Is he? No, no, he's not coming. Not on the Monday anyway ...'

Twenty minutes later they were still there, still accepting but postponing a drink, still repeating everything twice, still reminding one another at intervals that they mustn't stop because they were off to the Top Time Hotel, or over to Chirk to deliver a door; or because they were casting the summer performance of *The Tempest* in the leisure centre down at Pale Meadows, the usual story of incompetence and under-commitment on all sides. Every time a conversation wound down, it began again. When there was no one else to talk to, they shouted into their phones. Victoria loved it. She loved the liveliness of it. She still heard 'Moya!' and 'Voya!' in the mornings when the soft mist in the back gardens was beginning to fill with sunshine: but more often now at night, during the endless phone-in radio show of closing time, the pure, self-involved rage of which was absorbed and smoothed out by that light, persuasive call. When the voice moved away, you had the illusion that the drinkers followed. But 'Voya!' and 'Orright?', she thought, dispelled each other: somehow representing moods that cancelled out. The knack of 'Orright?' lay in pitching it as if the other person was at the far end of the high street, even when they were three feet away. It should sound brusque, cheerful, with a little musical lilt.

When she mentioned these and other conclusions to Pearl in the car one day, Pearl looked irritated and alert for a moment, as if something had puzzled her. Then she laughed.

'Go on!' she said. 'The things you think!'

'Does your father own a dog?' Victoria asked. She wasn't sure why.

It was a Sunday afternoon. The intention had been to drive down to Ludlow, calling at Shrewsbury and Church Stretton to scour the charity shops and antiques markets. They were waiting at a rural crossroads in fine rain, while, at the next crossroads along, lines of cars made their way into an empty field and bumped across the grass. Pearl stared out of her side window into the nearest hedge. 'That old bugger?' she said, as if she might find her father there, among the faeces, beer cans and discarded plastic bags. 'What use would a *dog* be to him?'

'I suppose I wondered, that's all.'

The waitress shrugged. 'He can barely take care of himself. None of them can. How would he take care of a thing like that?'

'It's only a dog, after all. It's a pet. Are you all right?'

'Of course I'm all right.'

Things eased up until they got to Ludlow, where the alleys and pubs were rammed with Barbour jackets and Boden frocks. 'It's a bit *Wicker Man* round here,' Pearl noted. 'Look at that

84

pair!' This, of a west-London couple who had clearly arrived in
a 2013 Land Rover Discovery that very morning with exactly
the same purpose as her, seemed wide of the mark: but since
the Childe Beckwith visit, she had an opinion on everything.
Her concern was to develop Victoria's taste. Her eye for a
bargain was ruthless. In the antiques markets of the county she
would reluctantly approve an Ercol table, but never any kind
of chalk-painted furniture, especially if it claimed to be French.
At Oxfam she revealed a keen personal investment in clothing
from the 1940s to mid 1980s, mix-and-matching items across
the whole period – as if it was indeed a period and represented
a single, logical semiotic sweep.

Though enjoyable, expeditions like these led to no great intimacy between the two women. They had a good time. They
always went home with plenty of things. But when Victoria
asked about her mother, Pearl would only grin wryly – as if the
question had been self-evidently rhetorical, with implications
they could both enjoy – and slowly push her empty glass across
the table.

Then she would lean back and say, 'Another one of those,
I think.'

At the end of the day, none the wiser, Victoria would drop
her off at the western entrance to the Gorge, where she lived
in a graceless-looking and repeatedly flooded terrace not fifteen
yards from the river.

'The bloody Severn,' as Pearl put it: 'your waterway of commerce, romance and mystery.' Originally, Welsh for most of
its course, it had flowed north and emptied into the sea near
present-day Chester. Of its progress after that, accounts varied.
In one, baulked by glaciation from the north, it was envisaged
as tunnelling out beneath the ice. Another model, Victoria

found, required that it feed a vast meltwater reservoir, which, overflowing catastrophically, left behind the vestigial lake now known as the Aqualate Mere: the largest natural body of water in the Midlands yet, eerily, nowhere more than a yard deep. Either way, the river made good its escape and sped away deeper into England, scouring furiously down to the Silurian bedrock until it had dug out the Gorge.

As a result – the Gorge scarps being so ripe with coal, iron ore and friable, thinly bedded limestones, with tars and fireclays to be had down at the south-eastern end where things began to level out – the Industrial Revolution was inevitable. In the beginning you could scoop up these resources from shallow pits; you could get at them with spades. Later, more investment would be necessary – agricultural profits parlayed into horse-drawn railways and long-wall mines, cheap labour shipped in from Ireland, squatter communities tumbling downhill towards the wharves at the base of the town. At the height of coal production they were shipping 100,000 tons a year: manufactured products followed. Brick and tile, glass both broad and bottle, kitchen goods. Fabulous castings for cannon and steam engines. Twenty tons per barge of clay tobacco pipes, pig iron and porcelain.

Victoria learned all this from the books in her mother's boxes. She sat in the sun in her garden. She made soup and salad. She lay in bed at night with a fine rain on the window and read that the Severn was a considerable river even now, the longest in Britain, bent like a paperclip since its encounter with the Devensian ice, turned back on itself to debouch a hundred miles south and east of its source in the Cambrian Mountains. It was a roundabout trip, just to arrive at the Bristol Channel: you don't expect natural engineering on that scale a mile from your house. One early morning seventeen thousand years or so after the river took control of its own journey, she sat thoughtfully on a memorial bench a mile or two behind the town, where the landscape chamfered off for its sudden descent into the Gorge.

Hawthorn saplings dotted the convex slope immediately in front of her. A little further down, everything vanished into a vast tranquil layer of mist, flat for miles until it encountered the woods on the other side of the valley, where you could see a glasshouse shining, farms and churches white, yellow and brown emerging along the contour. The mist was nearly the colour of milk, it was almost like a liquid until you noticed how it rolled and shifted against the sides of the valley. West and north, it opened out all the way to the horizon, dazzling under the sun, transforming the whole Shropshire Plain into an estuary.

Deep beneath, you sensed, the Gorge was still a work in progress; while the Severn – now a contraflow, a river beneath a river – whirled and eddied along with the energy of its own weight and depth. You would always wonder what might emerge from the mist, the future or the past. In the end, she thought, only vast sweeps of time would count, whether you were looking backward or forward – indeed, if you could tell which was which. There were no trees or roads or buildings down there. It was too soon or too late. Victoria imagined a dim light, diffusing thinly across both ancient and freakishly new forms of the landscape, which were strewn about without sense.

Puzzled by these ideas, because she couldn't tell where they had come from, she shivered and turned away; and not long later came across the waitress, waist-deep and naked in one of the pools in the fields above the power station. 'Over here!' Pearl called. 'Come on! Come in!' They waved at one another until Victoria was close enough to bend down and swirl her fingers in the water.

'Too cold for me,' she concluded. 'What a lovely morning though! I saw the valley full of fog, but the sun's beginning to shift it now.'

'Your mum would have been in here like a shot,' Pearl complained.

She began to wade ashore, her body smooth and muscular, her hair, recently done chemical blonde, slicked back and flat to her skull. She resembled a late adolescent in a 1930s Kodak print – strong-boned, sly, full of life and the secret about life everyone else already knew. For a moment something seemed to cling to her shoulders like a caul of thin fabric, white with air in the folds, transparent where it touched the skin; Victoria – who felt that the sky above the Gorge, though clear, was somehow confusing her – couldn't tell what.

'Aren't you cold?' she said.

'Why would I be cold?' And then, 'Mind the nettles!'

The pool was scruffy, of irregular shape, thirty or forty feet in diameter, ruffled a little by a breeze Victoria didn't quite feel. A pylon towered above it, clicking and buzzing. In the centre a few bereft-looking rushes with bleached leaves leaned together their feathery heads. An old willow, falling across one corner years ago, had sent up sturdy vertical branches from its half-submerged core ever since. Despite this history the pool seemed new, as if the clear water had seeped up from deep in the ground overnight and quickly filled some old hollow. It lacked boundaries: the surrounding pasture simply slipped beneath its surface, and in the shallows a handful of bright star-shaped yellow flowers could be seen living the submerged life as easily as they had lived in air. Further off lay a wire fence and then a blackthorn thicket, behind which the light sprayed up into the sky from the woods and the mist in the Gorge.

Pearl looked around proprietorially. 'Say what you want about Old Ossie,' she boasted, 'he had me paddling in every one of these spots before I was four. I own all this.'

'What *was* my mother like?' Victoria asked.

'She loved a good time.'

'You say that. But I just don't remember her that way. She was all nerves.' When the waitress didn't answer but only smiled as always, Victoria dipped her hands in the pool again and decided: 'You would literally never get me in here.' She looked down at the water's edge, at her own reflection and down past it to her white fingers among the submerged yellow flowers, and saw no reason to apologise for that.

'In the end I will,' Pearl promised. 'Because I never fail.'

'Aren't you going to dry yourself?'

At this suggestion, Pearl stopped and looked up as if she had heard something unexpected among the faded grey spars and glassy insulators of the pylon. 'Scabby great thing,' she murmured companionably after a moment, perhaps to Victoria; perhaps to the pylon itself, the way you might talk to an animal you liked. Then she went on gathering her clothes from where she had strewn them between its concrete feet, shaking her head over each item as she took it up and saying, 'I really wonder why I bought any of this'; and, 'I'd kill for two slices of toast with butter on it, and have it brought to me for a change.'

'You're not really a girl, are you?' Victoria brought herself to say.

Pearl looked away shyly and down at the water.

'Then I don't know what else I am,' she said. 'What else would I be?'

★

Their outings continued. They drove all along the Borders into Wales. They visited the gardens of Powys Castle and ate ice cream at the Devil's Bridge. Everywhere they went, Pearl sat up in the front seat of the Fiat like someone's grandmother, describing things as if Victoria couldn't see them too. They read out to one another the signs they saw. Fun Ride. The Grosvenor Chippery. Frolic Street. They had their lunch in garrison towns from Regency romances, Llangollen, Welshpool, Newtown, Builth Wells, places you've heard of but never been, mapped in 1812 and then forgotten. Hypnotised by light slanting through trees in stripes, they hallucinated lorries like coloured boxes at the top of a hill, crows with a black muscular stride, flat earth under some vast clouds. Blackened spires. Sunny dips and lifts, dogs barking in houses and gardens and outside shops, mystical June weather on hillsides, architectures of rain and sunshine, surreal tractor rallies in the middle of nowhere—

'Look out!' cried Pearl.

Someone's brand-new motorcycle, missing a corner on the A458, had rammed itself instead into the ivy bank at the side of the road.

Fifty yards away with his back to the wreck, which now lay ticking and buckled and contracting in a pool of its own fluids, its owner stood smoking hard and staring into the river below. He was OK, his friends said, he was fine. He was lucky enough, they emphasised, to have got away with it. But it had been a fucking stupid thing to do, and he knew it, and as a consequence none of them wanted to get too near him. They walked about stiffly, creaking in their leathers, helmets under their arms like heads, patient with him but wanting to be off and enjoying the rest of the day. They cleared some shattered plastic off the carriageway. With the toes of their boots they explored the gouges he had made in the recently renewed tarmac surface, all the while casting guarded looks at their own machines, intact for now, perfect in all colours, propped up in a shiny row in the lay-by.

'Thanks for stopping,' they said, 'anyway.'

'That poor boy,' Pearl mourned later. 'If I'm not careful I'll spoil my whole afternoon thinking about him.'

Victoria considered the smoked yellow ceiling of whichever unreconstructed seaside pub the Fiat had reached at its apogee, and to cheer her up admitted:

'I felt old enough to be their mother.'

But this, which wasn't entirely true anyway, didn't satisfy either of them; they diverted themselves by watching a man carry drinks on a tray to his children messing about in the sun outside. 'Look at him,' Pearl invited, with the air of someone pursuing an inflammatory argument. 'Root beer. He shouldn't have let them order that. It always sounds interesting when you're a kid but it tastes like Germolene. Now he'll get his phone out. See? Selfie to the ex, to prove they have a nicer time with him than her.'

'It's just a phone, you know. People just have phones.'

'Do they, though? Ossie wouldn't know what to do with one. None of our lot would.' Then she added: 'That poor boy, with his beautiful motorbike.'

'What's wrong?' Victoria said.

'Nothing is wrong.'

'You're not bored?'

'No,' Pearl said. 'What do you think is wrong? Only my life.'

'Oh your *life*,' said Victoria. 'Come on then.'

They exhausted the charity shops. Victoria bought deco side plates, Pearl a kind of old lady's blouse, violet, with a big bow. Holding it up against herself: 'This can be the core of my Margaret Thatcher look. Everyone should have one of these. I'm not saying pussy bow. I'm not. I'm not saying those words.'

At five o'clock, the sun went in, the temperature fell and a light shower blew in from the sea. They ate chips until it cleared; then all the way back to Shropshire it was sunshine again. By the time Victoria pulled up outside Pearl's house in the Gorge, travel had repaired their mood. They sat on for a while without speaking, until Pearl put her hand over Victoria's and said:

'Why don't you come in for a cup of tea?'

The house – an end-of-terrace originally as spacious though not perhaps quite as tall as Victoria's – had fitted itself tightly into the north bank of the river. Behind it the hillside steepened rapidly through coppiced woodland and old ironmaster estates. Deeper than the rest of the terrace, and with a bleak little parking space on the open side, it stood somehow foursquare and apart; had flooded once every February since 1802 – events that were preserved not as a smell but as something prior to smell, something more fundamental. In the same way, recent layers of fitted carpet and damp wallpaper maintained the record of dead pets, tobacco, takeaway food. A private hotel between the wars, it had lain disused until the construction of Telford New Town saw it divided into bedsitter accommodation for semi-skilled labour. Stuffy with the past yet endlessly restructured, it remained a memorial to disconnected use, a warren of low-ceilinged rooms where the light flowed slowly from wall to wall like silt. Once you had stepped inside and spent a moment in the hall you began to hear televisions in distant rooms, all tuned to different stations.

The two women stood next to each other, suddenly

uncertain what to do next. Looking up the stairs towards a landing she couldn't quite make out, Victoria said: 'It's nice.' She asked if there was a toilet.

'Of course there's a toilet,' Pearl said. 'Of course there is.'

They stared at one another, then Pearl said, 'It's just along that passage. Most homes have one these days. I'll be upstairs.'

The passage, which had plasterboard walls and was stacked with bulky plastic toolboxes of different sizes, led out into a whitewashed yard and thence to an old outside toilet with a rusty cistern high up. It seemed unused. When she had finished, Victoria found her way back to the stairs easily enough; but though she stood on each landing and called out, she couldn't find Pearl or catch anyone's attention.

'Hello?'

She returned to the ground floor and pushed open the door of the first room she came to. It was lit by a single fluorescent tube set in a false ceiling of warped plywood sheets. A very old Labrador lay sleeping just inside the door. Further in, some much smaller animal – a handbag dog with random tufts of hair, its eyes both yearning and foul-tempered – gurned up at her from a decaying rag rug. The room stank of them, then underneath that of acetone, dust and fruity human sweat. In the corner furthest from the door an old-fashioned hospital bed had been set up, adjusted to the partly raised position. On this lay a huge man in a pair of striped cotton pyjamas.

'Hello, dear,' he said. His voice was soft. His feet were bare. He said his name was Andy, and also gave the names of the dogs, which Victoria didn't catch. 'Have you come to see me?'

Hearing these words as though from an earlier, more optimistic phase of its life, the Labrador coughed suddenly and tried to get up, raising its head with some effort and scrabbling exhaustedly with its back feet. As if in response, the other animal began running to and fro in front of the bed, snarling and yelping at Victoria. When she remarked on this, Andy said: 'Oh don't worry, it's quite friendly, it'll go to anyone, that one. When you're shopping it'll go straight in your bag.'

'It doesn't seem to know what it wants,' she said.

Andy didn't look as if he ever went anywhere, although his bed was surrounded by freshly opened boxes of sports shoes. He was pathologically obese, but his feet were small and neat. They had an unused quality, like the feet of a child, and they were in good condition.

'I'll lose them in the end of course,' he said cheerfully when he saw her staring at them.

'I ought to go now,' Victoria said.

'Well, my door's always open.'

The Labrador, redoubling its efforts to lift the front part of its body up off the floor, peed itself copiously.

Not long later she found Pearl sitting on a windowsill on the second-floor landing, drinking from a bottle of Sainsbury's pinot and staring down at the Severn as if she had been waiting all day for something that never came. It didn't seem as if there would be any tea. Twilight was coming on, the water ran oily and purposeful; along the road in both directions the pub microwaves were serving the evening crowd from Telford. Out on the Wharfage a woman in a pale green evening dress hurried past, came back two minutes later, stopped and stared into the middle distance with an expression of rage on her face; suddenly hurried away again.

Pearl said, 'They're all so fucking weird here.' And, when she heard about the fat man: 'Those shoes of his? He says he's going to run a marathon but he doesn't get out of bed!'

'Perhaps he will,' Victoria suggested. 'Perhaps one day he will run a marathon.'

This fetched a look of contempt.

'Don't be a twat,' Pearl advised, 'if you want to get anywhere in this life.' She gave her blank sidelong smile. 'That smell in there? Ketoacidosis, and his favourite book is *Born to Run*? As for the rest of them ...' She shrugged.

'So I like the house,' Victoria said, though she didn't.

'I was hoping you would.'

They passed the bottle between them until it was empty. After a thoughtful silence, Victoria said:

'I think I'd better walk back up the hill. Rather than drive.'

'You do that,' Pearl advised.

She stared down at the Severn. Then, clearly talking to herself: 'Places like this seem nice for an afternoon. After that they're just a lot of history.'

Victoria thought she would say goodbye to Andy, but when she put her head back round his door, she found that she had somehow got the wrong room. This one was smaller, with floor-length maroon velvet curtains tightly drawn. Instead of carpet there was ancient wood-effect lino on the floor; the walls had been painted hastily a long time ago with a single coat of greyish-white emulsion. A number of men sat on sofas and armchairs in the dark, watching US sports TV via satellite, intent yet formless in the glow of a fifty-inch screen.

'Sorry,' she said. And then, raising her voice above the commentary: 'Sorry to disturb you.' Two or three men turned their upper bodies slowly towards her, as though they knew someone was there but couldn't quite make out who. One of them was Steve the roofer, whose face seemed paler now than it had when she brought him his tea every morning on the top stage of the scaffold. Suddenly he was smiling vaguely – the left side of his mouth dragged down – and beginning to get up, one arm outstretched to offer her something.

'It's all right,' Victoria said. 'Sorry.'

There were so many men, she now saw, that not all of them had found seats. They perched on the arms of chairs or sat on the floor with their backs against the wall. There were more of them than any room would be comfortable with. She wasn't sure they had actually noticed her anyway. It was hard to see what sport was being played – something with bouts of movement separated by discussion. She had the impression of teams struggling not so much against one another as with a structure of rules too complicated to understand. 'How the hell are you?' Steve the roofer said. He was offering her *The Water-Babies* again. 'Have you read this? A lot are.'

'I don't want it,' Victoria said, more loudly than she had intended.

'A lot are reading it.'

Going out, she met Pearl's father coming in.

'Do you all live here then?' she heard herself say puzzledly.

'You mustn't listen to any of this lot,' Pearl called down softly from her windowsill. 'They don't know anything.'

Wee Ossie stood on the doorstep and winked.

'Nothing's ever good enough for our Pearl,' he said.

9

The Pool of Tears

Victoria emailed Shaw.

'It's very English Heritage up here. I expect I've told you that before.' As soon as you entered the woods, a dozen foot-paths, signposted at the will of competing conservation bodies, went off busily in all directions, running precipitately into one another, stumbling over brand-new stiles, toppling into an overgrown quarry and out the other side. 'They're offering access. They're offering so much access you don't know where to go for the best.'

In fact, she often ended up beside the pool where she had watched Pearl bathe, and stood there wondering how she could make herself go in. She took off her sandals. She took off some of her clothes then, believing she had heard someone call their dog in the next field along, quickly put them back on again. She was puzzled by herself. On the surface, something seemed to splash and turn lazily; below it, the yellow flowers still lay preserved. They maintained their leaves, and a brittle look, and except for their curious habitat they were quite ordinary. On the way back she heard church bells. The day already had a waxy look, as if some very modern coating had been applied to it at half past seven that morning.

At home she sorted her mother's things: small mounted

prints slotted as tightly as old vinyl into cardboard boxes, top edges furred with dust; an ashtray with horses on it; seashells in a jar. This to go, that to stay. Nothing she could place securely in her childhood, or in some later house.

Among the prints she discovered Gertrude Abercrombie's 1948 oil on masonite *The Red Rook*, in which a set of steps, a simple yet anthropomorphic tree and a chess castle are seen standing, walking and floating respectively on water under a cloudy moonlit sky; and *The Colossi of Memnon, Thebes, One* by Carl Friedrich Heinrich Werner. The only thing she liked was a Felix Kelly capriccio, about eighteen inches on a side. It was already framed. Victorian chimneys confronted self-satisfied Jacobean architecture across a placid lake; trees leaned out from wanly lit surrounding heights. In the background, Wales had somehow been brought too close to Shropshire. She wiped the glass, knocked a nail into new plaster; stood back to look and saw, predictably, her own reflection.

'Why does that always happen?' she wrote to Shaw. And: 'I don't expect you to have time to answer, between the demands of the gig economy and the heady bustle of metropolitan life. Well, here it's been raining since 1301.' Storms had in fact swept up from Powys for a week: after each one, rain slopped off the front gutters of the closing shops, while refreshed jackdaws conducted their meetings in the invisible boardroom between the roofs. It was still summer but it didn't quite feel like it.

'I don't know what to think about Pearl,' she admitted suddenly, as if Shaw was in the room and was someone she could talk to. 'I'm not quite as settled as I thought. I feel as if I'm travelling in opposite directions at once – I arrive too completely then I don't arrive enough.'

★

Two in the morning, woken suddenly, she went downstairs and opened the shutters to look out.

At closing time she had heard all the usual noises, halfway between laughter and animal cries, as teenagers trudged up and down the hill, thin and done up to the nines, from the Long Gallery Bar to the Penistone Hotel, in the hope that a door would swing open in welcome, lights go up, and the night out begin again with a clean sheet. Every evening it took a long time for them to give up and go home. All the usual drunken scuffles had broken out, dying away into uneasy laughter and distance, then returning.

'Fuck off, I'll fucking kill you.'

This offered almost idly, but then, gaining energy: 'I *will* fucking kill you. The fucking lot of you.'

No one had believed these promises – not even Victoria – and now rain was striping down between her window and the railings, between the railings and the blacked-out window of the greengrocer's across the street, and she was tilting her head in the dim room to hear something familiar but new: she was ready to do foolhardy things. Though silent, the high street still seemed full of people. They were quiet, as if they had exchanged drunkenness for something else, something more benign but harder, perhaps, to understand. Everything else – shops, pubs, houses – gained a frail lambency from the light of a scudding, intermittent moon.

'You're dead,' she heard suddenly, right outside the window. There was no one to be seen. 'You're fucking dead.'

Then, interrupting, from much further off: 'Voya! Coom 'ere!'

What kind of word was that? To be honest, she thought, I'm sick of hearing it. But it was more that she was sick of not knowing who it was, always calling their girlfriend as if she were the dog.

Victoria found a coat and some shoes and went out into the street. By then it was empty again. A single figure could be seen, bending this way and that, looking into doorways, standing distractedly, slipping as if between imaginary pedestrians until it heard 'Voya!' again, or perhaps 'Vira!' – at which it stiffened attentively, head on one side, then ran on, through the little town and out onto Woolpit Road – a mile of retirement build cutting steeply through sandstone to the river – which smelled by day of wood treatment and car wax. At night you were less likely to be aware of the bungalows than the dark woods on the spur of land above them. There was no wind. The rain fell. Victoria soon found herself soaked to the skin. She could hear the voice call, 'Moira! Coom 'ere!'

Of its owner she had no more evidence than the voice itself, sometimes close, sometimes fading into the night; while the pursuer – stopping and starting, darting from side to side of the road, its appearance adolescent, its combination of stiffness and pliability a puzzle – remained quite silent. It was perhaps male, perhaps not; and from a distance it seemed to be dressed all in white, like a member of ABBA in 1979. Down they went, until it became possible to strike north through Workhouse Dingle – where by day, just off the newly installed Heritage Trails, bitumen could sometimes be seen bubbling up from the coal measures not far beneath – then stumble and slither precipitously down clay slopes, through the woods the eighteenth-century labour force had known as 'Suicide Coppice', to the banks of the Severn.

There things stuck. As if musing on something – some long-held simple idea about the world – the voice fell silent. The darkness deepened. The trees leaned out of their understorey of holly and bramble. A few watery farm lights still glimmered on the black slopes half a mile away on the other side of the river. During that moment of respite – a minute, no more than two – nothing about the pursuing figure puzzled her: it seemed, after all, to be only a boy, about sixteen, drunk, arms thin, blond hair sculpted with product softening in the rain; eyes a greenish colour where they briefly caught the light. He looked ordinary and confused. Victoria huddled down between the trees. Straps, leather belts and bleached ropes of every kind dangled from the branches. She could taste the rain on her lips, in her mouth.

Then the voice called out again, from the other side of the river, soft and sly. The boy began to take off his clothes.

'No wait, wait,' Victoria whispered.

He didn't hear. His body was so white as to look green. The moonlight, coming and going, gave him the unsteady outline, the flickering corona of an animation painted on glass. He was so thin! He stood up, took a few quick, awkward steps towards the river, turned to look back into the woods. Then he slipped into the water and swam quietly but strongly away with the current, towards the ancient Devensian mouth of the Severn, leaving his clothes – if they were clothes – in a shadowy pile on the bank, hard to make out except by going closer than Victoria wanted to be. There was a glitter of movement, like a fish coming up to take a fly; then nothing but the surface of the water. Over on the opposite bank, a jaunty figure could now be seen moving away into a light ground mist, hands in pockets, whistling and calling, 'Vira! Vita!'

'No! No!' Victoria heard herself reply.

Wherever she went the next day she could feel the dark complex folds of the Gorge, never more than a mile away, an invisible but unmistakable interruption of the woods and fields. If the boy had swum towards the sea, she thought, then the river must have reversed its course again: since this clearly couldn't be the case, she began remembering the events of that night as a dream. *In the dream*, she would think; or, *In my dream* ... In her dream it was as if the river now flowed north-west, into a vast shallow estuary which debouched thirty miles wide into the Irish Sea south and east of Wrexham. While the boy – if he had been a boy at all, and not something beautiful but unsexed, or perhaps sexed in some way Victoria would never understand – stayed with her, moonlight and rain a blurry, overexposed admixture down one side of his face as he stared intently into the water then back up at the woods; something more like a special effect than a human being.

A little less than a week later, a man came to her door at nine in the morning. In the time it took her to get down from the top floor, he had rung the bell three times and banged the doorknocker twice.

'We've just had the new pictures done,' he said.

Victoria had no idea what he was talking about. Though he was shorter than her, he stood bent at the neck a little, as if the doorway was too small for him and he had to peer under the lintel to look inside. He was dressed in a yellow short-sleeved shirt and he sounded a little like George Formby. He was in a rush. It was as if he had rushed to get here and now he was already rushing to get away. At the same time he was insistent. As soon as he saw she didn't understand, he raised his voice a few decibels and bellowed, 'The pictures? The new pictures?'

'I'm sorry?'

'The pictures!' he insisted, as if they had met previously, maybe in some pub, and discussed it all, and she had asked him to let her know the moment they were ready. 'It's the new aerial pictures! Of your house?'

'Ah,' Victoria said. 'No thanks. Really.'

He stood on the doorstep, acting as if she had forced him to look down under the lintel to get a glimpse of her. 'Are you going to close the door in my face?' he shouted as she began closing the door in his face, appealing not to her but to the street at large.

'If I'd let him go another minute,' she told Pearl later at the café, 'he'd have had his foot in the door and called me Petal.'

Pearl didn't seem especially interested. She seemed uneager to talk, as if she didn't know Victoria very well and wasn't yet sure she was worth it. 'That'll be little Tommie Jack,' she said eventually. 'People like him aren't what you'd think. As a kid Tommie always had the feeling that something nice, something like honey, say, was being poured in all round him but he couldn't have any of it. It set, and held him in place like glue, but it wasn't his. It would never belong to him. Do you know what I mean?' And then, as if these things were connected: 'What should I do about myself?' That afternoon she had her hair in a tall white-blonde pompadour – which, extending upwards the thin inverted triangle of her face, gave her an air of wide-eyed surprise – and her fingernails freshly done in an electric-blue polish called, she later claimed, 'Through the Looking Glass'.

'It's lively,' admitted Victoria. She went on to say she hadn't even cut her nails since she arrived in the town. 'They've hardly grown.'

'Something in the water, I expect.'

'It's a nice lively blue, that.'

Pearl spread her left hand and held it, palm out, away from her; shook her head. Victoria stood looking through the window as the acetone smell of remover diffused slowly through the moist warm air. It was a slow day, a dark afternoon in town. The radio, lost somewhere between *The River* and *Tunnel of Love*, played mournful Bruce Springsteen standards. Outside in the little car park, the light shifted and changed, dull and subaqueous.

'So where's Ossie today?'

'Only God knows or cares,' Pearl said. 'Today's had it.'

She dragged the chairs about, offered Victoria a cloth. 'If you just wipe that table – no, the one in the corner – we can close up.'

In an attempt to engage her, Victoria tried: 'I saw another weird bloke last night. It was down by the river.' At this, Pearl's head came up alertly for a moment and she stopped what she was doing. Then she said, 'Everyone's different when it comes to personal presentation.' And, standing with hips tipped forward and fists thrust into the small of her back, 'Want to see something you won't have seen before?'

Victoria said she didn't mind.

'Come with me then.'

A narrow staircase went up steeply from behind the counter. Victoria felt uncomfortable from the moment they got onto the upper floor. There were more rooms than she expected. A single passage connected them. None of them contained much: paint-spattered planks or sheets of wrapped plasterboard leaning against a wall. Piles of dust, food crumbs trapped in spiderwebs. Flakes of paint fallen year on year from the skirting boards.

Pearl stood at the end of the passage and called out. No one answered.

'Buggered off this morning, I expect,' she said.

She then proceeded from door to door, looking briefly into each room. The one she settled on had a sash window, flooding it with wet light and inviting a fall of fifty feet down to some shallow cobbled stairs in a corner of the Portway. A sour odour filled the air, hard to identify until you saw the aquarium tanks, four or five of them, half full of cloudy water and vegetation but apparently without fish, on a table by the window. Someone had ripped the wainscotting out years ago, then, tiring almost immediately of whatever plan they had, stacked it loosely against the yellowed plaster and left it there. Also on the table were arranged: a Napoleon mantelpiece clock ticking heavily but the hands not going round; several faded shakers of fish food; a photograph album bound in brown faux-velvet with faux-gilt borders, which, being opened and spread, made a single sharp snapping sound.

'So here's Tommie as a kid,' Pearl said. 'He sold double glazing before he sold photographs. And' – turning the page – 'here's the kind of pictures Ossie used to sell.' Children down by the Severn, swinging from a rope over the brown water; sunbathing naked in a little dry basin in the bank. Pearl herself, about to enter one of the pools in the fields behind the town. 'I was ten in this one. I could swim a mile and I already had the beginnings of tits.' Everyone holding their bodies at odd angles, one hip sideways to the camera – looking shy or sly, Victoria suggested, because they had screwed their faces up against the sunlight. 'Oh, we weren't shy any of us. Tommie had a wart on his eye once, or that's what he said.'

After that, picture after picture, dim and faded, taken back in the seventies, showed men by the sea, but no women or children. Children would have insisted on crisps, chips; women on a good time. 'This is Ossie and Steve on their holidays up by Morecambe.' Tapping each flat, endless sandy expanse with a varnish-discoloured fingernail: 'They were hardly more than lads. Tommie. Steve. Fat Andy before he was fat.' Andy didn't look much thinner. It was hard to see what they were there for – unless it had something to do with fish or dogs – or what they thought a holiday was. Pictures without women: discoloured Polaroids, for instance, of a smiling bespectacled man in his thirties, in a red and white scarf on a shingle bank in winter. Behind him on the beach two defecating whippets faced each other in the matching poses of china dogs on a mantelpiece.

'Who's this one?'

'I don't know. They went all over in those days. They knew all sorts.' Pearl shut the album suddenly, but allowed her hand to remain on it, as though the memories it contained were still moving about inside; as though she might be reminded of something else and open it again to look. 'No,' she said eventually. 'We weren't shy. We were a knowing lot.'

'I can believe that.'

'Oh, you can, can you? I expect you can.'

'Is it possible to get a wart actually on your eye?' Victoria said.

'I'm just going to the loo.'

She was away for longer than you would expect. Victoria tapped the side of the nearest fish tank; shuddered in expectation she couldn't explain. Nothing moved in there. The toilet flushed, then flushed again. When Pearl returned she reeked of old-fashioned scouring powder. Her fingers were sore and reddened around the nail bed, as if she had been scrubbing at them. She turned the pages of the photograph album again, offering it spread open to Victoria.

'I might be your double!'

'But you don't look anything like me.'

'So that's how you see it, is it?'

She shut the album abruptly and went over to the window. 'People like Tommie are more complicated than they seem,' she said, looking intently down into the Portway. 'How far down do you think it is? To the ground?'

They saw less of each other after that. It was nothing deliberate, only the way things worked out. Victoria began to have trouble sleeping. She blamed it on the heat and drank a lot of water in the night; but it was really a kind of puzzlement. 'I don't even know what I'm puzzled *about*,' she wrote to Shaw. 'It's all quite non-specific.' When she did sleep her dreams were odd.

One of them went like this:

She was standing at the edge of the Gorge, which was a hundred feet deep in white mist. Up out of the mist, along a limestone path beneath little aged apple trees, emerged a man and a woman leading a llama. The animal's coat, rough but at the same time preternaturally clean, had warm milk-chocolate tones. It wore a red headcollar with a tiny brass bell; stared about in an alert but dignified fashion as it walked, as if trying to memorise the topography for its own purposes. The three of them came on gravely, then turned away along another path before Victoria had a chance to say how delighted she was. They knew she was there. It was an event with all the formality of ceremonial or folklore: she felt like a groundling, a spectator, just enough of a congregation to see them into being.

The mist now mutated from a sea of vapour into a sea of water. At the same time it widened and stretched away northwest, glittering under pastel sunlight with a sense of dawn in a foreign country. The smell of salt came up the hill. Down there, perhaps, lay a fishing port, a harbour mole, stacked white houses and two steep cobbled streets. Time held all this loosely but carefully in its hand. She was to understand, Victoria knew, that she was seeing a future. People had found fresh ways to live. Or perhaps it wasn't, as far as the Gorge was concerned, a future at all, only an intersection of possibilities, unconformable layers of time, myths from a geography long forgotten or not yet invented.

The weather continued good, though it rained more often. Her walks took her further afield.

West towards Wyke and Hunger Dale, a green slot through the woods emerged into unused lanes, still surfaced but sub-siding here and there into moss and hardcore, caught between destinations no one ever chose. After that you were out onto dazzling upland fields, already warm at seven in the morning, not quite sure for a moment where you might be; or into a village where the nettles grew high on the banks, leaning over where the lanes were narrowest, and last year's muesli of oak mast, crab apples and damp leaves remained trodden into the ground under the trees. It wasn't anywhere you knew. In the afternoons, she could often be found in the garden. She put in sweet peas, hostas in pots and night-scented stocks. She repainted the old grey RHS bench a current but inappropriate pastel shade. She tidied up, but invited montbretia and fox-glove to droop over the margins of the lower lawn so that in the twilight it resembled even more a pond in an Edwardian faerie book.

Otherwise she spent the time clearing her beautiful house: sorting through, boxing up, running down to the local recycling centre in the Fiat with the things she didn't want. Carpets. Memorabilia from cheap Mediterranean resorts. Contents of a garden shed, contents of a chest of drawers, contents of a bathroom cabinet. Two boxes of best-selling romances, their covers plagiarised from aspirational photography in *Men's Health* magazine. She found a purple dildo. In the light of these distractions, her mother seemed to diminish and become undependable, at least for a time. The heavy make-up and karaoke evenings appeared chaotic and inappropriate. The home-made dresses scattered about the place, their fantastic lines slashed and broken by black and white stripes at odd angles, seemed less late style – less eccentrically inventive – than mad; products of a repressed sensibility, owned too late, running on the disintegrating platforms of age and existential panic.

Before she stuffed them into the recycling bin, like washing into a front-loader, Victoria stood in the sunshine wondering what she would do with herself now. She understood that she would move on but wasn't sure what that might entail; hearing thunder not far off, went home and stood in the garden waiting for rain. None came, and she felt cast away. Later, searching the remaining cardboard boxes for what she had begun to think of as evidence, she found old films on VHS, old music on CD; and, stuffed thoughtlessly between the bruised and cracked plastic cases, two or three envelopes of prints from a digital camera.

Most of them showed local views. They were proof of travel or arrival. The front of the house. Trees under hot light at visitor centres above the Severn. Floodwater in the low-lying car parks. Then, as if the eye had detected some quality in the landscape no lens could bring into focus, two or three shallow characterless dells overgrown with iridescent moss, further along the Gorge east of the town. A single picture had been taken inside: it was of her mother with a man. At first she didn't know either of them. They were just two people having drinks, leaning together with their arms around one another's shoulders, raising shot glasses to the camera. He was shorter than her. His face couldn't quite be seen due to flare; hers, full of life, looked a little shiny and lapsed, as if it had already received the benefits three or four vodkas can bring. Their surroundings were indistinct, the background colours overexposed and skewed to orange – though Victoria could make out spirit optics and Christmas decorations. It had the air of a bar or a restaurant.

Unlike the other prints, this one was both creased and crumpled, as if someone had folded it small, unfolded it, screwed it up, returned to it, smoothed it out, pored over it and folded it again. Victoria in her turn studied it a long time. Then she took it to the café, where she found Wee Ossie behind the counter and put it down in front of him.

'Is this you?' she said.

He turned it round and then back again.

'Nice, that, isn't it?' he said, as if they'd looked at it together before. 'Full of joy, your old mum. She took a good picture.'

He held the photograph to the light a moment, then handed it back. 'That would be the Long Gallery,' he said, as if giving her directions. 'You'll have seen it, opposite the market on North Street. I'm often there if you want to come along some evening.'

Victoria stared at him. His fingers smelled powerfully of nicotine and soap, his hair of some tonic last available from the town barber towards the end of 1974. She snatched the photograph off the counter and walked out. Barred from understanding the sea change in her mother's behaviour – first by memory, which offered only this discontinuity, these two separate women; and now by a loneliness she would continue to inhabit until she aged and died in her turn – she found herself experimenting with a new idea: *I shouldn't have come here.*

At the door she called, 'And where's Pearl hiding herself?'

The old man took out a comb, flicked it deftly left and right through the hair above his ears, and had it back in his inside pocket again before you could really see what he'd done: it was a sleight practised and hermetic, less grooming than language from another time.

'Our Pearl has always come and gone as she pleased,' he now declared. 'Some will take that as a virtue, some won't.'

Fuck you, Victoria thought.

10

Victoria's Progress

She bought a television and had someone connect it. She went to the pictures in Birmingham; returned by the last train, from the windows of which she could watch distant lights map out the human landscape: neon signs, flood lamps at security gates in the middle of nowhere, rural traffic lights glimpsed partway through their cycle at empty junctions.

Her spirits remained low. The weather wasn't a help. Daytime temperatures fell. The sky filled from the south-west. Storms swept through each afternoon, their behaviour so strictly patterned they were like demonstration models: it grew quickly dark; lightning flickered; hail battered the old windows, settling thickly on the pavement outside the greengrocer's, where braided streams of water instantly began melting through it like vast rivers observed by satellite. Twenty minutes later the pantomime had moved on, leaving a few sodden jackdaw feathers to collect as slick pulp on the orange tiles in a corner of the front area. Traffic hissed by, but seemed reduced. Inside, the rain had changed temporarily the acoustics, it had charged the air in the downstairs rooms so that her cushions and covers, though they remained dull and even a little grubby-looking, took on the pure painterly values and eerie depth of the objects on a Virago book cover in 1982.

Victoria crossed the river and walked further than she had expected. On top of some whalebacked outlier of the Shropshire Hills, she ducked and huddled out of the wind, determined to enjoy its spectacular views of the M54 and the Cheshire Plain. She had packed no lunch. Later, half a mile down the hillside in fine blowing rain, she thought she saw a woman walking ahead, making her way quickly between dark, glossy rhododendrons towards a house on the edge of fields. She was wearing a flower print and high heels. White gloves. By the time Victoria got there she had vanished inside, if she had ever been there at all. The grey four-square walls were home to yellow lichens. Coughing could be heard from an upper room. The small, sodden garden featured: one child's swing, an empty pond, a fire pit full of charred beer cans and M&S prosecco bottles. Over in one corner, rotting apples were strewn beneath a well-grown holly.

It was the kind of place, Victoria imagined, in which murders had been committed so quietly and savagely over the years, and under such careful disguises, that they were never discovered. When she got home, she described them to Shaw as crimes of passion committed without any passion: dead wives, dead husbands, dead children; dead pets.

'And why would there be apples under a holly?' she asked him. 'Windfall apples under a holly tree! I don't think I even understand the countryside.'

She joined the local history society, but found its members less interested in the history of the town than in the history of their complex territorial disputes with other local history societies. An older man with thinning hair and an enlarged larynx invited her to join the film club. Moisture crept into everything. The water table, hacked repeatedly since the advent of long-gallery mining, and now labyrinthine, came alive. It had its own motives, its oblique discourse with the world above. The house took note, and in the afternoons withdrew some of its earlier promise. It breathed. You heard the beautiful floorboards shift and creak. Victoria stood on the stairs listening attentively to these structural realignments, then at night lay thinking about everything. It was hard to believe so much time had passed since she arrived. She had felt such relief to be away from London. It had all seemed sufficiently like coming home – your own old-fashioned adventure with a black and red tiled hall and a foxglove by the back door.

Consequently, she now saw, she had expected to find her mother's boxes full of familiar items. They would be essentially sad but they would make little, reassuring vertical links through time, to remind her: *You certainly inherited your father's chin!* or, *Here's Tumble the cat. You won't remember, but you did so love him when you were three!* 'Of course I expected that from the house too. But it really wasn't any of those things,' she wrote to Shaw. For instance she was now able to admit that she had rather romanticised the state of the cellars. 'They're just wet.' 92 High Street was, the same as anywhere, a collection of metaphors and guesses.

'I'm at that stage where you're still in love but you aren't quite sure what with. Reality begins to dawn.'

And then: 'Lots of room for improvement here but no money.'

When she thought about Pearl it was with a combination of anxiety and exasperation that compelled her to leave texts on the waitress's phone – 'Look, where are you?' – and compacted itself eventually into a mood she couldn't explain.

The café had closed. For three days rain had dripped from the frontage. Ossie's bruised Toyota was absent from the car park outside. Victoria put her face against the window and cupped her hands around her eyes; then, having glimpsed little but furniture, stepped back into the road to reduce reflection from the upper windows: nothing could be seen through them, either. She wandered about the surrounding streets and jitties, only to emerge surprised at Geoffrey de Lacy's keep, beneath the great ruined overhanging prow of which a brisk wind was tearing petals from the bedding plants by the public toilets. Halfway down the slick dank slot of the Portway – unable to identify the rear wall of the café though she knew it must be embedded somewhere in the crust of ancient buildings above – she remembered her previous visit there, and was careful where she placed her feet.

'Are you upset with me,' she texted, 'because I don't know why.'

Later, down by the Severn, at the waitress's lodgings on the Wharfage, she battered on the door until someone buzzed her in. She had a clear memory of the hallway from her previous visit, but her sense of knowing where she was had already run out. She stood at the bottom of the stairs and called:

'Hello? Pearl?'

'Straight to the top,' a voice directed her.

'Who's that?'

'Straight to the top,' the voice repeated tiredly, 'and on the left. But you won't find her.'

It was a quiet voice that had something else to do, a voice that had long ago grown used to fielding similar enquiries. It might have come from any of the rooms Victoria passed on her way up. Entering one at random, she found Andy the diabetic, to whom she said without preamble:

'Where's Pearl? Do you know where Pearl is?'

Andy, dozing with his dogs, proved welcoming but vague.

'There's a lot of crying out when she's here,' he said

eventually, conveying by a sequence of shrugs and nods that they both knew what this might mean. 'Always a lot of crying out.' He didn't look well. Today even his aged Labrador smelled of diabetes. 'She hasn't been back for a day or two, I know that.'

While they were talking, Victoria heard the scrape of footsteps in the room above, followed by a terrific chaotic thudding.

'What's that?'

'They're clogging it tonight,' Andy said.

Able to make nothing of this, Victoria persisted: 'But Pearl? Someone must know where she went!'

'They'll be here, there and everywhere tonight. They'll be up and down those stairs.' In the dim light his face gave the impression of being quite heavily bashed about, as bruised and scabbed as if he had recently fought someone and lost. He chuckled. A breath of pear drops filled the air. 'They'll have fish and chips and everything.' Raising the smaller dog in both his swollen hands, he dandled it about in front of him. 'Especially fish,' he said. This thought made him laugh harder. Somebody had made an attempt to tidy up his room. Apart from a single muddy pair, all the brand-new running shoes were back in their boxes; the boxes were stacked like a rickety wall at the end of the bed. 'Andy's not feeling at his best today,' he told the dog, which only looked away uncomfortably, baring its minute teeth. And then, to Victoria: 'He won't get out of bed.'

'Thanks,' she said.

The top-floor landing had a thick damp odour, compounded perhaps from all the other smells in the house, which daily rose from floor to floor until there was nowhere else to go. All the walls and woodwork had been painted in the same shiny cream paint. The paint coated the walls. The smell coated the paint.

'Hello?' Victoria said.

Daydreaming about how the waitress might live, she now discovered, she had assembled many of the correct elements – classic jive and rockabilly albums stacked by a refurbished Dansette portable; a poster which encouraged YOU'RE ALLOWED; garment rails from IKEA jammed with boiler suits and donkey jackets – but imagined a livelier arrangement of them. A divan single bed was pushed against the wall, its old-fashioned bedclothes partly stripped. The sash window, glass and all, had been painted the same shiny cream as the landing walls. There was an electric fan, with a dish of water placed in front of it to increase the humidity of the already humid air. She mooched about examining these things. When she dabbled her fingertips in the water, they came away salty and warm. On the make-up table, where she would have expected a collection of ironic wig stands and discarded front-tie headscarves dusty with retro forties face powder, there was only a Dell laptop, switched on but asleep. Depress its space bar, she found, and a website called *The Water House* sprang to life on the screen, red ten-point text packed onto a black background, relieved only by two-line drops and brief greyscale video clips the content of which was hard to make out. Victoria leaned in and read:

'During the late 1950s, especially at high tide, figures might be seen leaving the Brent River and its environs – the boat-yards at the Thames confluence, past Wharncliffe Viaduct and the zoo, towards the A40 at Greenford.'

And then, after scrolling down at random:

'On the subject of PDE10A and the Aquatic Hypothesis, these notebooks offer only the following fragment, the context of which has been defaced to unreadability: "In the [illegible] known to earlier expeditions as the *sea organ* or *Apprehension Engine* – as well as in the canal system beneath the Temple of Inscriptions – were found buildings, *systems of mirrors*, 'moonlight collectors', and a type of *accumulator* seen at many peripheral sites in Yucatan cave complexes. In cases where [illegible] are depicted, [illegible]. There seems no option but to acknowledge that we have observed the signature of late horizontal traffic – adaptive introgression as recently as eleven thousand years ago – in the human genome."'

The website and its videos resembling pornography from a culture with a drifted value for the term 'sex'; the dish by the fan; the underwear discarded in a corner, the outer garments all over the carpet, each item with its arms or legs so tangled up in every other item that you had the sense of them continually separating and rejoining in some liquid medium when you weren't looking: it seemed all of a piece. Victoria couldn't place the waitress here. She stared about in puzzlement for a moment, then descended the stairs to wander the shadowy middle reaches of the house, calling, 'Pearl? Hello?' until she blundered back into Andy's room.

Neither Andy nor his dogs were to be seen in there now: only men, among whom she recognised many of the trades who had mended her house – the plumber, the carpenter, Steve the roofer who had so praised her dexterity and sense of balance when she fetched him his tea and a ginger biscuit in the mornings. Absorbed and breathing heavily, none of them seemed to recognise her in return. They thumped and bumped along in their work boots, first one way then the other around the periphery of the room; then, joining hands, lurching suddenly into the centre, packing themselves firmly together with their arms across each other's shoulders, while at the same time they threw back their heads with the effort of pulling away from the intimacy this contact implied. It was dancing of a kind, Victoria supposed. She wondered if the quiet, angry struggle at the centre sometimes hid another participant – someone taller – a figure perhaps huddled on its knees and bent over from the waist and thus invisible. But how would it have got there without her seeing?

There was no music, although the bare floor sometimes made a reverberant, almost bell-like sound as it flexed under the load. The bed had been pushed into a corner, the boxes of running shoes piled upon it. A small fire, she saw, had recently damaged the skirting board nearest the door, and a faint smell of the nearby river overlaid the smell of the dogs in the still air. Someone produced a flowerpot, which they tossed to and fro for a moment or two until it slipped and fell and smashed in the empty hearth; black compost sprayed about. The huge TV screen on the chimney breast above showed a female gymnastics competition from the 1970s, Olga Korbut, 'the Sparrow from Minsk', charming the world on the beam, her small hands ushering in the era of gestures both positive and elfin.

Meanwhile, Victoria, less alarmed than exhausted by the effort of giving meaning to what she could see, was backing out of the room.

'Excuse me,' she said. 'Does anyone know what's happened to Pearl?'

They stopped dancing, and stared; and, as she took herself to the front door of the house, gathered quietly, pushing and shoving each other, on the staircase above her. 'She'll have gone off again,' one of them said. 'Nothing's ever good enough for that girl.'

'Our girl Pearl,' someone else said from further up, to general laughter.

'Oh for God's sake,' Victoria said, and left them to it.

★

She walked back up the hill and, when she got home, switched on her own television. On the screen the prime minister, mouth slack and ill-looking, repeated something three times; Victoria switched off again. Then she took out the picture of her mother at the Long Gallery with Ossie, and – as if it could be played in some way – ran one fingertip like a Dansette record-player stylus along its complex creases and folds. How do you get knowledge about a state of affairs unless you already know where to look? How do you know what platform the knowledge is running on? She was trying to think her way into the picture's flarey orange tones, its memories of karaoke and cheap lights of vanished Christmas, when she heard voices in the street outside the house next door.

She thought she would go out and look, in case it was Pearl.

The air had brisk qualities, and the clarity of a different time of year. Above the greengrocer's shop, sunset was colouring a mackerel sky. The disturbance turned out to be a man and a woman who, having received no response at the door of number 91, were already making their way through Victoria's front gate to their next target. 'So glad we caught you,' the woman said. She laughed. Her name was Brenda, she explained. She was nervous, in her thirties, neat and well presented, with Marks & Spencer stylings. Her eyes were blue. The man was Tommie Jack.

The moment Victoria saw Tommie, she made it clear she wasn't interested.

'Piss off,' she said.

'We're just calling on people today,' Brenda told her, 'to share this.' She put a paper-bound copy of *The Water-Babies* into Victoria's hands.

Victoria handed it back.

'Are you an idiot?' she asked Tommie Jack. 'What is all this?'

'What we think we don't know, we sometimes do,' Brenda suggested. 'Don't you find that? I know I do.'

'Oh, great,' said Victoria, and began to close the door.

'They're the past, you know,' Tommie Jack said, dodging forward nervously. You could see that he hated and feared a closing door; he was wounded by it. He would rather have a door that didn't open at all. 'We're the future now. Now everyone will stand a chance.'

'Who's the past?' Victoria said. 'What do you mean?'

She shut the door and shouted through it, 'Can you hear yourself? This is just some rubbish religion!'

'You'll keep seeing the visions,' Tommie advised her from the other side.

This enraged Victoria, who stood in the hall trembling and looking down at the black and red tiles and trying to remember what she had been doing before. She cleared her throat. 'I'm not interested in that,' she said, more to herself than Tommie Jack; a response that seemed to be neither sufficient nor, anyway, true. She opened the door again, waited until they were safely up the high street, turning off by the flower shop at the top end of Cocksall Lane, then called: 'What visions? What fucking visions?' They stopped on the corner and looked back for a second, their faces white and stretched with anxiety, as if they were afraid she would pursue them through the town. Tommie Jack made a curious palliative gesture with one hand.

'*What fucking visions?*' Victoria called again.

She was thinking how the llama in her dream had made its patient, dignified way up the path from the seas of mist in the Gorge.

She went back inside and feverishly rearranged the living-room furniture. 'You bastard,' she said, although she wasn't sure who to. She made overdone fishcakes and fried potatoes and ate them with a fork; she ate a raspberry Dual from the freezer. She tried to read a bit of *Jacob's Room*, but got only from page 16 to page 17 before she fell into a deep sleep on the sofa: woke, much later, to the grey light of her iPhone, although it was clear enough that no one had called. She enjoyed seeing her books, shelved in the alcoves next to the old fireplace; she liked the Welsh blankets and bits of brocade thrown over the furniture to disguise that it had belonged to her mother. The shutters still lay open, and it was dark. Almost asleep again, she heard, spoken in a calm voice from close outside – as though someone had been crouched directly beneath her window ever since she had moved into the house, motionless, pressing themselves against the cold Georgian brick down there so as never to be seen – the words:

'Vita? Vita?'

It was impossible to move, one way or another, she found; towards the window or away from it.

'Coom on now, Vita,' the voice cajoled.

Victoria remained as still as she could until she heard it move off down the street. Then she struggled into her coat and ran out after it, into the fields behind the houses, where she stopped and hid whenever she heard it call. It was a clear night. The moon cast soft pixel light across the landscape, producing black, stubby, precise shadows, accentuating and elongating every rise and fall; the pylons, crackling and hissing, seemed to curve above her like pylons in a linotype illustration. In that remote place the voice abandoned her. She stared around.

Suddenly it was Victoria who was calling – 'Hello! Hello!' – to no answer.

After that, the great dark charcoal coppices drew her in: Bosle, Swiney and Leastnow; Factory, Workhouse and Suicide.

These old woods, draped over the mess the eighteenth century had made, were warmer than the exposed dip slope; their labyrinthine topography of track and knoll, prolapsed lime kiln and pennystone spoil hill, sprawled away silent and dark to the edge of the Gorge, where every winter on the scarp one more beech tree levered itself out of the mud and leaned tiredly into the catch of its nearest neighbour. Across the grain, syke to syke, Victoria's progress — if that's what it could be called — was by short steep uphill struggle leading inevitably to a kind of exhausted, cautious slither down the other side. Her arms windmilled. She was lost. She did not feel entirely in charge of herself. Eight deer ran past her from nowhere, down a narrow salient between two overgrown rock quarries. All she could do was watch as they flickered away, in and out of the trees, pale in the moonlight, on some business of their own. Enchanted yet anxious, a London woman in a lot of mud, she wandered about all night until the sinister half-light at the hour before dawn brought her to the edge of the woods again; from which she looked out this way and that.

The grassland beyond had the blanched and wind-dried appearance of early March, as if she'd cast off some months of life between the trees; the air had a smell she could recognise but not name, and moved across the sky like a cold grey fluid. A hundred feet up, the power cables swooped from field to field. From the base of the nearest pylon came a quick complicit glitter of water, the waitress's familiar bathing pool with its attendant collapsed willow and submerged flowers. Victoria, relieved to locate herself so exactly after the night of chaos, ran out of the woods as if she was greeting a person rather than a geographical feature; then turned round and ran straight back in when she saw someone approaching up the long shallow drag from the town. This figure, slow to resolve, became first a woman and then the waitress herself, whose shadow was long, whose gait a pure sexual trudge, relaxed yet optimistic.

'Pearl,' said Victoria, not loud enough to be heard.

She felt embarrassed. She was a mess. If she revealed herself it would be hard not to admit that she had been lost in woods all night, up to her ankles in it, aged forty and wearing her mother's hiking boots. Pearl had always made her shy; but it was some deeper reserve – innate, untouched by circum-stance – that kept her kneeling in the wet grass at the base of the blackthorn. The waitress, meanwhile, approached the pool and with a languid smile addressed perhaps to the water itself removed her clothes. She folded them neatly. She had lost weight since Victoria saw her last. Her skin was pale, her stomach displayed the perfect late-medieval curve. She whis-pered to the pylon, trailed her fingers possessively along the split mossy boughs of the old willow. Then she stepped into the water, smiled around again, and waded confidently towards the centre, vanishing segment by segment as she went, as if descending a short, invisible flight of stairs.

There was no drama. Thirty seconds later, only a few cir-cular ripples were left to show she had ever been there at all.

Victoria stared.

'Pearl!' she cried, and stumbled in after.

The pool was bitterly cold but nowhere more than eighteen inches deep. The water never came up further than her knees. She bent down and swirled about with her hands. 'Pearl!' The waitress, five foot eight without shoes, wasn't down there. Nothing was down there. There was nowhere down there for anything to go. Victoria lumbered backwards in a panic; fell. She pulled herself shivering out onto the grass, stared back in astonishment at the roiled surface with the little yellow flowers wavering beneath. What am I looking at? she thought. Then:

if someone drowned here, who would know? Who would find her, she meant, submerged amid the flowers? Cold, white, preserved forever without being aware of it. Ripples were still breaking gently on the margins of the pool: out in the middle, the water had felt briefly welcoming, as if the disturbed mud was releasing a year or two of stored-up warmth.

'Pearl! Pearl!' she called.

And from the woods nearby a soft conniving voice replied: 'Coom, Vita! Coom by! Coom by, Vita!'

By now the sun was fully up, stretching everything to the limit, explaining nothing. Where it touched the top of the pylon, the glass insulators seemed to ring. Victoria disarranged with her toe the pile of clothes by the water. She returned to her house and let herself in. She went carefully upstairs and stood under a hot shower looking straight ahead at the shower cubicle tiles. She ate two slices of wholemeal toast. Then she packed a bag and put it on the back seat of the Fiat and drove the Fiat towards London at a moderate but unrelenting speed.

She needed a familiar face, and since the only person whose face she could describe that way was Shaw, she stopped to call him from an empty lay-by. All she got was a bad connection. She sat on nevertheless, dialling and redialling while the Fiat shuddered in the slipstream of the high-sided traffic churning past. That morning everyone was in logistics; they were delivering the future today. Victoria possessed only the sketchiest idea of where her future might lie, although clearly it wasn't by the side of some dual carriageway in the Gothic regions of a county she barely knew. Road signs offered Sytchampton, Ombersley and Norchard Pole. She could see some cumulus cloud; a hawk, a hill, and at the base of that a railway line.

It seemed like a long journey thereafter. Shaw remained elusive, a memory she couldn't be certain about. At 7 p.m., parked illegally on Shepherd's Bush Road just north of Brook Green, she tried his landline. It was the lull between the rush hour and the evening rush. A measure of liquid gold and silver light, she could tell, remained in the wide air above the Thames: if you were over in that direction, you would be drenched in it. Drinkers would be making their way between the river pubs, arms bare in the exhaust fumes drifting down from the A40 to fortify the food and wine. Captivated for a moment by the sheer width of the river, they would be pausing to gaze in delight (but also, perhaps, with something like puzzlement at the precarity, the undependable rarity of it all) across the glittering tideway, at the fringe of schools and tennis courts on the other bank.

'Hello?' said Shaw loudly. 'Hello?'

He cleared his throat. He sounded puzzled that anyone would call him. He sounded as if he hadn't spoken to anyone for a day, or even longer.

'Oh, hi,' Victoria said. 'I expect you remember me.'

Three

II

The Sea Change

Of his childhood, Shaw could retrieve only scattered but very specific images. A frozen puddle. A sack of sand. Stacked window frames on a half-finished estate somewhere near the sea. Four years old, he had found objects of this type interesting because of some intrinsic quality, such as being transparent, or being a kind of tawny yellow; or having moved since he last saw them. He had looked out less for himself than from himself.

His contemporaries at nursery school, by contrast, were primed to act. They were already impatient to do things. Agency was their goal. But where, for instance, the end of each day brought for them the chance to fasten their own coats, Shaw encouraged his mother to fasten his, so that he could remain hypnotised by the shine and colour of someone else's buttons. Later, this would lead him to a metamorphic theory of personal development. Age ten or eleven, watching his cohort take control of its own destiny, he could easily imagine himself grown up: but less as the agent of self-change than as an organism which – having reached some gate level he couldn't yet be expected to recognise – would flip automatically into a thoroughly novel state. By then a voracious reader, he was still failing seven times out of ten to correctly recite the alphabet.

'Go on like this and you'll never get used to yourself or anything else,' his mother had warned him more than once. 'You'll always be reinventing the wheel.' Then, as if aside to a third party: 'And my God, won't that be as tiring for you as it is for everyone who has to deal with you.'

In revenge for assessments of this kind, Shaw had quickly learned to skip-read his own experience, maintaining through adolescence only the most lateral relationship with its problems. A short attention span had helped: if for a month or two he liked motorcycles, by Christmas it was horses. He didn't meet girls. He didn't make friends. With university behind him, he'd found himself able to skirt most events and encounters, problematic or not, by cataloguing them under 'sketchy and uninterpretable' even as they occurred. When he actually took in the things that happened to him, the work was done somewhere else, somewhere deep, if he had anywhere like that: his surface focus – indeed his entire personality – always seemed to be taken up somewhere else.

By the time he kept his first appointment with the medium known as Mrs Swann, a month or so after Victoria Nyman left London, this triumph of disconnection had hardened into a lifestyle. It would provide the sole viewpoint from which to construct an understanding of their subsequent relationship.

The way to Mrs Swann's cottage in East Sheen was on foot, up from Mortlake High Street via St Mary Magdalen and West Temple, over the railway footbridge, then across the cemetery where he had first met Tim. Rain, blustering in from the Chiswick shore, had forced him to turn up his collar. Now it varnished the thin old headstones, swirling into the north-east corner of the graveyard where a few trees clustered against the wall of the old Barnes fever hospital. His jeans were soaked. The wind had emptied a bin, spreading an uneven slick of sandwich wrappers and fruit peel across the waterlogged ground; the cottages, their tiny front gardens planted with stalky lavender and full of sodden rose petals, seemed untenanted.

Mrs Swann, who was opening her front door even as he knocked at it, turned out to be a completely different kind of person than her name suggested – younger than him, pretty in an overworked way, with large if unexpressive eyes. For a second or two he thought she had been startled by something she could see over his shoulder. Thirty-odd years of similar surprises, he judged, had made her cautious. At the same time – sudden, momentary but incremental, predictable in form but never in substance – they had granted her a stability, a sense of the world that people like himself lacked. Her face reminded him of someone, but he couldn't think who. Neither could he place her accent. She was taller than him. She wore a loosely waisted flower-print cotton frock and box-fresh Converse shoes. Popular with young married women in west London about five years before, this was a look she would favour the whole time he knew her, even when the summer ended.

He should come in, she said. He could call her Annie. But before they began she wanted to tell him something:

'I only do this because I have a family to support.'

Shaw expected more, but after a moment she shrugged as if he had missed some social opportunity now withdrawn, and settled him down on the cheap leather sofa in her front room.

'Annie,' he said. 'That's an interesting name, because—'

'You should face forward and look at the wall,' she advised.

She sat beside him and took both his hands in hers. Her hands were warm. 'No,' she said, 'don't look at me. Look at the wall.'

Shaw looked at the wall. There was a faint rectangular

discolouration of the wallpaper above the mantelpiece, as if a large painting or poster had once hung there. After a moment Mrs Swann leaned away from him, caught her breath suddenly and fell over at an odd angle, still in a sitting position, still clutching his hands. For five minutes, she whispered and shook. Shaw, who had forgotten to switch his phone to record, found he couldn't release himself. Her grip was quite noticeable. Every sentence or two, she seemed to struggle briefly inside herself. Her frock rode up. Not sure what his part in this pantomime might be, Shaw sat on in his wet clothes and stared hard at the wall. Nothing happened, although once or twice his concentration became so great that he thought he felt the room lift and tilt around him. A river smell, funnelled up from Mortlake and across the railway line by the gusts of wind and rain, filled the room suddenly then dispersed. After ten minutes, Mrs Swann began to snore; her grip relaxed. A little later she woke up and smiled.

'I hope that was what you wanted,' she said. 'Sometimes they get what they want, sometimes not.'

'Was I supposed to see something on the wall?'

She laughed. 'How would I know?' she said.

She looked down at herself. 'Oh dear,' she said matter-of-factly. 'That does sometimes happen. But I don't suppose the men mind.'

She offered him a cup of tea. She did everything tentatively at first, then with a sudden slightly disorienting smile, as if she had remembered all about filling a kettle or opening a drawer and looking about inside it for a spoon. Shaw watched her for a minute or two, then sat on the sofa feeling calmed despite himself, looking around at the thick dove-grey carpets and pine furniture, the oversized ornamental mugs from English Heritage depicting otters and kingfishers.

'I can tell you have vulnerabilities,' she called from the kitchen. And then, sitting beside him again: 'This is such a difficult service to offer. No one comes to the medium without a problem – but people often aren't sure what it is. The medium, in her turn, can't be sure what's being provided. She's absent at the most critical time. She's only a conduit.' She smiled. 'You'd be amazed,' she said, 'how much can be solved by simple changes of habit.' To this end she gave him some leaflets, most of which seemed to recommend replacing meat with fish in his diet, and a number to call if he needed any further advice.

'Some people find that their anxieties are actually increased to start with,' she said. 'That passes. But if you're worried about anything at all, just ring for an extra consultation.'

'I didn't expect it to be quite like this,' Shaw said.

'You expected advice, you expected insight. Perhaps you expected a voice from the astral plane. Well, some get that. But what you found was an ordinary woman with two children to support.' She touched his arm reassuringly. 'Everyone finds something different,' she said; and at the door as he was leaving, 'There is one thing. You should look after your mother.' The glance with which she accompanied this was complex – diffident and apologetic yet direct and somehow full of irony. 'After all, she looked after you.'

'I suppose that's true,' Shaw said as blandly as he could, though he wasn't sure it was. What could she know about his mother anyway? Later he told Tim: 'I'd call that an odd thing to say.'

Tim didn't seem interested.

'Annie's my sister,' he said. 'But we don't speak any more.'

'That would make you Tim Swann, then. You don't look like a swan.' And when Tim only stared at him, 'I was trying to turn it into a joke.' Adding after a moment, 'I suppose she's obliged to say something like that to everyone.'

Shaw woke up at 2 a.m. on a Wednesday morning, with the impression that his landline had been ringing. When he answered he heard, instead of a voice or a dial tone, a kind of electronic silence, very pure and artificial and expectant.

'Hello?' he said.

He said, 'Victoria? Is that you?' It wasn't.

For a while, Victoria Nyman had left him voicemail most nights, messages stored for him to find next morning – deft little instagrams that would catch him up on her day, her beautiful old house, the progress of its renovation. Life was a permanent adventure up there, she said. 'You can sit on the first-floor landing in the sunshine, read a children's book that belonged to your mother, then, just as you're wondering why nothing magical ever happened in *your* life, the carpenter tells you you've got wood-boring beetle.' After a visit to Telford B&Q she had described the racks of tools as 'male ornaments, collectible objects for men'. It was all very Victoria: self-deprecating and cheerful – deliberately brittle, perhaps. 'I've got to say I'm meeting some quite weird people.'

Shaw had never answered because he didn't want to encourage her into the habit of it; but the messages often made him smile.

'Victoria?'

The dial tone returned suddenly and he dropped the receiver. 17 Wharf Terrace was quiet for a change. Faint smells of someone's takeaway supper – raw tuna with sticky fermented soy beans, from Tosa in Ravenscourt Park – were borne up on the stairwell draughts to seep under his door. He stared out across the street, to where the London summer aurora, an inert yet somehow swirling orange, could be seen between the house-tops; then after two or three minutes – like someone who has taken a boiling saucepan off the heat and given it a little time to cool down – he picked up the phone again and dialled the number Annie Swann had given him after his seance.

'Sometimes,' he said, 'I feel as if I've never known who I was.'

When he woke the next morning, he felt calmer. He felt at ease with himself in some way. The sensation lasted until mid-morning, thereafter returning briefly at intervals.

In lieu of work, he continued to familiarise himself with the workplace.

Under the landward window he found a leather shoe, and a teaspoon covered with what seemed to be hardened yoghurt. At the back of the desk drawers he turned up parcel twine, age-baked Sellotape the smoky bromine colour of a Victorian medicine bottle; half an indelible pencil. From behind the filing cabinet he recovered some sheets of the *Brent Advertiser*, June 1984, folded carefully to display a story about a man who had faked his own death six years previously – an action which had reduced him in an instant to a carefully composed note and a pile of clothes on the towpath about a mile north of the confluence boatyards. In the intervening period, the *Advertiser* reminded its audience, he had been sighted up and down the river – most often reported naked and anxious – mouthing silently as if behind glass: sightings that had always been easy to dismiss. Now, he'd turned up again, rueful but unable to give an account of himself. All that time he'd been living with his wife, a chemistry teacher, in Acton. 'Harry tried to vanish from his own life,' she explained. 'You can never do that. I told him it couldn't work. I think we both wanted something new.'

The accompanying photograph had been faded and lacking in contrast, Shaw suspected, from the moment it was taken.

He stuffed the *Advertiser* back behind the filing cabinet; the other objects he returned carefully to their places (though out of dislike he threw shoe and spoon into the river). He had no sense that they belonged to anyone in particular, or to any specific style of occupancy. They could neither context the site hut's present nor explain its disconnected past.

Later, pissing off the end of one of the abandoned barges upstream, invisible among the tall weeds and strengthless-looking bushes that grew on every square foot of its decaying deck, he thought he heard something behind him. There were two or three confused movements further along the hull, followed by a fluttering or rustling just outside his sightlines; then a quiet splash as if something had slipped furtively into the river. He waited for ripples but they didn't show. He leaned out to look up and down the reach. Nothing. Anxious, he zipped up and pushed his way back towards the land through the vegetation. In there, among recent shoots and withered induviae, everything felt dry and at the same time rotted to a wafer. Small cream moths floated up from among the faded lager cans and shredded plastic bags. A fibrous mulch was replacing the old deck, but you could still feel the decaying timbers flex beneath.

Secure on the towpath, he looked back. Anything, he thought, could be living in all that warm, dense, airless, puzzling growth. But the surface of the river was compact and burnished all the way to Kew Bridge, where the piers split it into whorls and eddies which streamed off towards Barnes. It was one of those London mornings when the overcast distributes the light evenly across the sky. The sun never breaks through but you feel it there all day, wrapped around you, until your eyes tire with it and you take refuge in some bar. The previous week's bad weather had folded itself away into heat and humidity, but remained immanent somehow in the dull brassy glare that lay across the city. Everything was dusty again, but the sky could always open. The worst of July, the foretaste of August, when, up and down the river from St Margaret's to Putney, the red pelargoniums hang listlessly in their municipal baskets and you wait for the weather to break and you might as well have gone to Spain.

That lunchtime, for a change, he walked downstream to Strand-on-the-Green and ate a hamburger sitting outside a pub called the City Barge while middle-aged women in yoga pants by Liquido and Spiritual Gangster exercised their miniature dogs between him and the river. Shaw felt as if he was sick of all that side of things. The tide had turned. The water was beginning to slacken and churn. Midstream, Oliver's Island looked like a Victorian dreadnought abandoned in the quivering light, its slabby iron plates somehow turned to stone. I would never have to fake my own death, he found himself thinking. I've all but vanished already. Part of him welcomed that. Another part, larger but distributed so thinly across his personality that it seemed invisible, panicked soundlessly on a twenty-four-hour schedule.

Wednesday evenings he met Tim at the office. There they reviewed the video of Shaw's latest encounter with the medium. On a good day this comprised anything from five to fifty minutes of Annie Swann's sleeping face; on a bad one, an equivalent account of her bookshelves, ornaments, disarranged clothing, walls. While Shaw had quickly learned to free one hand from hers as the trance began, he could rarely free both; nor could he ease the contorted positions into which he was dragged by her subsequent collapse on the sofa. As a result, by the end of each session he was exhausted; and camera shake had reduced everything to a grainy, ill-lit blur.

If Tim found anything worthwhile in this record, he edited on the spot, uploading straight to *The Water House*, which like many similar sites was set in red ten-point Palatino, single-spaced on a black background – less an aesthetic than a promise, a brand: bad presentation as a guarantee of authenticity. Watching the edit over Tim's shoulder, Shaw glimpsed large unleavened blocks of text, then his seance material distributed as a sequence of small misproportioned close-ups between phrases like 'PDE10A and the Aquatic Hypothesis' and 'archaeological sites in Yucatan cave complexes'. Then suddenly, without warning, what seemed like a communication from a completely different kind of publication, 'Yesterday I watched a heron eat a live eel in bright sunshine on the South Pier mudbank. Today it was foggy: the mud was almost awash, the heron still waited there. I fear the hidden channels of the confluence and hate low tide as much as I hate the partly foundered lighters.' Shaw found this oddly intimate, as if he'd read someone's diary, and said on an impulse:

'You didn't tell me the blog belonged to you.'

'I was certain I did,' Tim said, smiling without looking up.

Shaw had no idea how private all of this was supposed to be. To what degree should he think of himself as involved? Was involvement part of his job description? He wasn't sure how to ask. He wasn't sure to what extent he was being invited to join in. He compromised by pretending an interest in the map on the wall.

It was about three feet by two, old and discoloured, curled at the corners, with rusty marks where old-fashioned drawing pins had been removed. The land was in grey, the sea white. If you looked at it long enough, there before you was a brand-new planet. It featured a sea shaped like the Americas, another sea like the eastern half of Russia. In between them, in the centre of the map, stretched this vast new continent which didn't even have a name. Blink and it was gone. You couldn't get it back. You were left with a featureless map of the world on which someone had marked naturally occurring clusters of a repeating DNA sequence sometimes found on human gene Kv12.2, code which had originated, he read later, 'more than 500 million years ago in the genomes of sea-dwelling species' and which played 'a decisive role in human spatial memory'. Why anyone would map that was unclear: it was an oddly specific way of looking at things, and not one you could navigate with.

When he saw Shaw looking at the map, Tim smiled to himself as if it was what he had expected. 'You're interested in that, too,' he said. 'Everyone is. Stay behind one night. Have a drink. Have a look at the documentation.'

'Perhaps I will,' Shaw agreed, in a tone he hoped would indicate a genial scepticism.

Privately, he wondered how long he could avoid the invitation. In the pub or at the dry-cleaner's, which was the only other place he seemed to go, Tim was always in earnest conversation. He was always trying to persuade someone of something. From the towpath at night you sometimes saw the site shed's landward window lit up, and heard raised voices from inside. Tim could be seen displayed like a character in a Hopper painting, or something on offer in an aquarium or an empty, brightly illuminated chiller cabinet. His body language could be read. A conversation could be heard. It was often defensive, as if he was talking to a customer; it was often one-sided, as if he was talking on the phone. But sometimes the customer was present, demanding less a refund, perhaps, than something more satisfying for their money than *Journeys of Our Genes*. What could Tim offer them, except vague ideas? He was, you sensed, manipulative, but not good at it. Sometimes during these exchanges he seemed to be pleading.

Shaw was taking too long about things, his mother said the next time he visited. He was acting as if he'd live forever. 'You aren't getting on with it,' she said. And then after a thoughtful pause: 'People never forgive that.'

It wasn't a new complaint, although what she wanted of him Shaw could never be certain. What's the proper speed for living? What's the appropriate density? What, even, constitutes a life? He had to agree that she had never taken too long about things herself. Looking through the photograph albums, it was hard to see her slow down at any point along the trajectory she had made her own. Up with the rocket, down with the stick: one emotional project replaced by another the instant the smallest thing went wrong. To Shaw at seven years old, this lability had been both her curse and her deep mystery – her cult. He had loved and feared it. When things were good she couldn't stop talking them up; the next day they had become too complex to manage, and she left suddenly, and might not be heard from for months or even years, after which there was a postcard, a tearful but stiff reunion which inevitably prefixed another parting. There was a new family for Shaw, members of which might or might not be present.

Up and down the south coast from Hastings to Ramsgate, every start was a false start. From shingle bank to sink estate she had pursued and been pursued by men with schemes. Later, west and north, all the way round to the Bristol Channel, lost holiday towns and permanent caravan sites through Aberystwyth to Anglesey, Liverpool to St Annes Bay, she found small, quick, lively entrepreneurs who reminded her of her father; men who like him could always charm her by talking about something they knew, men with a trade – estate agent, carpenter, sea-defence contractor – who also had dreams. They worked all day and at night schemed to build a go-kart track in a retirement village, a porn warehouse on a deserted peninsula. They knew the sea coast, perhaps they loved it; above all they wanted to stand some project of their own against its grandeur. They fought five years for planning permission, then stood proudly on the steps of a run-down cinema or at the bottom end of a sloping clifftop field from which a four-inch skim of topsoil had been removed, to have their photo taken in a football scarf.

Shaw kept in touch with one or two. Others his life turned up again at random, as if offering him, or them, a second chance at something indefinable – something of unknown value, perceived as an anxiety.

A retired teacher from Swansea had arrived one drizzly Saturday on the doorstep of the Maida Vale house-share where Shaw was at that time living in a nice double room with a woman called Jasmine. The teacher's name was Keith and in his prime he had taught creative writing to maximum-security prisoners on the Isle of Wight. He was in his middle seventies now, and already drunk when Shaw answered the doorbell. Three o'clock in the afternoon, late November, fifteen years or more since Keith had been his father: Shaw had no idea how he had got the address. What Keith wanted was even harder to understand, though he had brought along a file of handwritten poems under the general title 'Pleasing the Long-Dead Heart'. He ate dinner with them, watched TV, drank shiraz until he was paralytic, then Jasmine drove him to the station in her Austin Metro. In the car, he expanded further on his theory of the heart; put his hand on Jasmine's knee; described Shaw as wet. If she ever needed a real man, he suggested, she should look him up.

'He's missed the last Tube,' she said when she got back. 'I just left him there.' Shaw felt embarrassed for them both.

A few months later, Keith died under anaesthetic during a routine varicose vein procedure. By then Jasmine, as puzzled by Shaw as she'd been by Keith, had gone off with a tree surgeon. No one blamed her. There was a memorial service, held somewhere in the armpit of the Gower Peninsula, which Shaw didn't feel like attending; he kept the poems, though they weren't much good. Viewed in the context of their relations with his mother, men like Keith often seemed less errant than lost. What was missing from Shaw's memory was any sense of them as human beings: he couldn't at that distance return it to the picture.

'Bastards,' his mother would say, 'the lot of them.'

But what do you ever know about people? In an attempt to divert her and keep the photograph albums intact – in case, perhaps, he should eventually learn something from them, something about himself as much as her – Shaw often took her a selection of videos. These they watched together in the afternoon, on a forty-inch flat-screen Panasonic provided by the care facility. He chose films he thought she might have preferred as a young woman, available in digital remasterings with bonus material. *A Matter of Life and Death, It's a Wonderful Life, The Red Shoes, Strangers on a Train, I Know Where I'm Going*. But his only real successes were with *Brief Encounter*, through which she smiled and chuckled happily, and *Lady and the Tramp*, which she watched as if it was a nature programme. Most of the time she fell asleep, leaving Shaw to sit bored and angry through the relentless cycles of Powell and Pressburger or Ealing comedy.

Five o'clock, she would wake, look around, murmur, as if she was still in her own house, 'Oh dear, I suppose I'd better make some tea.' Then, anxiously, 'Aren't we going to have the photographs today?'

'We've had the film,' Shaw would have to explain, 'instead.'

'What film?' she replied this time. 'Don't be so stupid, I haven't seen any film.' And, as if running on from the same thought: 'Just don't wait for life to come to you, that's all. That's my advice. Your life will never forgive you that.'

On his way out, he stopped to look at the Arnold Böcklin in the day room, only to find it had been rotated with the rest of the art to another part of the building, its place being taken by several small John Atkinson Grimshaw prints.

Blurry, estuarine-seeming streets in the centre of nineteenth-century Leeds; a version of Hampstead set on vague bluffs above shallow water; ambiguous figures observed on a vast, sloping, otherwise deserted quay. Sea change, taking place in damp air, foul weather, at a distance, at night. Everything liquidised. Where it wasn't the moon shining on water, everything *looked* like the moon shining on water: it was hard to see what the artist had been thinking. Bathed in the transformational odours of care-facility cooking and floor polish, the traffic rolling in on the A316 like surf or tinnitus behind him, Shaw sat captivated until visiting hours were over and he was asked to leave. If all change is sea change, he thought on the train back to Mortlake, then he could describe his own crisis – whatever it had been – as distributed rather than catastrophic. Sea change precludes the single cause, is neither convulsive nor properly conclusive: perhaps, like anyone five fathoms down into their life, he had simply experienced a series of adjustments, of overgrowths and dissolvings – processes so slow they might still be going on, so that the things happening to him now were not so much an aftermath as the expanding edge of the disaster itself, lapping at recently unrecognisable coasts.

'Another thing,' he had once tried to explain to Victoria Nyman, not long after they first went to bed together: 'a crisis might not even be your own. Perhaps no one should be able to claim a crisis as personal. If you aren't expected to own it, a crisis can be a barely noticeable thing.'

'Remind me: where exactly would be the crisis in that?'

'I'm saying you'd be part of the whole thing.' And then impatiently, 'The thing whatever it was.'

'This is the thing, here.'

Victoria was still sending him emails. Increasing gaps in the narrative suggested she had become more interested in living her life than in describing it. She still loved her house, she said, though work was needed to parts of the roof and the cellars would have to be tanked. 'Why *does* a cellar,' she asked, enclosing the word between asterisks as if to contain as well as emphasise it, 'seem so romantic before you sign the contract?' She had met some pretty strange people. Was always in her car. Walking a lot too, getting to know the county, which was English Heritage from one end to the other. The local power station was closing next year. 'Meanwhile every old ruin for forty miles around claims to have hosted a meeting of Parliament in 1432.' What did he make of that?

She was full of a kind of skittish energy. Never a week went by when she didn't tease him, 'How are you and that fish getting along? Still lovers?' They were less like emails than the sound of a cheerful but indistinct radio programme coming from an open window a little way down the street. Sometimes he didn't read them for a day or two, sometimes not at all.

12

Any Port in a Storm

Late evening, making his way home along the river from the Fox Inn at Hanwell, Shaw needed to pee.

The river was up. Away from the towpath lights there was sufficient moon to cast a shadow. He headed for one of the more overgrown barges that lay in a line in the mud a few hundred yards downstream from the Brent confluence. It was larger than the others and perhaps his favourite, although he had only seen it by day, when the word 'Anabasis' could be made out stencilled on its bow in rusty white letters.

Access was over a concrete wall, between two lopped willow truncheons and down a new-looking aluminium ladder, then by a narrow plank fifteen feet above the rising water. Once aboard, you were greeted by a close, overgrown terrain littered with crushed and whitened beer cans, ragged plastic bags, underwear discarded as an offering; the whole smelling of herb robert and – more mysteriously – cheap pesto. All of this was familiar enough. But paths Shaw knew well in the afternoon seemed less amenable after dark, and he was soon lost among the disordered deck furniture, nests of wire and piles of sodden slats, the old curved hatch covers presenting as entries to an underworld. Thickets of elder and hazel, the latter black with last year's catkins, hung over the water. The structure shifted and creaked as the tide lifted it. Everything seemed larger than he had expected it to be. After a few minutes the sense of a void to his left convinced him the river lay in that direction. He arrived instead at the huge blunt landward side of the bow where the foredeck, rotted by decades of leaching soil acids, had buckled gently into the empty hull to produce a saucer-shaped clearing.

It was nothing much – a few square metres of cropped-looking turf with a springy but rotten feel underfoot. The edges were littered, but not the middle. Moonlight bleached everything, lending more of a sense of space than you would expect; it glittered prismatically off something Shaw took at first for broken glass, but which proved to be a precise row of three little Victorian medicine bottles embedded at angles in the turf as if it had grown up securely around them. Each chipped neck had been plugged with a swatch of stained tissue. They were hexagonal, square-shouldered. In their day, they had represented pain relief, life relief, relief from life's fevers and revelations; their utility now was unclear, though clearly not ornamental. The milky fluid so carefully stoppered up inside them resembled semen, though it was on second thoughts insufficiently thick. Moonlight lent it a greenish cast.

As Shaw stooped to examine this arrangement, someone burst out of the undergrowth beside him. The flimsy decking bounced and shook. He had a strong sense of being over-whelmed by events before he had even become aware of them. Something cold and muscular gripped his upper arm. He was enveloped by a smell he didn't recognise. He was lifted half off his feet and shoved out of the way. There came a moment of confusion as he tried to keep his balance; some further contact, which spun him around; then a naked figure, very pale, not as large as he had expected, parted the vegetation and ran off bent double between the stems. 'Hey!' he called, but it had already vanished. The hull dropped and wallowed on the riverward side; lifted again as if relieved of a weight. A dull splash followed, and after that a brief period of energetic thrashing which seemed too far out on the river. Silence. Shaw stared into the dark. It was a typical night on the Brent waterfront, traffic coming and going over Kew Bridge, laughter and vomiting from drinkers further along the towpath, a quick burst of music from an open door. He massaged his arm where it had been gripped. His fingers came away cold, sticky and wet.

'Jesus,' he said, wiping his hand agitatedly against his thighs. 'There was no need for that.'

The bottles were gone. He kneeled down and pried about with his fingers for a moment or two in the neat hexagonal sockets they had left behind; then, imagining the soil full of rusty edges, ecosystems of mulched-down condoms, gardens of microbes – weeks, perhaps, of his own piss – got up hurriedly, wiped his hand again and stumbled up to the towpath, directly over to the Watermans Arts Centre, the vile red brick and endless, ramified back parts of which confused him to such an extent that he became briefly lost and tried to open a fire door by throwing himself three or four times savagely against it in the dark, and was eventually able to gain access at the front of the building and find the downstairs bar and, breathing heavily, drink a whisky while staring around at the purple neon and unoccupied plastic chairs.

The next morning, in the aftermath of looped, unstable dreams, he went to see the medium.

Sea change had already entered this relationship. He phoned her most nights, misdialling repeatedly before he got through, watching between attempts the summer rain as it polished the roofs the other side of Wharf Terrace. By morning he always found it hard to remember what he had needed from her, although he recalled phrases he felt were typically his own: 'sensations of being dead' or 'rental accommodation'. He was ashamed. It had become a habit. He was failing to outflank some force in himself, eager for a reassurance no one in the world could provide, the nature of which surprised him even as he articulated it.

'The thing is, I don't really see where I am. Not now.'

In response there came only a yielding silence. Shaw thought of it as puzzled, calmly unproductive yet still somehow expectant — even intent. She was rarely the first to end the call. 'Sometimes,' she would suggest eventually, 'we just need to hear another voice'; leaving him to resume in a self-wounding murmur, 'I'm not like this. I wasn't always like this.'

'No one can live without change.'

The medium never referred to these conversations when they met. Indeed, sometimes she was so preoccupied that she hardly seemed able to identify Shaw as the person who visited her once a week.

At the Avenue Gardens end of Mortlake Cemetery, a woman sat on a bench, slowly eating some kind of wrap or filled pitta. Barnes Hospital, on the other side of the graveyard wall, advertised itself as providing 'the very best services for people with mental health problems'. Perhaps she was an outpatient, but she looked harried enough to be a nurse. When Shaw waved, she got up quickly and moved off. He had already half convinced himself it was Annie Swann, so that, knocking at her door a minute or two later, he was surprised to find her at home. The door opened directly into her front room. Light seeped in from the cemetery onto the wall above the fireplace, where it lay brown and inert.

'I thought I saw you over there.' Shaw said. 'I didn't expect you to be here.'

She looked vaguely in the direction he was pointing. 'You'd better come inside,' she said, 'and sit down.'

'I'm Tim's friend?' he reminded her.

'Tim?' she said. 'Tim hasn't got any friends.'

She laughed. Suddenly she crouched down in front of him and scraped around on the doormat. Shaw stared puzzledly at the top of her head. 'The person who lived here before me gets more letters than I do,' she said. She took the post into the kitchen and, after a minute or two's silence, called: 'It might have been me in the park, I suppose.' He heard an envelope being ripped open, a tap running, some pots being banged onto a draining board. When she came back in, she seemed more like herself. 'I call it the park,' she said. 'Not everyone wants to be reminded they live next to a graveyard! Now come on, sit down and we can get on.'

'I always feel a kind of calmness during these sessions with you,' Shaw said, 'a kind of repose.' He was trying to prompt her, but all she said was:

'That's good. That's very good.'

The seance had its rhythms. Shaw had grown familiar enough with them that he could gently detach his hand while Annie lay grunting and shifting in her altered state and wander round her house. All the cottages in this terrace were one-up one-down, with kitchens and bathrooms built out as extensions into small patio gardens, and steep little staircases which opened onto single bedrooms. Shaw mooched about up there. There wasn't anything new to see. He picked up a photograph of two children – who, if they were Annie's, didn't live with her here – and wandered into the bathroom, which smelled strongly of shower gel and toothpaste. The bath still contained three or four inches of water in which floated a little mechanical toy, a pink plastic figure of a man wearing a blue and white striped Edwardian bathing suit. Between them, toy and bathwater made a circumscribed, curiously complete world. The toy whirred agitatedly but slowly across the bath until it bumped against the side. Thereafter its progress was crabwise, tentative, until its clockwork wound down. It stuck to the margins. The water maintained a lukewarm tempera-ture, as if Annie had only that minute stepped out onto the bathmat. Shaw encouraged the figure into a circuit or two, then removed it, wiped it briefly on a towel and put it in his pocket. He replaced the photograph in the bedroom.

He often wondered how the medium fitted into her own life. The letters in the kitchen were all addressed to 'Annie S. Swann', in a handwriting he recognised. Only one of them had been opened. He was about to read it when he heard her call out from the trance. He went back into the front room and looked down at her. Then he stared up at the wall above the fireplace until it was time to sit down and hold her hand again.

'I do notice something about you,' she said when she woke up. 'You should listen more to the people you know.'

It was his turn to laugh.

'Who do I know?' he said. 'Who do you think I know?'

He was angry, and he wondered where that had come from. Remembering the social difficulties of his last few years, he complained: 'People try to help, but all they have to work with is their theory of you. You might as well not be there. In the end they're talking to themselves.'

'Even so,' Annie Swann said, calmly smoothing her skirt.

'I don't know anyone.'

Out in the cemetery again, he felt as if he was still going through someone else's belongings, and not even out of interest. The woman he had seen when he arrived was back on the bench, slumped and still eating. He couldn't place her. She was older than the mothers you saw in East Sheen during the day, in their compression tights and expensive running shoes; her posture wasn't good. Thin old gravestones leaned at sharp angles behind her; next to the bench a red plastic watering can lay in the grass on its side. Since his last visit to the medium a council emergency number had appeared on the noticeboard by the gate. What kind of an emergency, Shaw wondered briefly, occurs in a graveyard? The sudden need to bury someone?

It began to rain, and the day continued wet. He returned home, dozed in front of a film he had bought for his mother – *The Wages of Fear* – and in the evening met Tim Swann at the office to present the evidence of Annie's most recent trance.

Tim's response to these reports never varied. He seemed uninterested in Shaw's verbal summary. He would download the video, tap his fingers impatiently, sigh with disappointment, then lean forward suddenly as if something on the screen had caught his attention after all. After that it only needed a few keystrokes to generate a GIF file from ten seconds of the record and paste it into *The Water House*.

'Do you see what I see?' he asked Shaw now.

Shaw couldn't see anything much. Annie Swann lay on the sofa slowly opening and closing her mouth. She looked content. She was clearly asleep. Suddenly a timestamp began blinking on and off in the top right-hand corner of the image. While he was trying to remove that, Tim said, with a kind of calculated offhandedness:

'You're stuck here for a bit; why not have a proper look at the documentation?'

Rain poured down on the surface of the river outside. Both men were damp from the walk along the towpath. Neither of them had taken off his coat. They inspected one another like two animals meeting in a field, each trying to determine what was expected in the situation. Shaw recognised a short circuit, a reconnection, the inevitable outcome of their original meeting in the graveyard: something which should have happened there and then, and which he had been postponing ever since. He felt cornered by Tim; but he also understood that Tim felt cornered too, by his own needs. It was too late to suggest they went to the Earl of March instead – besides, he had grown nauseated with that pub's warren of small rooms, rammed from six in the evening with estate agents and middle-rank City bonuses – so, recognising that if he let the silence develop any further neither of them would know how to save himelf, Shaw said yes, that would be fine.

'Although,' he was careful to add, 'I don't have all that much time this evening,' as if honesty forced him to admit that any other evening would have been more sensible from his point of view.

'Just the short version, then,' Tim said encouragingly. 'The quick run-through.'

'Yes, great. The short version would be great.'

'That's great.'

The short version, perhaps two inches thick, turned out to be a download from the website, a sheaf of media reports, anecdotal observations and scientific abstracts touching on everything from the Turkish 'mystery city' of Göbekli Tepe to the sequence of uplift of the Hoh Xil Basin of the Central Tibetan Plateau; from ancient human migrations – tracked via mitochondrial haplogroup – to the Gnostic foundations of Stalinist science. Everything was either a truth or a mystery.

Truths and mysteries ran together, hardening into unconformable layers of time and data. Body parts were washed up in Southampton, England. Someone had invented an app designed to identify unknown locations by matching them with 'a library of sixty million images'. Two paragraphs from Wikipedia shed new light on metabolic by-products found deep in the Juan de Fuca tectonic plate. The first complete Neanderthal genome had proved to include DNA from at least one previously unknown human species; simultaneously, in Wiesbaden, Germany, a man of about forty was observed by passers-by to drag himself out of a canal then run straight out into heavy traffic on the nearby dual carriageway, where he was struck first by a black BMW E30 with UK registration plates then by a Peugeot painted Mediterranean blue.

The useless specificity of these last two facts seemed to sum up the whole collection, which was interleaved with Post-it notes − 'What is the exact nature of our relations with the inland cities?' − and personal memos, as if its curator's need to find narrative in the density of events left him unable to make distinctions not just between different scientific regimes and types of evidence, but between his obsessions and his life − although the latter was often revealed as a weak secondary growth on the former.

As soon as Shaw had read a page or two, Tim began leaning over his shoulder to make cross-references. 'Look at this' − leafing forward excitedly through three or four pages − 'and don't miss this! Do you see how one conclusion makes it impossible to avoid the other? Do you see how elegant it is?' None of it made any sense to Shaw. When he said so, Tim nodded wisely, as if a careful academic point had been made. 'What haunts me is exactly that! In the end, is logic in *any* sense the right method to be applying here?' Unsure how to respond – and in any case anxious that anything he said would only prolong matters – Shaw heard himself announce, perhaps more forcefully than he'd intended:

'Annie got your letter today.'

This produced a silence, startled and irritable on Tim's part, disorienting for Shaw, which neither of them seemed to be able to negotiate. Someone walked past on the Thames Path, shouting into a mobile phone, 'But did he feel all right? Well then, that's all right then.' The wind blustered downriver, booming in the rusty metal hull of the lighter and thumping the wooden walls of the office; the rain fell on a falling tide. In the distance, mid-evening traffic could be heard grinding its way out of Hounslow, west along the A315 and into Chiswick.

Eventually, Tim said: 'Anyway, I think you'll really like this too.' He was holding out a copy of *Journeys of Our Genes*.

'Brilliant,' Shaw said. 'Thanks. I'll take them both with me.'

'Take them both with you,' Tim Swann said, as if he hadn't heard. 'I've signed the book.'

On his next visit to the care facility, Shaw found his mother in the day room, in an armchair beneath the Grimshaw reproductions. Enlivened by some squabble with the staff over bed linen or a bath – they hadn't been quite clear which – she sat with legs tucked up to one side like a much younger woman. It was a posture of triumph, obstinacy and renewed confidence in her own options. Late-afternoon sunlight glittered in the side of her eye. She was soon refusing to go back to her room and watch *It's a Wonderful Life*.

'But you said you enjoyed it.'

She laughed. 'I never once said that.' Then, giving Grimshaw's *In Peril* a look of contempt, as if she had caught the painter out in some equally basic error about the nature of things: 'I don't think much of these, either.'

'What would you prefer?' Shaw said. 'Morecambe Pier?'

He took out Tim Swann's book, opened it at random and began reading aloud. When he read to her, his voice stunned her into passivity. He had nurtured this emotional advantage since he was six years old, a point in his life at which she had seemed to him like a sphinx or other savage mythological creature – charismatic, mood-driven, hard to parse, harder to defuse. It had been his only weapon in the asymmetric conflict between mother and son. Now, more of a nuisance than a danger, she half sat, half lay in waxy repose, staring out at the garden where a harried-looking thrush hopped about on the lawn. 'Don't think I don't know what you're doing,' she said. 'You're trying to get the right side of me.' As she listened, she kept an eye on the thrush's efforts among the worm casts. After about ten minutes she got to her feet, banged on the window and watched with satisfaction how the bird flew away.

'It hasn't got much of a story,' she said. 'This book of yours.'

Shaw admitted that it hadn't. Line by line it was as disorganised as *The Water House* itself. Stories reproduced from every type of science periodical appeared cheek-by-jowl with listicle and urban myth. These essentially unrelated objects were connected by grammatically correct means to produce apparently causal relationships. Perfectly sound pivots, such as 'however' or 'while it remains true that', connected propositions empty of any actual meaning, as if the writer had learned to mimic sentence structure without having any idea how to link it to its own content. It would be incorrect, Shaw thought, to describe the data as 'cherry-picked', since that would imply an argument they had been chosen to fit. Instead, they were part of an endless list.

Riffling through for something to keep her interest, he opened it onto a full-page reproduction of the map on Tim's office wall, done in three colours and with additional symbols, none of which he recognised.

'It isn't my book,' he said, 'anyway.'

In the paragraph beneath the map, Tim was asking himself: 'Who hasn't, at some point in their lives, dreamed of strange organisms? Infestations. Algal mats. Microscopic activity in crustal basalt, detected only via by-product, "perhaps the largest ecosystem on earth". Not precisely animals. And most often, it has to be said, the kind of things that grow in layers in a drain. They're soft. I also dream of that wiry, fibrous stuff you get in a bad avocado. In this case it's a dark red and it runs through everything.'

Shaw closed the book and shrugged. 'You know, we could always watch David Attenborough instead,' he said.

'I know full well what you're doing.'

13

The Swanns' Way

Annie Swann had other clients. Shaw never saw anything of them – although he once found a yellow plastic bag of CDs that she said someone must have left under a chair – except at the regular mass seance, which took place in the evening on the second Tuesday of every month.

For this event, most of the furniture would be relegated to the kitchen. The curtains were drawn and the sofa dragged in front of the empty fireplace. Although it was a different affair to the one he was used to, 'mass' was perhaps too ambitious a qualifier. The occasion was formal in an amateur way, as if the participants weren't really used to being with other people. The downstairs room would fill up from about seven o'clock with a dozen men wearing business suits or Australian oiled cotton jackets. Collar-length white hair and a navy-blue Guernsey pullover indicated a retiree. Each of them seemed to have a single prominent defect – a thickened jaw, one eye too large for the other – and while they presented as well off, Shaw thought they lacked the healthy patina and slightly overfed look you would expect of older west London. Packed into the tiny front room, forced to regroup every time the door opened to admit a late arrival, they shouted cheerfully enough at each other but lacked confidence. He recognised one or two of them, but he couldn't think from where. There were rarely any women.

After perhaps half an hour, during which she asked her favourite of the week to hand round glasses of medium-dry sherry and Waitrose nibbles, Annie would take her place on the sofa, smile vaguely around for a minute or two, then slip stage by difficult stage into the mediumistic coma. The men gazed uncomfortably past her at the wall above the fireplace. None of them spoke or moved, although sometimes a quick sideways glance might be exchanged. It was less pleasant, more of an effort, for her to produce anything in these circumstances. She was tired afterwards. There was a prolonged period of disconnection, a shallow delirium in which her legs twitched and shook. The men, released slowly, as if from a similar psychic bondage, coughed and shifted their feet. They regarded one another blankly; then, having stared at Annie for a while – in the hope, perhaps, of something more – left the house one by one, letting in the cold evening air. Shaw, who often stayed behind to make her a cup of tea and help drag the sofa back into its usual position, watched them drift away across the graveyard. When they had quite gone, Annie would smile tiredly, pat his forearm, touch his shoulder. If there was a kind of flirtatiousness to these gestures, she was, he thought, only trying unconsciously to make a bond with him. They were the mannerisms of a tired performer. It wasn't something she could see she was doing.

One evening after the seance he saw that the map from Tim's office, or one exactly like it, had appeared on the front-room wall. Fastened with a dozen or so equally spaced bright red drawing pins, it fitted precisely into the discoloured area above the fireplace. But when Shaw drew her attention to this – saying something like 'It might almost belong here' – Annie became irritable.

'It does belong here,' she said. 'It's mine. It's my map.'

Then, as if she expected him to argue: 'It's mine. It was always mine. If you want to help, just go and put the sherry glasses in the dishwasher.'

Shaw stared up at the map which, overpowering the dove-grey fitted carpet and 1980s pine furniture, now dominated the room. Here the early-evening light, undiffused by water, fell more directly than it did on the houseboat, revealing the paper to be stiff and fragile, furred with use, prone to curl at the edges. Close to, it had a faint smell, a little like old books, a little like used bathwater. There were random discolourations. Worn places, greyish and greasy, were distributed along the coastlines and in the middle of the oceans, as if generations of forefingers had drawn attention to locations the significance of which would always escape the unschooled viewer. When Shaw blinked, the sea obligingly changed places with the land.

Later he said, 'You shouldn't tire yourself like this.'

Through the window he could see the last client to leave – a man in mustard-yellow cords and a maroon pullover who had stood through the whole seance with what looked like a shoebox under his arm – still loitering near the entrance to the graveyard. After a minute or so he was joined by two women in calf-length trousers and another man with startlingly white hair. All four of them were in their sixties, well preserved, with fluting voices and an assortment of tics. One of the women had a pair of dachshunds on a single leash. After a discussion they got into an Audi estate. There was some slamming and reopening of doors, then the car moved off eastwards along South Worple Way towards the White Hart Lane level cross-ing. Shaw watched with a sort of incomprehension.

'Who are these people anyway?' he said. 'They only take advantage.'

'You're very nice,' Annie said, 'but a bit naive.'

He pondered this judgement over chicken and ham-hock pie at the Earl of March. The pub seemed emptier than usual and something in the air was making his eyes itch.

'Don't look at me,' the girl behind the bar told him. 'It's whatever they've put in the lavatories. It's been like it all day.'

'I wasn't looking at you,' Shaw said.

A few days after the map turned up on Annie's front-room wall, he met Tim Swann at the river end of Barnes. It was a Saturday, more like early spring than summer, and the sky was widening above the Chiswick shore. Tim presented as vaguely as ever. He wore the sleeves of his yellowish cotton-corduroy jacket rolled to the elbow. He had done something that left him with a mild uniform redness on one side of his face. He was staring into the display window of an estate agent, one of the crocodile of a dozen or so that slithered its way up the high street from the river, and he had encumbered himself with a couple of damp-looking carrier bags which he held up for Shaw to see. They were heavy enough to have left inflamed creases across the palms of his hands.

'Always get to the fishmonger early,' he advised.

Then, as though he might buy something if only property would act a little more sensibly: 'Look at these fucking prices.'

Shaw joined him at the window and they talked for a bit. Then Tim said he had to be in Hammersmith. They walked up as far as Barnes Pond together. Sunlight glittered on the traffic sawing its way round from Church Road into Station Road. Mallards could be heard squabbling on the little island in the middle of the pond, while over in the Essex House car park the farmers market busied itself inevitably towards lunch – anxious bankers from France and Scandinavia vying for the last of the hand-made pasta, free-range meats from Somerset doing as well as ever. Between eleven and twelve the green had filled with strolling project managers, their children and identical chocolate Labradors turned out for a walk in the Cotswolds; now toddlers crowded out the margins of the pond, shyly offering ends of artisan sourdough to the geese and seagulls in the shallows. 'Darling,' someone called, '*please* don't let them bully you like that!' Tim regarded these activities with barely suppressed irritation, a tension which expressed itself in sudden small movements of his shoulders or the corners of his mouth. 'The Mort Lake, or "Dark Pool",' he said. 'If they knew anything about the history – if they knew the thing John Dee knew about this place – they'd keep their bloody children at home.'

Though he had no idea what was implied here, Shaw suspected some reference to *The Water House*, or *Journeys of Our Genes*. He could only shrug. He had given up trying to read either of them. 'Do I know anything more than them?' he wondered, in a tone he hoped would indicate that he did but that the issue of what *could* be known was perhaps more complex than anyone else might assume. 'I'm not sure I do. You're the one with the ideas.'

Tim chuckled. 'Quite right,' he said.

They stared thoughtfully across the pond for a moment or two. The traffic locked up, moved again, locked up again. That morning everyone was in too good a mood to use the horn. 'If they knew why the Dark Pools had emptied themselves overnight in 2001 they'd keep the kids at home,' Tim said. 'Oh yes,' he added, smiling grimly to himself. 'You're wondering why I use the plural there.'

'Is that your bus, by the way?'

'Christ.'

Shaw watched him struggle off between the Maserati
Biturbos and Pashley beach bikes, swapping his bags of soaking
fish from one hand to the other. As he went he called over his
shoulder:

'We'll need you up in the Midlands again next week!'

They caught a train to Wolverhampton on the Tuesday. It was
later in the day than Shaw expected, and more crowded. The
train stopped everywhere: after each stop people would wander
helplessly up and down, banging their luggage on the seats as
if lost in some much less linear system and asking: 'Is this the
quiet carriage?' Piles of luggage built up quickly in the aisle,
caused blockages outside the toilet. Shaw sat in a window seat.
Tim sat opposite, watching the gently rolling partly wooded
landscape grey a little in the distance under rain. There were
lines of poplars closer to, and, racing along in the foreground,
low damp pasture which gave way to standing water then small
fields overgrown with brambles. A strong smell of partly digested
beer filled the carriage. Shaw asked Tim if he wanted anything
to eat. Tim looked at him in what seemed to be amusement.

All the way north, Shaw could hear a couple talking in the
seat behind his.

With a little inadvertent sigh of pleasure the woman said,
'There must be some meaning to these clouds!'

They were complex, layered, torn about by winds, bathed
in a dull metallic light; but the man next to her wasn't interested. 'Where's Michael? Where's Michael?' he kept saying
into his phone, his voice too quiet and too close to Shaw's ear
to be comfortable. 'Don't forget now. Don't forget!' All with
a kind of hidden urgency, as if fearing surveillance – 'Where's
Michael?'

Then, in a different tone, disappointed but dismissive at the same time, 'You won't forget him? All right. All right then. Goodbye for now.'

'I prefer my mint tea made from real mint leaves,' the woman said.

'Eat?' Tim asked Shaw finally. He looked around. 'What would you suggest?'

A local cab, a Toyota smelling of dogs and fish, awaited them at Wolverhampton. The driver seemed to know Tim already. He was a small man in a slick-look Castrol rally jacket from the 1970s, his face reddened, lined and folded from sixty or seventy years of Midland life. Some kind of infection caused him, every time he approached a traffic island, to take out an old-fashioned cotton handkerchief and carefully wipe his watery eyes. Once, he looked back over his shoulder at Shaw as if they were sitting at nearby tables in a pub and said, 'Those hawthorn brides, they aren't so fine now, are they? They seem a little tired for all their airs!' After that, he kept staring and nodding until the Toyota began to creep across into the opposite carriageway. Tim leaned forward briskly from the back seat, cupped the top of the driver's head in one hand and adjusted it to face forward.

'Just try and focus,' he said.

'It's much too late for hawthorn,' Shaw appealed to them. 'The hawthorn's finished long ago, surely?'

Ring-road landscapes of takeout and tattoo parlour gave way to suburban garden centres and sports fields, which in turn gave way to sandy heath and woodland – English Heritage country, where every hamlet claimed to have hosted a meeting of Parliament in the fifteenth century. After five or ten minutes of this, Shaw began to see signs he recognised.

'This is Kinver,' he said. 'This is where Helen lives. What are we doing here?'

Tim laughed.

'All will be revealed,' he said. 'I don't doubt.'

'You seem angry,' said Shaw.

It was raining by the time they arrived. The village lay as impermanent-looking as an industrial estate under the street lights; further up the valley, squalls blustered across the scarp, blackening the ancient sandstone above Helen's house, bullying the shrubberies below. Shaw and the cab driver stood soaked and ill at ease while Tim held his finger on the doorbell. Eventually she let them in.

'Hi,' Shaw said.

She was thinner than he remembered, dressed in three-quarter-length compression tights and a Lululemon top. He smiled at her but received no smile in return. The door slammed behind them. It was colder inside than out; a moth bumped around the hall. The driver, finding himself in the living room, stared with a kind of amused disbelief at the Georgia O'Keeffe flower prints on the wall. Since Shaw's last visit, the furniture seemed to have been rearranged at random. His sense of Helen now was as someone who had leaned on her certainties once too often. She bumped around the room as vaguely as the moth, then took Tim off into the kitchen, from which she could be heard warning him, 'Annie won't stick for this.'

There was a silence, then Tim shouted suddenly: 'Annie can keep the fucking map, if that's what she wants. But we'll have everything else.'

The driver laughed and tried to catch Shaw's eye.

'"They can *keep* the fucking map",' he mimicked.

Shaw, embarrassed by the accuracy of the imitation, stared away and through the French windows. Out there in the streaming rain, halide construction lamps sprang to life and in

their sudden actinic glare Helen's garden pond could be seen
to be surrounded by piles of builders' equipment and materials.
Exhaust fumes drifted through the cones of light. A miniature
JCB began grinding its way up and down the lawn, executing
sudden, jerky turns, while three blurred bulky figures in hi-vis
rainwear and safety glasses assembled a hydraulic breaker and
connected it up. They seemed slow and untrained. After a hurried conversation during which Shaw was ignored, Tim and
the driver went out to help: all five men began to lever up the
pool surround. When this proved more difficult than expected,
they used the excavator bucket to smash it to pieces. Fragments
tumbled in but seemed to take some time to sink, as if they
had entered a more viscous medium than water. At the same
time a wild thrashing about began in the centre of the pool. He
heard Tim shouting, 'Wait! Wait! This isn't going to work!'
The excavator ground to a halt, tilted over slowly with its arm
extended at a curious angle. The surface frothed and spurted
up; the lights flickered, dimmed and went out, but not before
Shaw had seen the workmen discard their tools and clamber
down awkwardly into the water, while Tim and the driver
urged them on. There was a long silent pause, then they all
stumbled back in through the French windows and struggled
about between the John Lewis armchairs with a bulky object
wrapped in blue tarpaulin. It was dripping wet.

Helen, contemptuous but essentially subdued, regarded these
events from the living-room doorway. Her hair was slicked
against her head, as if she'd been out in the garden too.

'You shouldn't be associating yourself with this,' she told
Shaw.

'I don't even know what's going on,' Shaw said.

'Then why did you come?'

There was no answer to that.

'I feel as if you're hoping to attach your anxiety to someone else,' he said. 'I don't blame you, when people come into your house like this.' Then he heard himself add: 'I'm living without explanations, if you can understand that.'

The workmen had abandoned their attempt to carry whatever was in the tarpaulin. Instead, they were dragging it along the hall towards the front door. A rug caught beneath it. A small table was knocked over.

'Oh for Jesus Christ's sake,' Helen said.

'Sorry,' said one of the men.

Because he couldn't think of anything else to do, Shaw followed them out.

'Haven't you got any idea what's going on here?' Helen shouted after him. 'Don't you care? Just ask yourself why you came here!'

'I don't know,' Shaw said, more to himself than her. 'I don't know why.'

He stood on the doorstep watching them deal with the tarpaulin and its contents. First they tried to manhandle it into the boot of the cab. As a result there was some feeble thrashing about and the tarpaulin came loose. An arm flopped out, the hand at the end of it clenching and unclenching; it was so white it looked green in the illumination leaking from the house. Shaw thought he heard low groans. 'So that worked out as well as could be expected,' the driver said. Eventually, after some effort, everything was forced into the back seat. By then the tarpaulin had gaped open into a shape like a Georgia O'Keeffe flower. Whatever it contained was always obscured by the struggle, but you could still see the hand clenching and unclenching fitfully. Water continued to pour out over the sills until the doors were shut.

The workmen wandered away to the back of the house; as

they went past Shaw heard one of them say, 'I'd begin again. Start the whole batch again from scratch.' Meanwhile the driver, whose part in the undertaking had left him bent double in the rear footwell, clambered over the seats into the front and started the engine. Tim got in and sat beside him. They looked over at Shaw but through him too. Shaw stood watching the Toyota drive away. Then he went into the house and asked Helen if she would take him to Wolverhampton.

'You came in a cab,' she pointed out, 'so fucking leave in one.'

Then she added: 'I'd like to know how much it's going to cost me to have that pool repaired.'

14

The Little Swimmer

For a week or two after that it was difficult to find anything
to say. When Shaw arrived at the office in the mornings, mist
was lifting off the river in threads. He would sit for a while
watching the sun dismiss it while he disentangled himself
from the previous night's dreams. Tim arrived later, if at all.
Conversation with him when he did appear was vague, hard
to enter or to exit. He had a more-than-usually preoccupied
air. Shaw, anxious to know what had happened that night in
Kinver, could find no reason to ask. He didn't want to seem
curious. Every day that passed made it more difficult, until
after a fortnight he felt unable to bring the subject up at all.
Confused and reluctant, he missed an appointment with Annie
Swann; then another. Tim didn't seem to mind.

St Margaret's Day of the Dead came and went, its cele-
brations ushering in deep summer, the city's burden of heat
and humidity. Things were quieter than usual at 17 Wharf
Terrace, especially at night. His cycles of insomnia reversing
unpredictably, Shaw slept too well or not at all. He dreamed
of the pre-Roman landscapes of the Brent confluence, over
the leech-ridden intertidal mudflats and treacherous alder carrs
of which an echoing voice repeated insistently: 'Those osier
brides are here again.' It was his own. Three in the morning

he found himself watching *Night Moves* with the sound turned down – replaying Act Two over and over again as he tried to identify the exact point at which Gene Hackman's private detective Harry Moseby fails to understand he has become a function of everyone else's scheme of things. Or else he sat by the open window, listening for movement in the room next door, looking at his own hands.

One morning at the Earl of March he wound up the little plastic swimmer he had taken from Annie Swann's house and dropped it into a pint of London Pride, where it bobbed and clattered its way around the smooth but unrelenting inner curve of the glass.

'So what do you think of that?' he asked the barmaid.

'Not much,' she said. She didn't think much of a thing like that.

Shaw fished it out and held it up so that its arms rotated energetically in the air. 'It worked better in the bath this morning,' he admitted.

The barmaid dried a glass.

'*So* disgusting,' she said. 'You've got to drink that pint now.'

Eleven a.m., and the river was down to naked mud, with here and there a faint iridescence as if something was seeping up from beneath. Dogs ran up and down the towpath. Sunshine slanted in through the dust onto the uneven parquet floor. There was a thick, not-unpleasant smell of flash-fried steak and last night's beer. In a corner at the back, a man struck up a conversation with the two older women at the table next to his. 'I go to Hastings for the fish,' Shaw heard him say. 'Because I know they'll always have some fresh fish. I go down early, for the day.' He seemed pleased with his own acumen. He usually drove down there for the day, he said, from Richmond. You could always get some fresh fish if you got down early. 'How funny, we come from Brighton,' one of the women said quickly, perhaps to head off further repetition; all three of them laughed at the coincidence, partial, fuzzy, yet somehow perfectly apt. They opened a bag of crisps and spread it out between them.

When Shaw shook the little swimmer, its clockwork seemed to hesitate a moment, then rush on. Golden drops of London Pride flew off its arms and legs into the light.

'Want it for your kids?' he offered.

'I don't,' the barmaid said. 'I don't like it, and my kids wouldn't either.'

'All kids like toys,' Shaw said.

They watched the swimmer wind down.

Later, he made his way to Kingston along the towpath, then back across the royal park, intending to finish his day at the Idle Hour, a slacker pub hidden in the veinous maze of alleys where Little Chelsea loses confidence and is absorbed without pity by the outskirts of Barnes. Instead he found himself on South Worple Way, not far from the medium's house.

The old burial ground lay empty and dark. The surrounding houses – including Annie Swann's – seemed untenanted. They seemed closer and taller than usual. They seemed to lean in on the cemetery. All the windows were unlit. As he watched, a BMW rocked out of its parking space beside the recycling bins and was driven almost silently away. As if released by this event, a fox slipped across the road, through the railings and into the cemetery. Shaw followed. He could make out nothing in there but graves. Benches. The litter bin. Then a hard little point of light, shining out of the leaf litter at the base of the psychiatric-hospital wall where he had first met Tim Swann.

'Tim!' he called. 'Is that you?'

Shadows thickened as he made his way between the leaning headstones. Something was going on down there, in the trees, in the mud, among the discarded food wrappers: as he began to run towards it, the light was occluded by a grotesque shape, human in form, thin but clumsy, first stumbling agitatedly to its feet then staring back over its shoulder as if it had seen something approaching from deeper in the graveyard.

'It *is* you!' called Shaw; and then, 'Tim, it's me!'

Swann hesitated a moment, then, making the gesture of someone who can't stop to talk because he needs to pick up his dry-cleaning, struggled off towards the exit. A line of figures streamed silently across the graveyard behind him.

Even in the dim orange light, Shaw recognised them as clients of Annie's, regular attendees of the mass seance. They looked as surprised to find themselves there as Shaw did. Tripping over their dogs, bumping into one another, their arms struggling and flapping, their well-worn Barbour jackets billowing out behind them, they bore down on Tim Swann. By the gates he slipped, saved himself, sped on round the corner by the recycling bins. He had an unathletic way of running, upper body arched tensely, head thrown back and to one side; under one arm he was clutching a long plastic tube, the kind of thing in which you might transport a poster or an architect's drawing. The night was so quiet Shaw could hear him breathing, even from there. Annie's clientele, flat-footed yet curiously quick, pursued him down the empty street, over the railway line and through the allotments, past the Idle Hour, all the way to the edge of Barnes Common, which spread away east, sandy heath and large silent houses colourless in the radium light. There, they appeared to lose him. As a result there was some shouting, musical, anxious and apparently wordless. Subsequently they ran up and down the irregular footpaths, looking behind

171

chestnut trees and under the clumps of gorse and blackthorn; while their little dogs – silent and energetic, bodies elongated and snaky in the shadows – quartered the woods alongside Station Road.

After a few minutes, a second group of people joined the search, arriving in ones and twos from the direction of Putney. A generation younger than the seance regulars, with broad socio-economic similarities to Shaw's fellow tenants at 17 Wharf Terrace, they seemed correspondingly more active. In repose their faces had the raw look of people who have become, too early in life, estate agents or wellness coordinators. The men arrived on bicycles with names like Venge Elite; the women were dressed for athleisure in close-fit body-warmers featuring a discreet hi-vis detail. They had equipped themselves with powerful single-diode head torches. It would be difficult, Shaw thought later, to describe the two parties as 'opposed'. If they had differences, they also seemed familiar with one another. There was discussion between them, and that was familiar too. They were trying to decide what to do with Tim Swann if they caught him. By then there were twenty or thirty of them, milling about the metalled pathway by the old tennis courts. Their voices, assertive yet not entirely confident on one side, polite and fluting on the other, rose and fell in the cooling air.

'Really, the best thing ...'

'I'm sorry, but I think you'll find ...'

With simple, firm exchanges like this it seemed their differences could be resolved. But without warning, a third group appeared, oldish hard-favoured working men with Midlands accents, dressed in yellow site helmets and hi-vis wear. A fierce struggle broke out. Someone was pushed to the ground; someone else fell on top of them. Before long they were clawing inexpertly at one another's cheeks, which stretched like plasticine and came away in lumps. Shaw felt dizzy when he saw that. He wasn't sure what he was looking at. Arms rose and fell. For a moment, he thought he saw the taxi driver from Kinver. An astonishingly fat man toiled away in the middle of it all, treading on anyone unfortunate enough to have gone down, his feet like canal boats in brand-new Mizuno running shoes, while two dogs barked energetically around his legs. Smaller scuffles eddied away from the main mass, energetic at first then dispersing across the common towards the residential backwaters the other side of Rocks Lane. 'Coom by, lads!' a tenor voice called clearly. 'Coom by now!' Distance distorted the combatants' faces further, magnifying their little deformities. The longer the struggle went on, the quieter it seemed to become, until it was like looking at an old woodcut, the aesthetic of which disconnects the modern viewer forever from the original meanings of the scene. Shaw was unable, somehow, to believe that anything bad was happening: it all seemed part and parcel of Tim Swann's existence, along with a bag of wet fish or a voice overheard on a train to the Midlands, hard to parse yet somehow perfectly ordinary – even humdrum – in its own terms. He stood for a while at the edge of the woods, uncertain what to do next, watching gangs of two or three hunt one another across the open ground; then, because Tim showed no sign of reappearing, turned and went home.

In the night, he was certain he heard them again, struggling quietly in the street outside. But when he looked, nobody was there, and it was just a fine drizzle glistening on the opposite pavement.

A rainy afternoon at the care facility off the A316. Shaw's mother sat watching her favourite Attenborough box set. She seemed well. Shaw occupied himself leafing through the photograph albums, while two and sometimes three generations of other people's visitors, on their way to sit speechlessly in groups beneath the seascapes in the day room, pushed unoccupied wheelchairs up and down the corridor outside.

'But how are you really?' he said.

She held up her left hand, studied the back of it briefly; then, angling it so that the late-afternoon light caught a landscape of dunes and striations viewed from some miles up, showed it to him.

'How do you think I am?' she asked. And, indicating something on the screen he couldn't quite see: 'Look at that! I never get tired of that!'

'I meant, in yourself,' Shaw tried to explain. 'How you are in yourself.'

In addition to the albums, two shoeboxes contained photographs that couldn't be placed. No one knew – that's to say neither Shaw nor his mother knew – who had taken them, or when. Or perhaps they were simply out of step with her life. Some were stuffed into old yellow Kodak envelopes; a shifting population, determined by this or that pressure of memory and sentiment, she kept wrapped in a batik scarf. Among the latter, that afternoon, Shaw had found a beach scene taken during one of her absences. Overexposed, divided asymmetrically by an ironed-out crease, it showed a curved strip of sand, some low, tired-looking waves, and a stretch of railings against which leaned a boy he thought might be himself.

The first few years of Shaw's life, they had lived on and off with his great-aunts Rose and Mabel. Rose and Mabel kept their house dark inside. It was terraced, capacious, not far from the promenade, with a garden narrow as an alley and barley-sugar brick edgings to the vegetable bed. All Shaw could recall from that time was watching with his mother as snow fell very slowly, the size of pennies, into the sea; later, during her periods of nomadism, he would stay with the aunts again, sometimes for months, once for an entire year: a cheerful little boy, always running errands, always welcome, always learning how they lived.

Rose and Mabel were big soft women, Jehovah's Witnesses who encouraged him to study *The Watchtower* when he came home from school. He read about a woman with a hole in her cheek from 'cigarette cancer'. He read about a man who survived a bullet in his brain. Another had a surgical window in his stomach. What was Shaw to understand from that? He couldn't think of them as entirely human. Had they been cured by the Witnesses? Or were they simply examples of some way of being he had failed to grasp? As he turned the pages he could feel a kind of sticky slowness in the passing of time. He ate his tea in the aunts' kitchen, where the shallow ancient sink smelled of carbolic soap. Each time he left the house to go down to the sea, he experienced a sense of relief. On the afternoon the photograph was taken, he remembered, the cloud had lifted suddenly in the west.

Two o'clock on a mid-December Sunday. Shaw stared down at the sand from the promenade car park of the Lifeboatman pub. Wet light shone off the council benches. Dogs hurried about. Restored 1960s motorcycles leaned together in a row, their aluminium fuel tanks dull with beads of water. The dismounted motorcyclists crowded round a boy who couldn't start his machine. He had a blank determined look. His thick forelock was dyed bright white blond, the rest of his hair cut so short it seemed shaved: the blond swag flopped and flailed up and down as he jumped repeatedly on the kickstart. From the steamed-up window of the pub, a toddler watched in wild excitement, laughing and screwing its face up in expressions impossible to interpret. Someone in the bar could be heard shouting: 'You know what coastal towns are like.' Eventually the engine caught. Blipping the throttle, the boy swerved violently back and forth across the beach, throwing up fountains of sand.

I wanted to be that boy's friend, Shaw thought, someone with a haircut like his who would need no encouragement to jump on the pillion and, full of rum and black, laugh all the way back to London in the dark while the shuddering headlight beam captured a banked curve, a fox in the hedge, a road sign at an odd angle. But that was already impossible and in this picture I'm the one wearing the maroon school blazer and grey trousers, standing on the sea wall looking down. Life goes on in front of that one – and behind him in weather-blistered chalets, health-food stores, parked Fords – but not somehow, though he's always welcome, always obliging and cheerful, in him. He watches and listens. Inside the Lifeboatman the barman rings time on an imitation ship's bell above the spirit optics. Over by the sea, jackdaws pick at the tideline, shiny and sharp-looking. Oafish young gulls stand motionless and unhappy until one of them finds – washed up among the faded Fanta cans and tubey weed – a human forearm so white it looks green.

This they begin to peck at, first speculatively and without much hope, often walking off after a few attempts only to return out of desperation or boredom; then with growing energy.

The boy on the motorcycle also seems to have found something, which he waves about in the air. Shortly afterwards, fifteen or twenty people, mostly middle aged or old, rush out of the pub, where they've been eating Sunday lunch. Inside, the roasts and pot pies are already cooling and hardening. The tide's coming in or going out. No one seems to understand what they're looking at yet. When they do, they'll all run over there. But that's not in the photograph.

Shaw sat in his mother's room, turning the picture the way she had turned her hand to catch the light. It was late afternoon. Tea trolleys could now be heard in every corner of the care facility. Coastal towns are suicide towns, he thought: although it's rarely an actual suicide that people commit in them, more a fading-away, an adjustment of values, the step change to a less energetic state. For his mother this transition had always presented as its opposite: a lucky accident, a holiday unpredict-ably prolonged, a chance at a new life – though with hindsight each new move would appear not so much an act of choice as a loss of concentration. He went over to her now and showed her the photograph.

'Do you remember this?'

'I can't be bothered with that now, Mickey,' said his mother. She gave him her most lucid smile. 'Whatever it is.'

'I'm not Mickey,' Shaw said. He went out of the room and down the corridor a little way and shouted, 'I'm not called fucking Mickey.' Then he went back in and picked up one of the shoeboxes and emptied it into her lap. 'You asked me to fetch these,' he reminded her. Prints of all sizes – their aspect ratios and styles of glaze clearly identifying the decade in which they had seen the light – fanned across her skirt and slithered onto the floor around her feet. 'I have to get your carer to fetch these every time I come here. So you might at least show some interest.' In a more conciliatory tone he added, 'I think this one might be me.'

'Who looks at those old things?'

'You do.'

She pushed his hand away. 'I'm trying to watch TV.'

'You weren't there, of course,' Shaw said, 'so I don't know who took it. You were never there.'

'I couldn't bear to be held back.'

'And what was your solution? Get a family, abandon it, get another?'

'At least I took you with me.'

'No you didn't.'

She turned up the television and shouted over it, 'I always took you with me. I'd never leave you in some shithole like this to die.'

'Fuck,' said Shaw. 'Fuck.'

He stared for a moment or two at the world of David Attenborough, millions of cockroaches crawling over a mound of bat guano in a cave in Borneo, then left.

Aunt Rose had passed away first. She had been the Witness, it turned out. They held her funeral, non-denominational at Mabel's insistence, in a crematorium a mile or two outside the town, by the roundabout where the main road curved off towards London. Mabel, her saggy, powdered features looking as if they were made of cloth or plastic (something, anyway, not flesh, too disappointed or muddled to be flesh), sat in a pew at the back, whispering loudly. The music got stuck and repeated itself for twenty minutes before the conveyer belt jerked into life and her sister's coffin vanished through the velour curtain.

'It was always arguments,' she told Shaw as they were leaving. 'Arguments, arguments, arguments.'

During the reception she wandered off. It was often difficult to find her after that, even when she was there. Shaw would have to make himself more useful around the house, she said; and although his mother took him inland not long after, and he

never saw Mabel again, he did help put the *Watchtower* magazines under the stairs, baled in twine, for collection. 'I never
approved of that sect,' Mabel said, 'and it was wrong of her
to claim I did.' Shaw remembered the heavy smell of talcum
powder; the slow, glutinous tick of an alarm clock in the night.
Thirteen, perhaps fourteen years old, he had felt as if the front
room, with its brown furniture, chenille tablecloth and green
carpet, would, if he wasn't careful, absorb him, a clever boy
who had nevertheless been caught and would henceforth have
to be the man of the house. On rainy evenings, rather than go
back there, he'd sheltered in the public toilets.

To Shaw, the skirmish he had witnessed on Barnes Common
felt not simply 'like a dream' – some easy but unsettling
sequence of actions, some suspended peculiarity of the light
– but like one of those dreams the content of which doesn't
quite connect with your waking experience of it. Asleep you
feel one emotion; awake, another. In the dream you're guilty
of some furtive sexual lapse; on waking, and for the rest of the
morning, all you feel is a growing anxiety about an errand you
think you might have forgotten, an email you ought to have
sent.

Tim remained silent on the issue. He had turned up at the
office as usual the next day, and, though preoccupied and
withdrawn, seemed unhurt apart from a few inflamed-looking
scratches around his wrists and a bruise low on the side of
his neck which sometimes made it difficult to turn his head.
Presumably he had spent the night pushing his way into some
patch of gorse or blackthorn until he was sure his pursuers
– having dispersed to a density at which they no longer felt
territorial pressure – had stopped fighting among themselves,
separated their dogs and gone home. Had he been trying to

steal back the map? It was no easier to discuss the incident than it had been to bring up the events at the house in Kinver. Later, Shaw would be surprised to what degree this frustration contributed to his rage.

Business, meanwhile, remained slow. Telephone queries were down on the month; everything else was down to zero. They were dispatching *Journeys of Our Genes* at the rate of a copy a week, often less. Tim seemed uninterested, though he sometimes opened a browser window, brought up *The Water House* and stared for a few minutes at the screen as if expecting news. In an impulsive attempt to gain his attention, Shaw said:

'I read your book.'

This produced a faint smile, as if *Journeys of Our Genes* reminded Tim of some aberration they had shared in their teens.

'What did you think?'

'I quite enjoyed it,' Shaw said.

'Mounts up, doesn't it? The evidence?'

'I don't know if it exactly mounts up.'

'Well,' Tim said.

'I notice the map's gone.'

'What map's that?'

'Your map,' Shaw said. 'The world map. The map of the world.'

'Ah, that one. Yes, yes it has. For the moment anyway. I don't think we'll be needing the seance results either.'

'But—'

Tim shook his head. 'They were a bit of a blind alley, truth be told. Didn't you feel that? I know I did.' He scratched suddenly at his left wrist. 'Annie has her uses,' he concluded, 'and I'd be the last to deny it. But spiritualism was never the most important of them.' He chuckled and added: 'There's always been a bit of a tussle over the map.'

Shaw felt too depressed to try and tease out whatever meaning might be hidden in all this. It hadn't been much of a job, even when you took the seance reporting into account. He couldn't see, he said, what might be left if that went.

Tim received this assessment in silence, then suggested: 'Prison libraries, you know I bet that's a lively market. Why not look into it?'

Shaw had his doubts. Inside a week, restless and without anything to do, he was thrown back on inner resources that turned out to be flimsier than he remembered. He increased his visits to the care home until his mother, already destabilised by the incident with the photographs, first asked the management to have a talk with him, then refused to see him at all, instead leaving a message for him with the staff. 'Mrs Shaw did seem rather anxious that you read this,' they said, handing over the carefully folded piece of paper on which she had written, 'I don't want you to talk to me any more.' He stared at these words, then out of the office window at the cars going by on the A316.

'I see,' he said; though he didn't.

At work he kept up with his favourite porn sites or busied himself trying to pick the lock of the door at the back of the site hut. He downloaded electronic books, the majority of which turned out to be even more unreadable than *Journeys of Our Genes*. At home he trawled listlessly the Powell and Pressburger back catalogue, or slept. He was settling down to *Black Narcissus* one early evening, before what he hoped would be a nine o'clock pie supper at the Earl of March, when the landline rang. It was Victoria Nyman.

'Hello, stranger,' she said. 'What happened to you?'

15

The Sunken Land Begins
to Rise Again

Shaw hadn't spoken to anyone since the day before.

He cleared his throat. He was suddenly aware of himself; astonished that he recognised her voice; puzzled that his own presence sounded so loud in the room. 'What happened to *you*?' he managed to reply.

Victoria considered this for longer than he would have expected.

'Not much,' she said eventually. Then, as though studying some half-familiar object from a distance: 'A quiet sort of life, mine, if odd.' And with gathering energy: 'I've been everywhere today, mind you. I forgot how to get on the M40, and then where to get off it. Now I'm parked illegally outside a restaurant just north of Brook Green. It used to be a sort of upmarket chippy.'

Shaw cleared his throat again. 'Are you lost then?'

'No, no. I told you.' She raised her voice. 'Brook Green.' Another pause, then: 'We could meet up somewhere!' And when he didn't answer immediately: 'I mean, we don't have to.'

'No, no,' Shaw said. 'That's great. That would be great.'

Once the arrangement was made and the connection broken, he found that he had walked the landline phone over

to his window and was staring down Wharf Terrace towards
the brewery. He could hear great wooden blocks of music
tumbling from the open side windows of a passing SUV. On
the river a fours coach bawled instructions through her loud-
hailer. Traffic was building up on the Mortlake Road over
towards Barnes, as the White Hart junction held then released,
held then released its evening emissions of Range Rovers and
Audis. Next, he propped the handset back on its stand and
stared at that: cream plastic, ageing quietly to the colour of
cigarette tar. At 17 Wharf Terrace it was the hour you listened
to people's radios up and down the stairwell: bright, eerily
professional voices issuing from closed rooms as if everyone
had a news presenter to supper.

He met Victoria outside La Belle Hélène, embedded in its
windy plaza on the Chiswick shore. When he arrived, she
was leaning against the river wall, gazing doubtfully at some
expensive houseboats, through the glassy neo-modern upper
structures of which, at high water, you could watch the sun
glint on the tideway. They studied one another. She hugged
him more desperately than he would have expected. 'Hello,
stranger!' she said. She was wearing a blue drill boiler suit with
elastic nurse-clasp belt, and carrying a Sainsbury's plastic bag.
Her hair had been cut in a high fade then dyed Daytona yellow
by processes she would later describe to him in detail.

'My God,' he said.

'I was just going to say the same.' She held him at arm's
length. 'But you look so *thin*!'

'I've been working quite hard,' Shaw said modestly.

La Belle Hélène was beginning to fill up. Once inside,
Victoria became thoughtful. 'I remember you always liked
this place,' she said, as if she had concerns but didn't want to

spoil anything. Instead she ate two or three olives and some bread; then drank half a Campari and soda, which seemed to cheer her up. 'I might have the soft-shell crab and salmon tartare. Oh, and look at this. Tortiglioni with grilled manouri and truffle sauce!' She sat back. Sighed. 'Sometimes I do miss London,' she admitted. She bent down suddenly and rifled through the supermarket bag, coming up with a rectangular package wrapped in an artful imitation of brown paper.

'I forgot,' she said: 'I brought you this!'

When he got the wrapping off, Shaw was surprised to find a copy of the old children's book *The Water-Babies* – bumped a bit at the corners and a little like damp and dust to the nose, as if it had been stored in someone's loft; but otherwise in nice condition.

'It belonged to my mother,' Victoria said.

Shaw leafed through some pages at random and read:

I once had a sweet little doll, dears,
The prettiest doll in the world;
Her cheeks were so red and so white, dears,
And her hair was so charmingly curled.
But I lost my poor little doll, dears,
As I played in the heath one day;
And I cried for her more than a week, dears,
But I never could find where she lay.

'It's nice,' he said. 'Thank you.'

At this, she laughed as if she had expected some other response, and looked away. 'Not a favourite of mine, Charles Kingsley,' she admitted. 'But I thought you might like it. I mean, like the joke of it. It's the one book most people re-member from childhood, don't they?' Shaw – who from that deep in childhood recalled only the Mabel Lucie Attwell fairy books – wasn't sure they did. He cleared his throat.

'I like the illustrations,' he said, and thanked her again.

'Let's eat! I'm really hungry.'

'So. How's your life going?' he asked, after they had ordered.

'Well, I have a really interesting new haircut – although to be honest who doesn't these days – and I'm here with you.' She topped him up from their half-bottle of Fleurie, but didn't seem to be drinking much herself. 'Along with everyone else in the world, it would seem. Was it always this crowded in here?'

When he took too long to answer, she said, 'Anyway, this is less a haircut than a personal essay about haircuts.'

'By "your life", I meant in general,' he pointed out.

'Oh God, let's just eat and not go into that. How's yours?'

'The veal is quite good.'

'I always loved this room,' Victoria said later.

It was ten o'clock and there was no milk. Shaw struggled to get the window open. River damp had swollen it night after night into its frame.

'Does the air smell in here?' he said.

If he added up the number of rooms he'd occupied since his arrival in London, it came to ten; a figure which, compared to his experience of rooms, his memories of rooms and the air in them, struck him as being on the low side. He felt as if his life must have pushed him further into double digits than that. Perhaps during his crisis it had: at night when he closed his eyes he sometimes saw rooms in Wembley, South Tottenham and Archway – rooms in places he wasn't sure he'd ever been, ungentrified and ill-lit, their doors forever loose on the hinge, their windows forever stuck shut or open – evolving and devolving around him like failed forms of life. What he meant by that, he wasn't sure, except perhaps that they resembled the temporary casings bodged up by some inept larva on the bed of a stream. Of them, 17 Wharf Street was, to Shaw's mind, the least ept of all.

'You were only here once,' he reminded her.

But Victoria had already moved on.

'Oh, and your *fish*,' she cried, as if only then remembering she'd given it to him. 'Your brilliant fish!' The fish stared solemnly at her from its popped lapis eyes. The Thames airs, Shaw now saw, had taken their toll: its lips were dull, its Peruvian silver flanks darkened with oxides, its body less flexible. 'How are you two getting on?' Victoria wanted to know. 'Still good friends?'

Shaw gave up on the window.

'I don't think I've got any alcohol,' he said.

She put the fish back carefully on the shelf. 'I'm not drinking that much. I never really did – only with you, because your panic made me panic.' She came over to the window, looked out onto Wharf Terrace briefly to make sure her car was still there, then put her arms round him without warning.

'And are you still in a panic?' Then, releasing him and turning away: 'My womanly senses tell me you are.'

'I could go out and get something,' Shaw offered.

They had instant coffee instead, and sat on the bed a little apart as if they didn't know each other. All the rest of the evening she seemed to him to be hiding her expectations. 'You never answer my emails,' she said once. Before he could think of a way to answer, she took his cup away and pushed him back on the bed. 'I don't believe you even read them. You're *so* missing out. I'm having real adventures up there in the provinces.' She began to struggle out of the boiler suit. 'What's our secret,' she said, 'people like us? How do we close all the shutters so completely? Don't even try to answer. Neither of us knows what I'm talking about.'

Shaw, recognising this as a moment of weakness, asked: 'Did you really see a corpse when you were thirteen?'

'That's just something I used to tell people to get their attention.'

'Did it work?'

She shrugged. 'Oh, I don't know.' Then: 'It worked with you.'

Around two o'clock in the morning she said:

'We're both thin now. How are you getting on with your mother?'

His mother was driving him mad, but there was nothing new there. 'She's not talking to me at present.'

'It's up to you to make the effort, you know.'

'I can't think of a short reply to that.'

She laughed. 'You can. You just don't want to risk upsetting me when things are going so well.'

Then, after a pause: 'And the job that's tiring you out so?'

Only computer work, he told her: 'Just a few hours' computer work and filing a week, really.' There was some travel, 'Although even to say that is to lay it on a bit.' But it was satisfying enough in its own way, and fun because the office was on a boat. 'I need to read a lot too,' he said. 'Mostly science stuff from the web.' Anyway, it meant he got a walk along the towpath every morning and evening; and from the deck he could see downstream as far as Kew Bridge. 'You should come and look round,' he suggested. 'I can give you the tour. It's handy for the river pubs.' He was aware he wasn't telling her anything, and perhaps she was too.

'I've had enough of water lately,' she said. 'Thanks.'

She wandered across the landing to the lavatory, where he heard her peeing, moving about, running a tap. Everyone else in 17 Wharf Terrace, he thought, was hearing her too. When she returned it wasn't to get back into bed but to stand square at the window, slide up the sash without effort and lean out as far as she could. 'I keep thinking it's raining,' she complained. 'And is the light always this sort of blue here? As if there's an ambulance going past?' Then: 'Oh God, I bet the whole street can see my tits.'

She ducked back into the room; shivered. 'Why do you still live here if you've got a job?'

'It's not really a job,' he admitted. 'It's what everyone has these days.'

Victoria was restless after that, and toured the room. She didn't seem to remember much about it. She examined his things: cheap coats and expensive computer bags humped on the back of the door; a postcard-sized print of Ippolito Caffi's *The Eclipse of the Sun in Venice, July 6, 1842* he had Blu-Tacked to the wall a month or two before, puzzled and attracted in equal measure by its mismatched crowd gathered at the side of the Grand Canal, its mysteriously illuminated quadrant of sky. Every so often she would hold something up for him to see and ask him what it was, and he would reply, 'It's a wind-up toy,' or 'I don't know, I got it in Birmingham.' She opened the wardrobe, closed it again. 'I never keep clothes in there,' Shaw explained, 'because it smells of moth repellent.' It was one of the emptiest reassurances he had ever given anyone.

By then, he was on his feet too. He wanted to clutch at her, bring her to a halt, bring both their lives to a halt for a moment, for what reason he wasn't entirely sure; but he just stood where he was.

'You're ashamed,' she said, coming close and kissing him briefly. 'Don't worry, everyone is. We're all ashamed now. But any gig is a gig.'

At this, a tremendous crash came from the room next door, as if someone had pushed over a pile of luggage. This gave way to separate thuds and scraping sounds, like something being dragged across an uncarpeted floor; followed by a curious unfocused murmur, which broke off suddenly. A phone rang in there, and a voice Shaw didn't recognise said clearly, 'That's of no benefit to us. We should hold off at least until next month.' Silence for a moment, then, 'No,' and the sound of the phone being replaced on its cradle. Someone crossed the room and went quickly down the stairs. The stairwell lights switched themselves on and off briefly from floor to floor; the street door banged open, letting in thick breaths of yeast from the brewery; footsteps rang away down Wharf Terrace in the direction of Mortlake rail station.

'Oh my God,' whispered Victoria.

'That's always happening,' Shaw said.

They stood there not quite sure what to do. Shaw felt derailed, but when he wondered out loud what Victoria was making of it, all she said was, 'This place is awful. You really ought to find somewhere else.' She touched his hand. He felt odd that they should be standing there naked, not quite sure how to react to something that had happened in somebody else's life. He felt she meant to be kind, but also that things seemed vaguer to her than he would have liked them to be: she was thinking about something else. He could forgive anyone that.

'Why did you come down here?' he asked suddenly.

This seemed to break the tension, because she laughed and said: 'For the sex, of course. What did you think?' Then: 'I wanted to tell you something.'

189

'What?'

'Oh God, who knows?' she said. She was continually giving up on herself. It was a style. 'When you're me, you don't even know where to start,' she complained, and hugged him. 'I'm cold now.'

Just before dawn, Shaw heard the street door swing open again and bang against its stop. Cold air forced its way up the stairs, then whoever had come in began their ascent, an unsteady progress adorned with clearly audible breathing and punctuated by periods of rest. After a time, the top-landing lavatory flushed, and 17 Wharf Terrace lay silent again. By then, Victoria was dead to the world and didn't notice. She looked tired, he thought, even in her sleep; with her crest of peroxided hair across the pillow, she looked subtly defeated.

It had started to rain. The quenched air outside the window smelled autumnal – rubbish bins, diesel particulates, something unidentifiable from the river. Shaw fell asleep too, and dreamed of finding a room he'd once lived in – a place he'd forgotten, clean and light, with modern furniture, a repository of all the things he'd forgotten he owned. When he woke, it was mid-morning. Further rain, moving north on a stream of warm air from the Continent, settled itself over west London like an unaired tent. He wondered what had happened next door the night before. It was a Thursday, he thought. Victoria, it turned out, was already gone, leaving a dreamily regretful note folded like a bookmark into the volume she had given him.

'I had such a nice time,' she had written. If he felt like it, he should come up to Shropshire for a visit. The one thing she had up there was plenty of room, and now the roof was fixed he could *easily avoid pneumonia.* 'You ought to take care of your mother,' she went on to say. 'After all, she took care of you!'

Then, less certainly: 'I'm glad you kept the fish. I wasn't sure you were keen on him.'

It was signed, like her emails, 'Your friend Victoria.'

As an afterthought she had added: 'You give too much power to other people. We don't know what to do with it.' This assessment – poked into the thin paper with one of Shaw's favourite Muji pens, leaving comma-shaped holes and tears as a kind of random emphasis – only confused him. 'I'm not one to be giving advice, but that's what you do.'

The first few chapters of *The Water-Babies*, which he skimmed before he went to work, confused him further. He didn't remember reading it as a child. He found himself an-noyed by the little chimney sweep's constant yet somehow unearned sense of guilt.

The tide was down in Brentford, where Tim Swann's barge lay squarely on the mud in a shallow, compacted scoop, the shape of which had been perfected day in and day out over the years. Above it, the sky demonstrated turbulent qualities, as if unknown chemistry was working itself out up there; the weather, Shaw thought, would soon change again. He took care on the strip of rain-polished deck surrounding the site hut. He made sure not to drop his keys, because to descend into that mud and try to find them would be beyond anything he'd ever made himself do in his life. Safely inside, he found that someone had been there before him. Wet footprints crossed the floor, clustered in front of the desk as if whoever it was had stopped to consult the computer, and made for the side door, from which they did not return. Shaw pushed at the door, but it was as firmly locked as ever. He studied the foot-prints – large, shapeless, partly evaporated – then left the office and worked his way precariously around it until he arrived on the river-facing gunwale. There was certainly a door out there

– plywood, unpainted, delaminating – although he couldn't be sure it was the same one. He banged on it angrily with the heel of his fist, as though to attract his own attention. Then, manoeuvring himself to face outwards, he looked across the river. All that could be made out through the rainy air was Brentford Ait; the confluence, with its maze of old channels and docks, just visible off to the right; and a fringe of trees on the far bank beginning to move briskly in the wind.

The sky now had a silvery look of better weather on the way. Halfway through the afternoon, as the tide reversed itself and the barge began to float, Tim Swann arrived on the tow-path from the direction of Chiswick, wan and haunted-looking among a group of shouting schoolchildren. The rain stuck his clothes to him; his face had taken on a glistening appearance. He didn't have much to say, only sat down and uploaded fresh content to the website; after which they spent the evening in the back bar of the Earl of March, listening reluctantly to eighties synth-pop while Tim ate minute steak and chips.

'So you were in earlier, then,' Shaw said.

'In where?'

'In the office. Earlier.'

Tim looked puzzled. 'I'm in all hours,' he said, after a moment.

Four

16

The Water Under the Sea

Victoria Norman drove her Fiat the long way back to Shropshire, abandoning the M40 to its faith in Oxford as the sole locus of truly human activity since 1167, and dawdling instead across the Vale of Evesham into the Wyre Forest; after which she allowed the Severn to lead her home. She knew that from now on she would need to be careful with herself. She had stopped only the once, to eat a sandwich while she watched two red kites circling, wings as flat as planks, over some sloping fields near Tilbury Hollow.

Evening arrived home before her. As she drove up the hill, the residue of sunset lay between the roofs and chimneys in predictably Munch-like smears of reds and oranges, like a poster in student lodgings long ago. When she opened her front door, she found that the circuit breakers had tripped again while she was away. Later, she ate baked beans on toast with aubergine pickle; turned the television on then off again; then, upstairs in bed, in what she thought of as her mother's room, tried to read a book the pages of which smelled somewhere between floor polish and avocado. She examined herself in the mirror. Wrote a text to Shaw. Deleted it. Driving makes you tired but keeps you awake. It feeds every kind of restlessness, switching on some gene which then becomes quite hard to switch off.

She decided that the hall would need replastering after all, but that there was no world in which she could afford to tank the cellars. She wondered if she should get a cat or a dog. She understood that most of these thoughts were a way of not thinking, and thinking that, fell asleep.

By late afternoon the next day, the air had softened and a fine, clinging rain had settled in; from the park at the top of the town you could watch it swinging in across the Shropshire Plain. It was like a lid on the world. Full of an energy she would have been hard put to explain, Victoria wandered about until she was soaked, ransacking charity shop after charity shop for something she might send to Shaw to amuse him. Somehow she fetched up on the pavement outside Pearl's café, which, behind its steamed-up windows, proved to be bustling, noisy and harshly illuminated. The door wouldn't open.

She put her face up to the glass and saw that the interior was crowded with trades – an electrician, shopfitters, two specialist glaziers working right at the back on something she couldn't make out – but none she recognised. Young, tall and muscular, not yet deformed by the work but already familiar with it, they were like the sons of the men she knew. Their clothes fitted them better. The glaziers had come in a van, and so had the shopfitters; the rest had lined up their expensive motorcycles outside, all leaning in the same direction, all the same bright colours slick as unchipped lacquer in the rain. Inside, they loped about, full of agency. Work was a substance to them. It was the medium in which they swam. It was new and it was what they liked. They had a liveliness around it. Their heads bulged with yellow ear defenders.

Under their influence, everything familiar about the café had gone. They had ripped it all out. The neon sign was gone, leaving only trailing cable above the door. Even the smells of stale fat and hot meat had gone, hauled away with the dismantled catering equipment; instead, the air in the street immediately outside reeked of sawn wood, sophisticated adhesives and cheap sealants; it was reverberating to the shriek of the angle-grinder, the snap of nail guns, the thud of music. You could hear this work they were doing broadcast itself across Hightown until, reflected by the ruins of Geoffrey de Lacy's keep, it echoed away, dispersing like cross-ply ripples in a bowl of water.

'Excuse me!' Victoria called. 'Hello!'

She battered on the window with the heel of her hand. Their attention thus distracted, all they did in return was shake their heads and silently mouth at her. It was like watching fish through discoloured glass. They wanted to get on.

'Closed, love!' they were calling. They were only boys.

'What are you *doing*?'

'Closed!'

Five o'clock, and the square was already in shadow. The local businesses were emptying. Two or three pedestrians passed through, sloping stiffly forward into their errands like figures in a 1920s watercolour. A car left the little car park, then another. Halfway across, turning back for one more look, unable to decide whether the moment had been sinister or comic, Victoria thought she caught sight of a movement in one of the café's upper windows. A female figure seemed to pass across, from left to right and then back, its posture relaxed and domestic. But there were reflections on the glass to be taken into account, and the air in between was so dark with rain that it was hard to be sure. Nevertheless, she returned and banged at the café door again until she had persuaded one of the boys to come over. He slid his dust mask up onto his forehead, took hold of the old-fashioned sign hanging on the door, pointed to it, then made sure it was turned over to CLOSED.

Victoria watched helplessly as he rejoined his friends, laughing and shaking his head, resettling the mask, blipping the motor of his power tool.

At that time of year you could almost hear the water rising under everything. It filled the ancient drains and sub-cellars. It filled the capped wells and forgotten sewerage culverts, the late-eighteenth-century mining galleries and goafs abandoned beneath the early-Victorian town houses, the half-closed shafts that opened suddenly in people's gardens, proving upon examination to be choked with lumps of worthless pennystone like fossilised children's heads – stealthily but determinedly forcing its way, as it did winter after winter, between the layered mazes of the old subterranean workings.

Nothing down there could really be said to flow. Nevertheless the groundwater rose and fell. It dripped and seeped. It percolated through the fractured beds beneath the coppices – through the demented, unpredictable, immeasurably fortunate geology, fuel for the industrial light and magic that had once changed the world: the iron money, the engine money, the steam and tontine money, the raw underground money hidden in unconformable strata, secret seams and voids, in jumbled shales, fireclays, tar, coal measures and thinly bedded limestone – to exit as seeps and springs above the heritage museums and leisure trails and decommissioned railways; while associated subsidence gnawed quietly away at the superficial architecture of the Gorge, peeling the narrow lanes slowly off its wooded slopes. The Gorge channelled the river, yet was in itself only a sponge, storing vast acquifers, drop by drop, in the decaying matrix of its own history. In town, meanwhile, the newer pavements displayed a tendency to shift and ripple; while at 92 High Street, the three-room basement, with its brick barrel vaulting and late-nineteenth-century kitchen range, began to weep and smell.

All through the house, Victoria's newly fashionable chalk paints and distempers yellowed overnight with damp. She sat listening to the rain, the dogs barking next door, the weird buzz of the kitchen fluorescent fitment. There was always a lot of wet coughing outside the front window. Old men, exhausted and complaining as they exchanged the news, turned out to be young men when she looked. Uneasily at first, she returned to the fields behind the town; and a few days later found herself beside the pool where she had last seen the waitress.

It seemed more extensive. The wind ruffled its surface, the rain dimpled it. She stared at the tuft of rushes in the centre: nothing. The petals of the submerged flowers looked a little duller. Some sort of mist or vapour was hanging over the woods. Victoria huddled beneath the pylon as if it might provide shelter; struggled with the impulse to take off her shoes and wade into the water. She was trying and failing to remember – to admit to – what had happened here. But after all, what *was* there to remember? Things being what they are, people don't walk into a pond as if they are descending the Tube station steps on a slow Wednesday afternoon at Oxford Circus. They don't vanish that way when you are watching. Pearl had understood quite well that she was being watched. And not so much by Victoria – who with her pretty latte-coloured car and London stylings had always been less than a player – as by the owner of the voice among the waiting trees. All along Pearl had been aware of that half-hidden gaze; she had sought its approval, felt and welcomed the weight of it. She had come to the pool that morning to be seen.

This understanding caused Victoria to feel faint. She reached behind her, put one hand flat on the pylon, allowed it to take some of her weight. Its quick pulse went through her, and she looked up instinctively between the glass insulators to the grey sky. Rain poured down on her upturned face. The wind dropped. When she examined the palm of her hand, it was covered with rust.

'Scabby old thing,' she whispered.

Wherever she went after that someone could always be seen exercising their small dog in the middle distance. Later she discovered Ossie's Toyota abandoned in a lay-by off Pale Meadows Lane.

It was no longer recognisable as a taxi. There was an air of senselessness about it. One tyre had deflated. Dried mud a thin grey colour painted the bodywork as if someone had spun the front wheels trying to drive it up through the coppice behind the lay-by. Even the windows were spattered. The old man's Castrol jacket, colours wrenched in the curiously distributed interior light, hung over the back of the driving seat; on the rear ledge he had abandoned a yellow site helmet and a hi-vis tabard showcasing the logo of some local builder; two or three items of old-fashioned porno on thickly glossy paper. 'You want to be careful down Pale Meadows at night,' she remembered him warning her. Perhaps he had ignored his own advice.

Originating as a small limestone quarry tucked into the side of the hill, the lay-by was used less for parking than as a turning place: puddles of dirty water lay across a surface deeply grooved and broken up by mid-weight commercial transport. Clumps of fern grew out of the cracks and niches in the quarry wall. The meadows themselves had been spruced up into sports fields a generation ago. It didn't appear that they had ever been pale. Believing she heard voices, she looked up and down the lane. The air was dark and rain-stained – it was easy to feel as if someone was coming when no one was. She banged loudly on the roof of the Toyota, in case Wee Ossie was sleeping inside. Nothing happened except that she imagined him curled up with the appalling economy of a small mammal in some corner she couldn't see. In the end, she walked briskly away across the playing fields and found her way home through the Low Town.

She was sick of both father and daughter. She could feel herself shelving the entire experience – it wasn't the right thing to do, but it was happening anyway. I need to be clearer about the world, she told herself. I need some respite. Standing by the pool that morning, she had heard herself whisper, 'But I don't know what you mean!' as if the waitress were still present and available for argument; or as if there existed somewhere some description of events they could agree upon. Once home, she made a list of things she intended to do the next day, the first item being to have breakfast in her garden.

But it turned out too wet for that, so she sat by the window on the first-floor landing with her laptop on her knees and ate cornflakes out of the packet while she answered emails. She was short of money. She was like everyone else now, revising their contacts book, making distress calls, looking for work they could do from home. Every so often she peered out through the glass at the sodden lawn, the overgrown rose arch, the yellowing clumps of montbretia. So much needed to be tidied down there. Suddenly everything had a sad, entangled appearance.

Shaw hadn't been in touch.

In London she'd found him as emotionally absent as ever. If the depth of his anxiety had puzzled her, and his favourite restaurant had repelled her, his room, with its bleak handful of things, had made her shiver. He would always choose to live that way, next to a shared bathroom with uninterpretable stains: not as an economy but as a way of keeping his head down, dipping below some radar nobody else was primitive enough to detect. But you mustn't let a person know that's how clearly you see them. 'People assume they have a swim bladder,' she wrote to him, 'some basic assumption – less about themselves than about the world – that keeps them upright and afloat. Then they find out they haven't.

'The thing is, I always want to tell you about my life but somehow I never can. Isn't that weird?'

This time she'd failed because as soon as she got south of the Chilterns her own anxieties had seemed, for a moment at least, reassuringly far away; because Shaw's very listlessness had been demanding enough to catch her attention; but most importantly, perhaps, because neither of them, in the end, would ever be able to tell the other anything. The difference between them was that she understood this and he didn't. Victoria recognised her own impediment but couldn't work around it: Shaw, she suspected, didn't even know he had one. As a result, already shaken by the waitress's descent into the pool (if indeed that was what it had been), she had further destabilised herself by her attempt to lean on the least reliable occupant of the contemporary London Basin.

Down in the garden, a fat pigeon raised one wing vertically into the rain to flush out parasites; prospected the result briefly but decisively with its beak; then, leaning to the other side, repeated the procedure.

'It's often there,' she told Shaw, hoping to entertain him, 'sitting on next door's fence, waiting for them to top up the feeder.' She had always thought of birds, she said, as living quite furtively in the foliage. 'But here's one leading its life in a spirit of transparency, in all weathers and for anyone to see. It's very keen on sex if there's another pigeon available.' The bird settled, ruffled itself up, settled again. 'There's something impressive about that. It wouldn't do in my case. I could never relax.' She examined this statement and after some thought acknowledged that it didn't say what she had hoped. 'So you do see, don't you,' she wrote instead, 'I like you, but I'd feel better if we were having any sort of conversation about anything. I suppose everyone thinks that. I'm never even certain I've got your email address right, and you don't help with that.'

Quite suddenly she surprised herself by finishing:

'Am I going to stay here much longer? I'm not sure. It's so dark lately, and the house is so damp.'

A month of rainy days followed, one after the other with a sort of careful, well-judged malice. Lights came on earlier in the town. There was a sense of bustle at the ends of the afternoons. At Halloween Victoria caught cold and for a week walked around deaf in one ear. She felt cooped up in herself. Nothing anyone said to her made sense – she could hear people, but there was something wrong with the way she heard them.

'Soon be Christmas,' the shopkeepers told the customers as they waited to be served. Victoria wanted to join in but couldn't think of anything to add.

'Orright, pet?' everyone asked.

'Orright!' she said. She was orright. It was just a cold, which she kept at bay by drinking shiraz in the evenings. She often thought she should go to the Long Gallery for a change, and take whatever they had on offer there; but the tribute bands and the karaoke – the groups of drinkers barking and whistling across the street to one another at closing time, working themselves up onto some plateau of outrage from which there was no clear retreat – put her off. Up the hill behind the rest of them, at a quarter past eleven one Thursday, came Tommie Jack, who looked unwilling, hump-backed and as bulky as if he had been made to shelter something beneath his coat. He wasn't keeping up. By the time he reached the top of the hill they were long over it and heading down towards the river. Since he'd come to her house the second time, Tommie Jack had put Victoria in a bad mood whenever she saw him. She ran to her front door and slammed it open.

'Selling something?' she heard herself call after him. 'Selling any pictures of little boys and girls swimming?'

Tommie Jack looked over his shoulder in not quite the right direction and tried to smile; but tonight his face seemed too large and round to manage easily. It was somehow moonlike. 'Hey!' cried Victoria. She always interpreted him as a threat; at the same time she felt stronger when he was around. She got one arm in her own coat, pulled the rest of it awry across her shoulders and ran after him, crying, 'Hurry on now, Tommie! Tommie, your friends are leaving you behind!'

Down towards the old iron bridge they went. It was dark much of the way, though you could see revealed in fits and starts the line of street lights in the Gorge, also the oriental neon of the Lavender House takeaway and yellow windows of the Top Time Hotel. Tommie Jack would hurry on ahead, then, tiring suddenly, drop back. At that she would catch at his forearm and pull him forward, crying, 'Keep up, Tommie! All your friends are getting away!' In fact his friends were gone as if they'd never been, vanishing into parked cars or up the hillside jitties to their homes. Tommie shook her off and ran panting across the bridge. Victoria's coat trailed on the ground as she pursued him along the riverfront until they arrived at Pearl's house.

By the time they got inside, his eyes were wet, his face

collapsed and sore. He was in tears, and Victoria had no idea any more what she was doing or why she had bullied him that way. She pushed past him, and ran upstairs to the waitress's room, calling out:

'Pearl! Pearl! Bloody, *bloody* where are you?'

'You won't be seeing her any more,' Tommie Jack said in a soft tired voice from behind her.

When she turned round to confront him, he had gone.

In Pearl's room things were the same as before – except that the mattress, stripped off its divan base, had been first propped against the wall, then left to slump down until it bent into the shape of a rough sleeper in some badly illuminated city square. The laptop was gone. Face powder dusted the floor. Of the posters, there remained only YOU'RE ALLOWED. Pearl's make-up table, empty but for a flat dish of water, had been dragged from its original position and placed crookedly beneath it. 'Where are you?' Victoria asked these objects. Without thinking, she dipped her fingers in the water, to find it as cold and salty as the sea.

'Where are you?' It was an accusation. It was, she understood, a way of saying, 'I expected more.'

She had already decided to speak to Andy the fat man, because despite himself he seemed reasonable and kind. But the air outside his room stank so of dog shit and diabetes that she had to breathe through her mouth; and every time she moved she heard shuffling noises within. The dogs growled nervously; their blunt claws clattered on the floor. There they were, she imagined, dragging themselves upright, ill, confused, half blind, following the sound of her movements through the wall. And it was as though someone else heard her too: even as she was making up her mind to end this dismaying interlude, she heard a calm, firm voice announce:

'That girl represents the past, with her special website and thong knickers. We're the future. We're the future now.'

Tommie Jack was still where she had left him when she came into the hall, lounging halfway between the front door and the base of the stairs, inert as an animal abandoned to its own devices. He was grinding his teeth. The light fell on him somewhere between grey and yellow; his eyes were dry, as empty and reflective as a sheep's. He moved suddenly and laughed.

'The inland cities are ours. We shan't be needing Pearl any further!'

'Do you even know what you're talking about?' Victoria said. 'Because I don't.' And, turning her back on him, she strode away down the hall.

Instantly he seemed to be standing in front of her again, with his face on one side and thrust up close to hers, shouting: 'You're the stupid one! You're the one who doesn't know what's going on!' Then he had slipped out of her reach somehow, using an intricate motion of the body she couldn't comprehend, and entered one of the ground-floor rooms without her seeing; and when she looked around, all the old trades were there again, arranged on the stairs behind her like iron filings thick on a magnet, packed together in their ill-fitting fleeces and chainsaw trousers, looking down. 'A lot are finding comfort in this book,' someone said.

Up near the iron bridge, the Top Time Hotel was closing for the night; the cabs from Telford took on their passengers; the lights went off one by one up and down the riverside. Rain had blown through Snowdonia from the Irish Sea the day before, and the day before that; the Severn was full of water with a fast and oily glint. Everything seemed meaningless and unsatisfactory, and now she would have to walk all the way back up the hill again in the dark.

★

After that, mornings went slowly; the afternoons seemed to rush away. She didn't know how to feel better. Music tired her out. At number 92 the light fell with optical clarity, and she saw every chip, dent and irregularity of the paintwork. Soon she was wondering if she should sell up. She didn't know where she could go, except back to Dalston. Looking around on these rainy days, she saw not only what she had failed to do, but also where she had gone too far and done too much. She felt as if she had disturbed the privacy of the old house, the deep sense of self that had attracted her to it in the first place. She was compelled to remember how she had dumped so many of her mother's things.

'I loved it here to start with,' she wrote to Shaw, then didn't know how to finish. Apropos of nothing she asked, 'What will you think of me if I just change my mind?', admitting, 'I must seem a complete idiot to you.'

Pearl's café reopened in the second week of November, as a home aquarium store trading under the name 'Shropshire Fish Supplies', which, appearing in blue, green and purple neon above the door, was repeated by a matching swing sign on the pavement. Inside, the long interior wall of the old café now presented like a bank of huge flat-screen TVs, each tuned to a different scene in an undersea Disney cartoon. Among the weeds, it was possible to identify forms that might be fishes, difficult to make out, rather bigger and slower perhaps – perhaps less filmy-finned and colourful – than the kind you might expect to find in a living-room aquarium. They turned a little back and forth, as if – while not admitting to any relationship with it – they could afford to acknowledge the other world, our world, where, enveloped in a kind of soft green-tinged shadow that seemed to have leaked into the shop from the tanks, Tommie and Brenda Jack sat behind the counter, a distance apart.

They looked well on it. Brenda kept the till while Tommie wrote something in a book then raised his head suddenly as if he'd been called and – making his way around a central pedestal display of nano tanks (ten litres or less), lit up the colour of mint gel toothpaste like quantum computers in see-through cases featured by some futuristic Apple Store – went upstairs to the second floor. From the counter they also ran the shop's website, an online underwater adventure of aquascaping ideas and tank decor. For a period, this business made the little square popular again, especially after school and on Saturday mornings, when the children came to bang on the tanks and startle their occupants.

'For God's sake,' Victoria told herself, looking in once through the window then walking away across the square.

It was closer to Christmas than she would have liked, and nothing more had happened since her visit to Pearl's room. In the end you had to concede that the waitress had probably grown tired of waiting around on the edge of the Midlands for her life to begin and gone to meet whatever future she could find. You were bound to admire that; you were bound to see it as a positive. She took herself home and, after a cup of tea, put the house on the market.

17

The Unreliability of Forms

Though she had several viewings in the first week, no one wanted to buy.

Decent and cheerful people, often from as far away as the next town, made appointments. They were families with dogs or children. They all loved number 92, and what she'd done with it, and Victoria loved seeing it through their eyes. They weren't so certain about the garden.

Victoria's garden still opened out to you the way it had all summer, but now it began to open on something different, something she liked less, although it was easily as demanding. Looking out from the staircase at night, she half expected to discover a brand-new view. Moonlight still tranquillised the lawn, which remained as flat as water. But the stars she half hoped to see weren't reflected there. By day, she stood just inside the kitchen with the back door open, watching the rain soak the browning clumps and nests of vegetation which had within her living memory been such a mass of flowers. Walls, paths, every built surface was shiny with water, full of a sky too white to be the one they were reflecting. She should tidy up, she knew, if not for her viewers then for winter. She should replace the old roses. It was all very sad. It was worse the other side of the arch. In late spring she had welcomed, on behalf

of the summer's butterflies, a buddleia; now it only reminded
her of choked lots viewed from London trains. The arch had
turned into a gateway which she avoided.

There were other problems. Despite its size, she found herself
agreeing, the house didn't really have many rooms; big rooms
are hard to heat, and the cellar was wet, and the constant rain
only emphasised these kinds of issues. A house like hers, she
understood – a house which has endured a few things, seen a
few things through; which, though lovely, shifts and resettles
with the climate, and makes its own noises in the night; a
house with very old timbers, which is 'like a ship', whatever
that might once have meant; a house in which you should
never use the word 'subsidence' in case it echoed; a house like
that, with all its associated expenses – might be too much to
take on. Nevertheless she felt hurt.

'I suffered the builders,' she wanted to remind them, 'for
this. They thumped and banged carelessly all day, they were up
and down my beautiful stairs. They made good the roof. The
loft is fine now, because I suffered while they ate the chocolate
biscuits. Why, that floor up there's so new! You could sail that
loft of mine out of harbour on tomorrow's early tide.' But they
were already puzzled enough by her, she could see; especially
the children.

Leaves off the willow, berries on the hawthorn. Victoria kept
away from the fields. She kept everything at a distance; drove
the Fiat as far afield as Runcorn; forgot her appointments.
November, meanwhile, gave up on itself without warning,
and suddenly the town had been dragged into the first week
of December. The Christmas lights went up; someone towed
Wee Ossie's Toyota out of the lay-by on Pale Meadows. One
morning the rain turned briefly to snow. Two inches had fallen
the day before in the Welsh uplands. Down in the Gorge, the

Severn turned one shade darker fawn than a Labrador dog;
flood warnings multiplied up- and downstream. In the old toll-
gate car park, Victoria watched tour coaches split apart at the
front like candy-red pupae; puzzled but laughing, late visitors
from California and South Korea hurried away from them in
twos and threes across the iron bridge and along the Wharfage,
only to find flood barriers in place and the river rising between
them and the industrial past they had come to take selfies with.
Victoria stared that way a moment; shivered; plodded her way
back up the hill into town, only to find that a water main had
burst in the high street.

Vast feathery geysers erupted through the road. Prismatic
colours flashed in all directions. The water collected in front
of the ironmonger's before racing away like a flood between
the bungalows of Woolpit Road towards the river. Everyone
was hurrying out of the nearby shops, smiling with a kind of
delighted alarm. The children, and even some of the men,
shouted and ran about, and had to be restrained. It seemed to
her as if the whole town stood there for a moment, wondering
if the world would end, or only take some simple, beautiful,
amazing direction.

Big or small, these events seemed all of a piece; they seemed
to point to the same thing. But you couldn't see what it might
be.

Like much in the new economy, Shropshire Fish Supplies
endured yet didn't prosper. Quickly more of an incident than
a business, it was one of those small-town events that has its
day. The little square soon went back to sleep. Footfall was
the problem, although in the dark evenings the shop still had
its visitors. That couldn't be denied. You would catch sight
of these people from behind, silhouetted against the window

they were staring into; and your lasting impression would be of shoulders that, when they weren't hunched against the early-winter weather, were long and steeply sloping. A bell rang as they went in.

Wee Ossie was now seen behind the counter more often than the Tommie Jacks. His Toyota reappeared in the car park, in its customary position tight up against the gritting bin, at a bit of an angle. The mud had been jet-washed away, the deflated tyre replaced; to balance that, someone had bashed in the rear window, as if whatever had happened in the quarry needed to be understood as part of an ongoing process. The old man closed up late, and always had some difficulty with the door. That was how Victoria Norman came upon him, ten o'clock one evening, bent double but trying to keep off his knees as he struggled with the lock.

'Have those two gone already?' she said. 'I thought they fitted in so well.'

He had to smile at that, he said. Tommie and Brenda, if that was who she meant, were away.

'I can see,' Victoria said.

'They're up at Kinver, on business of their own: we shan't be seeing them again. Not so soon at any rate. Not so soon.'

For a moment, they both gazed into the shop. The tanks glimmered or shone: at this point along the flattening commercial arc of the business, they contained more tank decor, that curious built environment in which everything is sunken or drowned, than fish. There were drowned cottages, drowned bridges, drowned castles, drowned temple columns and oriental towers. Sunken villes of mixed structure dispersed themselves on beds of gravel that contoured away into the calm green mirrored infinity of each tank. There was an aesthetic of glow-effect pebbles, mushrooms in vibrant purples and greens;

a conspiracy of 'ancient stone heads', sunken submarines and sarcophagi.

Down there, where scale meant nothing and even water could be depicted as drowned, postmodern treasure chests dwarfed the houses, overflowing with vast coins and strings of pearls. Everything was vividly simulated, luminous, tropically coloured, encrusted with plastic algae to signal slow, deep marine change: it was as if the fish tanks had transformed themselves into dioramic representations of the famous but now lost coral reefs of the world, designed by animation artists who had never seen one.

Victoria pointed. 'That waterfall?' she said. 'It's made of plastic. Doesn't that give you such an uncomfortable feeling? Water shown flowing under water?'

She felt herself shiver.

'It does me,' she said. 'It gives me an uncomfortable feeling.'

The old man bent down without a word and began fiddling with the lock again. His eyes were sore. His nose was running. She clutched at the shoulder of his Castrol jacket and tried to pull him to his feet, the way you pull a toddler upright in a mall. She was determined to capture his attention.

'Where have you been?' she said.

As soon as he was touched, he stopped what he was doing and stared ahead of himself, but not as if he were looking at anything. He became motionless. He seemed startled by the turn of events, and at the same time satisfied. While he kneeled there, the rain redoubled, falling through the shop light in long white strokes. It made frying sounds where it fell, and emulsified the hair on top of Wee Ossie's head. The yoke of his coat was soaked; underneath the fabric he felt thin, but his trapezium muscles were as solid as bone. He had, she thought, no temper. Despite that he was full of force: when he wanted to shake her off, he would.

'Don't ask and I shan't tell,' he offered.

'You can just stop evading me,' Victoria said. 'I promise you there's nothing to gain. I only want to know what's happened to Pearl. I want to know what happened to my mother before she died. I want to know what happened here.'

His face glistened white under the slick of rain. For a moment she thought he would hit her. But all he did was pull away, eye her for a long time, then say:

'Everyone gets an answer in the end.'

'Oh, fuck off. Just fuck off.'

Instead he patted her forearm. 'Don't worry so much, pet,' he advised. 'You'll do all right when it comes to it. They all do.'

At a loss because this seemed so empty of meaning, she could only watch him run nimbly, shoulders hunched, hands in pockets, across the square in the rain to his car. 'Have you got a dog?' she heard herself calling after him in her worst metro voice, pitched exactly between the mortgage in Dalston and the aunt in Clapham. 'I've seen you, haven't I? Out there in the fields, and in the town at night, with your little dog?'

At first Wee Ossie seemed to ignore her. The rain battered the roof of the Toyota, flew up again as a hard vapour in the light from the neon sign. He stretched across its tailgate to knock out a few remaining fragments of the shattered rear window; then, with a curious slithering motion – in which both agility and awkwardness were stored as potentials not quite expressed – hauled himself in through the hole. His little hips struggled. His little feet kicked and thumped, then withdrew neatly. Once inside, he turned himself around and stuck out his head, shaking it briefly in a sort of mystified contempt – as if no one could be quite so wrong about something as Victoria – before he disappeared for good.

'You'll do all right when it comes your turn,' she heard him say, just before the engine started.

The discomfort of this encounter drove her out of town, along the A5 and deep into Wales. As a result, she missed so many viewing appointments that the estate agent stopped sending people round. Victoria went to gee him up, at his neat shop-front in Hightown. Man and premises smelled of polish and sales. 'You have such a nice *place* here,' she said, sighing and looking around. Determined not to be drawn, he concentrated on the office desktop. 'Let's see,' he said. 'Let's get up to date on what's happening.' She had plenty of interest, he said: plenty of interest. There was plenty of interest but they were finding number 92 a bit priced up. 'They're finding it a bit priced up for the work they'd have to do.'

'But I've done a lot of work,' Victoria said, looking stubbornly out of the window into the street. 'I know the garden's a mess but my roof, for instance, is perfect.'

She could feel him sitting there professionally at his desk behind her, courteous, unjudgemental though he had plenty of his own opinions, more like a doctor in his nice suit than an estate agent. Places, she thought, force you to live the life that goes on in them. You think you're camped at the edge of a place, but all the time it's drawing you to its centre. 'Did you know your town has been occupied since 1086?' she said. 'When it was known as Bolsoe?'

He seemed to consider this. Then he suggested:

'You know, people often handle the sale themselves these days. It can work out a lot cheaper.' It did him no harm, he explained, to be open with people about how things were.

'Your mother, for instance, handled everything herself, online.'

My mother couldn't handle her bus fare, Victoria thought. Not when I knew her. 'I'd rather someone else had the bother,' she said, as offhandedly as she could. 'We should all spend less time on the internet.' By then she was at the door. She felt, though she liked him, that this had been all too much of a lesson, patiently dispensed. 'If I promise to do better, will you start sending people again?'

At least he had compelled her to think about the garden. Before she could change her mind – or remember too clearly the last time she had been there – she went back to Childe Beckwith. There she found the car parks deserted, the manor house closed up, the family in Barbados – as they had been every Christmas since 1956 – renewing themselves even as they reviewed their ties to the old slave and sugar assets, while at home the cedars closed over darkening lawns and the wet, lucid sandstone flags reflected skies a Roman legionary would have recognised. You could hear the peacocks, but only ever from a distance. Obviously there wasn't much going on in the rose garden: the plantings had drawn in on themselves, the underlying structure of things stood out like bone. Victoria avoided the pool. Dawdling through the Elizabeth Berrington Gallery, past faux-bronze hare and prolapsed watercolour fox-glove, she forced a smile. Nevertheless, her mood remained low; the afternoon hardened.

Before she left she walked across the estate, up through plantations of specimen trees until she reached the highest point of the little toy ridge the eighteenth-century landscapers had put in to advantage the view. From there you could stare past the manor, where someone had left a tipped-over lawn chair on the café terrace, and between the lugubrious folds of land towards Cramp Pool and Beckley. Unless you were willing to enter the Ionic temple, there was no shelter up there. Rain blew across the twin ornamental lakes and up the slope into her face. From the shop, after some thought, she had ordered one 'England's Fair' and one 'Maid of the Cotswolds', bare-root centifolias to be delivered to her by post from some other location. Even as she paid, she had been failing to imagine how such dry, bleak-looking sticks might thrive for someone else, in a garden no longer hers. She leaned into the wind and closed her eyes; opened them again suddenly.

She had heard a cry, from down by the lower of the two lakes; and now glimpsed a single motionless figure in a dark-blue donkey jacket, facing out across the water. It remained for a moment, then – head down, hands in pockets – walked rapidly off via the rhododendron clumps and soft ground around the sluices, in the direction of the disused icehouse and adjoining pet cemetery. She could see a single low-wattage light burning in a room on the second floor of the main building.

'Pearl!' she heard herself call. 'Pearl, is that you?'

But how could it have been? Whoever it was didn't slow down or look back or acknowledge her; and soon the lakeside was empty again. She ran down the slope anyway, until she was standing beside the water in her turn, looking for footprints in the greyish mud. It was hard to avoid a mounting sense of uselessness and fear. Nothing was being solved. She was losing what she wanted. There was a general failure to keep up her spirits.

Later, in the car park, she sat listening to the rain on the roof of the car, while the sky towards Clee Hill rhythmically gathered then distributed a rosy quality – not quite a colour – as if, off beyond the Beckwith yews, something was filling and refilling the receptacle of a winter sunset she couldn't quite see.

★

The estate agent proved as good as his word. For a few days nothing happened, then viewers began to turn up in a steady stream. They came from the dormitories around Birmingham and Wolverhampton, looking as if they had been made nervously competitive by the life they lived there. To slot their medium-sized cars into a small gap directly outside the house was a matter of pride with them; otherwise she found it hard to say what they might want for themselves. Runs of sharper days, with early fog leading to bright sunshine, would always bring them out. A thin woman arrived late one Saturday morning, hollow around the eyes from diet and CrossFit, hard to age, her look centred on black compression tights and a savagely hauled-back ponytail. Her name, she said, was Helen. As soon as Victoria opened the front door, Helen was walking in, summing up the hall, heading for the stairs.

'I've got about twenty minutes,' she said. 'Don't you find these old tiles a bit hard to look after?'

Much of Helen's conversation seemed too intense for the circumstances, as if it was always hinting at something else. After each exchange, she would regard Victoria askance, with her head a little on one side as if to say: your turn now. It was both compelling and frustrating. She came from Kinver, she said, and her work covered most aspects of special-populations health and exercise. Victoria, who had no idea what this meant, followed her from one room to the next, reviewing her own life choices with a kind of terrorised embarrassment and saying, 'I've had quite a lot of work done on the roof,' or: 'I think these floorboards are original.'

Helen didn't seem to hear, although a faint irritability sometimes crept into her expression. 'There's quite a nice property underneath it all,' she was prompted to admit, after they had

completed a brief tour of the garden. 'But these days you'll
need to be offering more.'

'I bought some roses,' Victoria said.

'It's not roses people want, though, is it? Not in this market.
I don't know what things are like here, but over in Kinver we
want a breakfast bar.'

'It was just to cheer things up, really.'

Helen gave her tight smile; then, on leaving, stood looking
up at the sunlight falling across the old frontage. 'A breakfast bar and a tanked cellar,' she said thoughtfully, and, when
Victoria failed to respond, shrugged. 'Of course, the weather's
on your side today.' She got in her car and started it up, then
wound down the window as if she'd come to some last-minute
understanding. 'I think you might have set your asking price a
shade too high,' she said. 'Especially at this time of year.'

Her Audi could be seen all over the town in the week thereafter, pulled in to the kerb in unlikely places while Helen, one
elbow resting on the driver's door window ledge, leaned out
to 'Orright?' someone or talk the local prices down. Victoria
tried to avoid her. Acknowledged from a distance across the
high street, Helen would smile and shake her head complicitly
as if she was still in Victoria's house and they both understood
what she was talking about. She seemed to know everyone.

The closer Christmas approached, the less Victoria knew
what to do. The Childe Beckwith roses arrived, only to remain
in their packaging, unplanted. One day was dark and a fine rain
hung without falling; the next, you could see your own breath
in the bright sharp air. The town, expanding its idea of itself,
sang carols, held its Midnight Festival of Lights and Tractors.
Like landlocked factory ships, the enormous machines ground
up and down in their marine layer of exhaust fumes. Dogs and
children ran loose. A chocolate-coloured llama stood patient

all evening in its pen at the base of Geoffrey de Lacy's keep. Dignified in its braided, coined and ribboned collar, unmoved by the fireworks or the U2 tribute band, it was waiting to be led ceremonially away down Woolpit Road to the river. For a moment everything seemed illuminated less by the street lamps than by mythic intersections, liminalities jumbled together from traditions that hadn't yet been invented.

The next morning, Victoria came upon Helen sitting with another woman in a café called Bethany's, which was positioned strategically two doors down from the Little Wedding Shop in Hightown at the top of the Portway. Bethany's, with its aesthetic of home-made bunting and Christine Keeler plastic chairs, was small and seemed quite new. On the counter a sign read: A BALANCED DIET IS A CUPCAKE IN BOTH HANDS. Neither Helen nor her companion, an oldish woman wearing a fitted maroon wool coat, looked as if they belonged there, or with each other. In addition, Helen seemed angry. 'I don't know why people aren't a lot more disgusted with themselves than they are,' Victoria heard her say fiercely and with a peculiar clarity. 'They stiff a lot of other people over their mortgages, pensions and insurance, and because they have good hair, and what they do is always right for them, oh no, *they* can't go wrong. *They* aren't doing anything wrong.' She stared ahead of herself angrily. 'I don't know why *I* should feel ashamed,' she insisted.

The other woman, clearly at a loss, looked down at her teacup. 'So anyway,' she said, 'in the end I had it tiled like everyone else. I've rather given up on it now.'

They stared at one another like animals of different species meeting in the same field. For a moment or two more, Victoria watched them struggle to communicate, then she went over and stood next to Helen's chair.

'What did you think of offering?' she said.

In the end, the distance between their positions was more easily closed than she had expected. Victoria needed to allow for inheritance tax. Helen didn't want any of the furnishings and fittings but would, as she put it, bear the cost of getting rid of them. 'It's more of an investment for me,' she said complacently, 'than somewhere to live.' In the end, they could agree on most things. Victoria would return to Dalston with a small profit and as little baggage as she had brought with her; she would go back to her old life, and desperately miss everything she had found here at the beginning, and wonder what it had been or why she had given it up. She understood that she had been hoping for continuity – some sense not so much of selling the house as handing it on. With Helen, though, there would only ever be the transaction.

At Bethany's your turkey dinner with sprouts and roasties came in at five pounds fifty pence. There were adverts for Kelly's of Cornwall ice cream, and music which reminded Victoria of really horrible nights in Lewisham in the 1990s. But the wi-fi worked, and she liked the hot chocolate, and Bethany herself stood behind the counter most lunchtimes, calling out, 'Thank you, cheers,' to the departing customer, raising her voice on the last syllable to turn it into 'goodbye'. Sometimes, looking out at the weather, she would shiver and add quietly, 'Rather you than me!' She wasn't Pearl, but she was kind enough.

That afternoon, Victoria began to sort through the things she didn't want to abandon during the move back to London – things of her own, things of her mother's. In the latter category she came across a little 1970s handbag notebook, two inches by three, thin paper ruled feint in thin leather covers, with smart gold-stamped edges and its own tiny pencil in the spine; the kind of thing you might unearth from an antiques market in Ludlow or Church Stretton, something no one had seen for a generation or used for two. All the pages but one were blank; and because several pages had been torn out in front of that one, what was written there seemed to begin in the middle of a thought.

'... but my awful old fingernails haven't grown since I arrived.'

Victoria, who felt odd quite suddenly, dropped the notebook on the bed. She went to the window, where she leaned on the sill to look out. She went back to the bed, and then back to the window again: the rain was falling on the lawn.

'That's five months,' her mother had written. 'I haven't had to cut my fingernails once in five months. I wondered if something was the matter with me. P said it was the chlorine at the swimming pool. It's very strong. Or that I might have made a mistake. But I caught her looking at her own nails in the bathroom, and when she saw me she closed the door. She was washing her hands. Spreading her fingers and washing the gaps between them. Nothing's the matter, she said. Nothing. And closing the bathroom door on me, just like that.'

Then, a little way below:

'Who makes a mistake about when they last cut their nails? But in another way she's right. Because as long as I have P, nothing will ever be the matter again.'

Victoria took the notebook to the lavatory and dropped it in, and was thoroughly sick on it before she could stop herself. She closed the lid and flushed and flushed until everything had gone down.

She thought of her mother – up on the top floor alone, examining the crossed lines on the palm of her hand; switching on the bedroom light at three in the morning to copy out one of her favourite poems, Rupert Brooke's 'Peace'; scribbling away – in handwriting that seemed tired, hurried, and from an outside perspective a shade infantile – in the absurd little book. Or perhaps carefully smoothing out the photograph of herself and the waitress's father she kept folded at the back of her complicated combination purse and wallet. The photograph, Victoria assumed, would have been less faded then. In the scattered glare of the bar behind the two figures, it might still have been possible to discern a third – whitened and flared, taller than both – although not well enough to be certain whether it was a man or a woman.

Wiping and wiping at her mouth, she wrote to Shaw: 'How can you ever know anyone? To me she was just old-fashioned, already too nervous to do anything about her life long before she married or had me. I was so angry with her about that, I never even came to her funeral.'

She sat on the bed and stared at the floorboards between her feet.

She wondered what he was doing for Christmas, and thought of calling him, and offering to drive down there, and even picked up her phone. But what do you say to someone you never see from one month's end to the next? – 'I'm just phoning you quickly, between giving blood and having my hair cut. Oh, God knows. Birmingham or somewhere like that.' Instead she watched herself write, 'I'm so tired.' And, quite without expecting to: 'Winter in a strange house! All those years I would have killed for a place like this. I don't even really know what I mean.'

Though she was suddenly nervous about falling asleep, she did.

★

When she woke again, out of a dream in which someone was calling her, the moon was up and the rain had stopped; she didn't know what time it was. She went downstairs and sat at the kitchen table with a cardigan round her shoulders, wondering if she should make something to eat or just go back to sleep again. She turned on the radio, but the news wasn't good. Two in the morning, and though she could feel the town all round her it was quiet outside. Two or three days before Christmas you expected some gaiety. She was drinking a cup of tea when she heard a thoughtful voice from not far behind her say:

'Vita?'

She looked out into her garden, where the shadow of the rose arch in the moonlight lay obliquely across the upper lawn. There was a figure out there. It was staring away from the house. She rapped on the window. 'Get out of there!' she shouted. 'What are you doing down there!' But she already knew. The figure half turned, then, without seeming to move, approached the rose arch, where it reached up to touch two or three hesitant winter blooms, turning its white face to her as it did so. It was waiting for her. 'Don't you dare!' Victoria called. She rapped on the window again, and ran to the back door and looked angrily out. At first the garden seemed empty. It seemed longer than it had been. The air was warmer out there than in the house. It was so warm that it might be July. It was so warm that if she went out there she wouldn't need a coat or shoes. The moon lit the rose arch, which seemed too small, too far away, too like an illustration in a book.

'Coom on, Vita,' encouraged the figure in its soft, conniving way.

One minute it was ducking to pass beneath the arch; the next it was back on the lawn, and everything was stretching too far away again, and the shadows on the grass were all too long. These shifts of perspective had a fluid, organic, easily achieved quality, as if she had been given a new way of looking at things. At the same time they were as devastating and transformative as the easily achieved vomits and fevers of an illness.

'Coom on then, girl.'

'Is that you, Pearl?' called Victoria. 'Is that you?'

The lawn was like a green pool on a summer night. It wasn't too large, it wasn't too small; it had the appearance of a surface you mustn't try to walk on. Plantings of gladioli, along with huge hollyhocks and night-scented stocks, curved over the smooth turf as if they were leaning out over water. Despite the houses on each side, she experienced such a sense of seclusion that she found it easy to remove many of her clothes.

'Vita!' the voice called. 'Victoria!'

Under the rose arch, the lawn began to gather itself and brim and curve. It took a sheen. It glittered solidly in the moonlight: Victoria now heard water falling away quietly on the other side. A dragonfly could be seen there like a flash of light, hunting across the grass! Without thinking – but never hurrying – she took off the rest of her clothes and with not the briefest look back sank down into the lawn and began to swim to the other side, where she sat beneath the arch at the top of the worn and slippery steps in the scent of roses and stocks, listening to the water and staring for a moment into the lower garden and the gathering dark.

'Is this what happened to my mother?' she asked the waiting figure, softly, almost sadly. She thought of all the beautiful things she would lose, but of all the things she might gain too; and took the steps down.

'Those that wish to be clean,' the voice said, 'clean will they be.'

At the very last Victoria heard herself say, 'Send me to the water,' and after that nothing.

18

Adaptive Introgression

A week or two after Victoria's visit, Shaw thought he would email her. All that strange evening, he thought, they had been failing to explain something to each other, never quite finding a way to act it out. They both had voids in their lives, they were jigsaws that would never complete. At the same time everything about their encounter had made his present lifestyle seem tentative yet no longer temporary: evidently fucked. Anything he could have told her about that – for instance that he'd like to invest more in himself and do things with a better heart – would have been too much of a revelation for both of them. Not so much about Shaw's circumstances as about himself. It would have been, in some way, too obviously an admission: although of what, he still wasn't certain. Now he wrote:

'Thank you so much for *The Water-Babies*. From our perspective it's hard to understand Tom's world.'

This seemed vacuous, so he began again. 'It was so nice to see you. We should ...' But the possibilities lodged in the last two words stalled him so completely that he stood up, shut the laptop, and over the following month or so tried not to think about any of it. London closed in around him. He wondered if he should move. He thought about finding a new job. At night he had dreams of Annie Swann, curious adventures which began well – as, unabashed and affable, she let her skirt ride up – but quickly went off in less pleasant directions.

He missed his Wednesday evenings with Annie, though it was true that she had spent the main part of them unconscious. They had been both relaxing and, in a comfortable way, exciting. The dreams seemed to reflect that, although he wasn't certain what else his unconscious might be suggesting. Around the time of the skirmish on Barnes Common, she had stopped answering his night-time calls; not long after, he had stopped making them. Now, with the idea of signing on as a private client, he tried again. No response. 'It's just that I don't know what either you or Tim want from me,' he was startled to hear himself plead, as he broke the connection. Two evenings out of three, on his way between the Earl of March and the Idle Hour, he knocked on her door. The cottage was dark and she never seemed to be in. Then one night about a month after their final seance, from deep inside the cemetery where he had stopped to poke around in the earth by the hospital wall, he thought he saw a faint light in her bedroom window.

Her gate hung askew, her narrow little front garden smelled strongly of wallflowers and stocks. Her front door was open a crack.

Shaw knocked. 'Hello?' he said.

When no one answered, he looked up and down the street, then pushed open the door and went in.

The downstairs room was full of outside air, which seemed to have been taken up by the carpets and soft furnishings. Street light picked out the larger items of furniture; slanted starkly across the bookshelves and a mirror.

'Annie?'

He crossed into the kitchen, touched the side of the kettle

with the backs of his fingers. Not quite cold. It felt as if someone had been there until about an hour ago. He slid one of
Annie's kitchen drawers to and fro, testing it for quietness and
ease of use; unwrapped a new pack of dark chocolate digestives
and ate one. He stood at the foot of the stairs licking his fingers,
uncertain what to do next. He thought he heard the faintest
sigh, really little more than an exhalation, from the bedroom.

Tim and Annie were up there, moving quietly around on
the disarranged coverlet of Annie's bed. Tim's trousers were
down, but he still had the rest of his clothes on. Whatever
they were doing imposed its own kind of silence on the room,
although once or twice, as he pushed into her, Annie grunted
softly. She was looking hard away from him. He was looking
at the wall. Their lips were moving; in the dim light of the
bedside lamp, their flesh had the whiteness and surface of a
freshly cleaned bath. It didn't look like sex for recreation.

Shaw stood in the doorway. He became convinced there
was another person in the room with them, then recognised in
a single pure instant that it was himself. Events seemed to have
paralysed him, casting his consciousness into the old root of his
brain whence it struggled to escape. He heard himself shout:

'Oh fuck off! Just fuck off!'

As he stumbled down the stairs, Tim called something after
him. He recognised the voice but not the language spoken. In
the lower room the air was thick and resistant. After a minute
or two he managed to settle himself and went out into the
street. He felt surprised but dissociated, as if he'd just experienced some neurological episode. There was a glue taste fading
in his mouth. When he looked up he could see the bedroom
light in the window; he wondered if it had been him who
switched it on. His mobile rang and a voice said:

'Lee?'

It was Annie.

'Yes,' Shaw said. 'Who is this?'

'Lee, you mustn't ...'

Shaw said nothing. His lips were numb.

'Hello?'

He left a letter of resignation on Tim Swann's desk, retaining for his own use the keys to the office. When he returned in a fortnight he found the envelope unopened and coated with a fine patina of dust the texture of which felt both gritty and viscous. It was a warm afternoon, quiet but for the lap of water on the hull. Sunlight rippled obliquely off the river, danced on the wall in the rectangular space left by the absent map. Shaw tried the second door: still padlocked. He tapped the computer keyboard, wiped the screen with his sleeve. His last footage, he saw, had been posted as a GIF at *The Water House*: Annie Swann reduced to a charmless blurry upskirt embedded between quotes from *Journeys of Our Genes*. 'Denisovans are the shit,' PorkSord121 applauded below the line: 'Ha ha lolz first again fuckas.'

Shaw followed the GIF through several iterations then, signing in as the site administrator, added a message of his own: 'STFU NONE OF THIS IS REAL.'

His mother still wouldn't see him.

'Get on with your life,' she told him on the phone, 'and stop being such a cunt'; refusing to answer thereafter.

The care-facility management, unwavering on issues of patient privacy, recommended a chat with her in-house psychologist. 'Perhaps she feels you need a rest from one another,' the psychologist suggested. Otherwise, he had nothing to offer. Shaw's mother had puzzled him, he noted, by insisting that one of the facility's extensive collection of art prints – Arnold

Böcklin's *Sea Idyll* – be moved from wherever they now kept it and hung over her bed. 'We were happy to oblige. No one else likes it.' Then: 'Mrs Shaw didn't used to like it herself.' In all other respects her behaviour met the standards expected from her age group. Her memory was – relatively speaking – fine. Recently she had begun to participate more, enjoying her weekly visits from the hairdresser and, especially, from the pedicurist, a young woman with whom she got on well. It was felt to be a positive step. 'You mustn't take things to heart,' he advised. 'Try again in a week, perhaps a month. She'll have forgotten by then.'

'I don't understand any of this,' Shaw said.

'They can be a trial, can't they?'

Shaw agreed they could be a trial. 'What do you mean by "a rest"?' he persisted. 'A rest from each other? I don't understand where that comes from. Is it the dementia?'

'Hard to be sure, really.'

'You're not being very helpful.'

A smile; a shrug. Shaw looked down at his own hand. An inevitability about the pattern of lines on it made him say: 'Sometimes I wonder about myself.'

The nakedness of this plea frightened him to such an extent that he left the psychologist's office immediately and caught the wrong train home. Around Strawberry Hill and Twickenham the river passed in and out of view in curves of perfect sentimentality: houseboats maintained to look shabby-chic, exotic trees with leaves beginning to turn, curious slender tranches of what could only be described as parkland a single house wide, glimpses of money like light twinkling off water. West Londoners invaded Shaw's carriage at every opportunity, their adult compromise with the clothes of teenage children worn a fraction loose but the right colour to an angstrom.

Arnold Böcklin, the Swiss symbolist known best for his dream paintings of the English Cemetery in Florence, had produced *Sea Idyll* quite late in his career. In it, three figures − a woman and two children − were depicted sprawled on a lumpen, almost-submerged rock barely large enough to accommodate them; while a fourth − perhaps a man, perhaps some more powerfully ambivalent creature of myth − emerged waist-high from the water nearby. Their tenure on the rock seemed anxious and marginal, their poses awkward and strained. The woman, in yearning towards the man, was carelessly allowing her baby to fall into the sea; while the dwarfish older child, its enlarged buttocks stuck up into the air as a result of some deformity of the spine, appeared to be trying to mount her from behind.

It was too fraught to be any kind of idyll. A sense of confusion − of failed allegory − infused the drab palette, the peculiar anatomy. Shaw fell asleep thinking about the agitated gestures of the woman, the smiling but curiously unreceptive expression of the older male figure; his dreams were filled with sounds both human and marine. At two in the morning the phone rang. A throat was cleared at the other end.

'Tim?' Shaw said. 'Hello?'

When no one spoke, he decided to go next door and have it out.

Music came up faintly from the second floor. The landing had captured the heat of the day, which hung beneath the skylight thickening with yeast smells from the brewery across the road. Reminded obscurely of the trial of Patrick Reed, who had seen green children springing up wherever he pissed, Shaw went to the bathroom and spent a minute or two examining the lavatory bowl. Nothing. He flushed anyway, then looked into the mirror over the sink. A year ago, he wouldn't have recognised the person he now discovered there.

Tim Swann's door, heavy with fireproofing and loose against its rickety latch, was unlocked. A light burned inside. Shaw stood back a little, out of a fastidiousness he could neither gloss nor suppress, and called:

'Tim? Hello? Tim, are you there?'

The room was empty, though decade after decade of tenants still seemed to be dissipating in its air like an oily residue mixing in water – a process incomplete since the 1750s, sustained by the endlessness of human need. Everyday objects – an armchair, a single bed, perhaps a gas stove – had reverse-stencilled themselves onto the bare floorboards in irregular patches of grease. That was it. Tim had gone. Perhaps he'd never lived there at all, but used it for some other purpose. Shaw, who was prepared to believe that, went to the window and let up the yellow cotton blind. Two men deep in conversation could be seen disappearing along the opposite pavement towards Mortlake, their shadows cast huge and filmily onto the brewery walls by the kind of late-night city light that, while failing to relieve the darkness in any way, seems to pour in from every direction at once. Otherwise Wharf Terrace presented itself with only minute differences from his usual point of view. He had expected more.

A few defeated-looking cardboard boxes lay in a corner. He raked listlessly about among them – almost immediately discovering, under some computer junk entangled in its own wires, three warped Eastlight box files labelled respectively 'Recovering the Rites', 'The Mort Lake' and 'Our Relations with the Inland Cities'.

The first was stuffed with old receipts and railway tickets; the second contained a journal of sorts, printed single-spaced

on foolscap; the third, smelling strongly of cumin (and under
that something Shaw couldn't identify, though he thought it
might be Vicks Vaporub), proved to be empty. He tipped out
the tickets and stirred them around on the floor – Worcester,
Leicester, Grantham, Rugby. Grantham again, then Birmingham
Central. Midland journeys running back twenty years or more.
He paged through the journal at random until he read: 'After
that, we watched the creature wade steadily into Barnes Pond,
never once deviating or flinching as it disappeared below the
surface. Yet that water is nowhere more than twenty inches
deep.' In the margin someone had added: 'When they use the
words "under water", we should be clear they don't mean
them in a conventional sense. It is perhaps as close as they
allow themselves to saying something else.'

Recognising this style of delivery from *Journeys of Our Genes*,
he skipped a few pages, then a few more; then was ambushed
so suddenly by his own name that for a second or two he failed
to understand what he was seeing and had to leaf back to find
it. 'Poor Shaw!' the journal said. 'Compelled to believe he
doesn't believe in anything, in case he unearths from himself
the one belief – the one deep consolation – he daren't relinquish: *that he was always one of us.* So much of his attention
bound up in the work of denial that what happens to him can
never really be experienced, only stored, and interpreted later
as symbolic. So marginally conscious that the endless return of
the repressed is all he has to work with.'

At this, all the objects in the room seemed to tilt a little, to
settle towards one another. There was a faint, objective sigh
in the air – the sound that inanimate things might make if
they relaxed – a smell of dust. Shaw kneeled on the floor and
closed his eyes, taking what he hoped were measured breaths.
Feeling only a claustrophobic vacancy, a sense of expectation,

of someone waiting for him to do something or say something, or understand what might be done or said, he grabbed the first items that came to hand and blundered out of the room, slamming the door behind him. Next door, the air felt nauseating and resistant. He looked down at his hands to find that he had retrieved two ribbed Victorian medicine bottles and a postcard of Lincoln Cathedral in 1971, on the back of which had been scrawled, 'Box found in great Egypt ruins.' His landline was ringing again.

'Fuck you,' he told it. 'Fuck the whole lot of you.'

He locked up, switched on all the staircase lights and clattered down to Wharf Terrace, not caring for once who he offended.

Three in the morning: a flat night without stars, just a bit of moon the colour of fish skin, a few clouds, humid air more like Valencia than London. The Thames was high. Shaw walked downriver until he could cross at Barnes then double back along the northern bank between the allotments and the mud, between the darkened pubs and garden walls of Strand-on-the-Green, to where the dark water swirled along the riverfront and around the heel of Oliver's Island, until, perhaps forty-five minutes later, he got to the office. There he found not Tim but Annie, slumped in the typing chair with her back to the door, her head at an odd slant as if it had quite recently fallen to one side and become too heavy to lift. She was staring at her brother's map, pinned up in its original position on the wall above the desk.

Shaw touched her shoulder.

'Annie?'

No response.

It was nothing like the mediumistic trance. She knew he

was there, but she didn't seem to be there herself. This focused absence had its effect: Shaw began to stare at the map too. Fine spots of blood had sprayed across it here and there. He remembered a crowded gastropub: potato ravioli with wild mushrooms; someone he hardly knew, laughing and shouting above the noise, 'More people are born on sea coasts than you imagine!' He could recall the pub but not the occasion. And however he blinked or squinted at the map he could no longer make the land and sea switch places. The effort tired him, yet he kept on with it.

Every so often he glanced sideways at Annie Swann. On her cheek a light sweat glinted: beneath it, as if optically clarified, her skin looked older than he remembered. Her flesh had a softness, a sponginess. The skin lay fragile and papery over that. If you were to press it with your finger, he thought, an indentation would remain. It would fill slowly. Annie was old at the surface of herself, very, very much older somewhere underneath. She looked at the map, Shaw looked at the map; the land was the sea, the sea was the land. For a while that was how things remained. Then Shaw felt as if he had been released, perhaps by a decision of hers, perhaps by some circumstance neither of them could control. But freedom from thinking about the map only encouraged him to think about the padlocked door at the back of the office: he stumbled around opening drawers and looking under the furniture until he found something with which to lever it open. After a moment Annie said:

'You won't need that, Lee.'

He looked across at her in surprise. Her head hadn't moved. Her voice, hoarse and vigorous, seemed to be located somewhere else – still close but not in the room, not in her.

'Lee,' it repeated. There followed a clogged chuckle, but though he waited, nothing else.

The door opened onto a littered space somewhat bigger than a toilet: cleaning materials on shelves; plastic storage bins with sturdy fasteners and see-through lids; a lump of styrene packing material from the river, eroded and anthropomorphic; rubber boots; an overall on a hook. The storage bins were full of body parts – some intact and recognisable, others roughly chunked – translucent bloodless joints as inoffensive as uncooked chicken. He felt no more than a brief disgust. Beneath the faint smell of bleach in the air hung another even fainter smell he couldn't begin to describe. The parts, when he counted them, added up to a single human being. It was male. It was about fifty years old.

Shaw stood for some time looking down. Eventually, unable to think what else to do, he dragged the bins across the office under the eye of Annie Swann – whose head, seen now from in front, still didn't seem quite settled on her neck – and emptied them one by one, piece by piece, into the Thames. He wasn't disposing of them for her, he thought: he was distributing them. Whatever had been worked out, it had been worked out between Tim and Annie. Were they even brother and sister? One of them would always win, but perhaps nothing would ever be settled. They were both mad in their different ways; or perhaps in the same way. Shaw had been a kind of witness. They had needed him for that, and now all they needed him for was this. The last thing into the river was a forearm, with its hand lightly clenched. The fingers seemed to extend when he threw it, as if acknowledging him. The dawn was coming up, grey but with a promise of light in it. It was breezy and cold.

By the time he had finished and got the bins back in, Annie was gone. Before she left she had opened a new page at *The Water House* – presenting him, he suspected, with some final, formal invitation. It was the same unreasonable stuff, in the same unreadable format. Shaw adjusted the font size. 'Human genetic bottleneck,' he read; then, a few lines down, 'Previously undiscovered subspeciation at 1.5 million years.' Someone had scrawled the same figure on the notepad by the computer, underscoring and adding question marks before and after.

19

The Farthest Shore

He went home and slept in peace for the first time since he had arrived at 17 Wharf Terrace, to wake full of energy. He felt liberated. He felt that he knew who he was. He went down to Mortlake High Street, where, at the corner with White Hart Lane, he had macchiato and home-made granola among the Little Chelsea wives crowded into Orange Pekoe; then made his way upriver by graveyard and Thames Path.

Strong sunshine scoured the house fronts along the river curve, transforming gable ends into blocks and triangles of light, drawing attention to an aluminium cowl here, a sagging phone cable there, making a point with the yellow registration plate of a passing Audi. Wind shook the stationary water drops on everything. Landward, the crows were working out happily above St Mary Magdalen, loosening up in twos and threes, doing air-pocket work, breathing into their stalls and sideslips, wingsuiting around Richard Burton's tented mausoleum. Mornings like these, Shaw thought, were the only times London could be said to have fresh air. Down on the towpath between the recycling centre and the National Archive, he realised he was on his way to work. Thinking better of it, he went to visit his mother instead.

'You took your time,' she complained.

He stared at her. 'You didn't want me here. You sent me a letter.'

She laughed until she coughed. 'I never did!' she said, in the tone of a younger woman who learns only now of some bravura socio-sexual faux pas achieved with the aid of alcohol a week, a month or a year before. It was one of her most effective impersonations. For a moment she seemed full of life. 'I never did!'

Shaw laughed too. Then he thought about her other children, who – matter-of-fact and with enviable practical skills yet somehow still waifish – ended up abroad, placing themselves unerringly at distant points around the coasts of Canada or Australia so they never had to meet one another again. All those globalised half-sisters and -brothers who never got on; all those dads in their red and white football scarves photographed on November the fifth, grinning out of a poorly scanned Kodachrome slide, excited and fatuous in the bonfire light, a decade too young for their age: all of that had become such a trial to her in the end. It had made her less available to him. Things were difficult enough without the demands the little Shaw might make, as, half in and half out of her life, he trailed about behind her. Somehow *he* had become the embarrassment, not those fathers and half-siblings; a day-to-day burden requiring more energy than she was able to give.

'Your father died of an enlarged spleen,' she said now, as if that was a virtue.

'Which father?' said Shaw.

'You say these things but you don't mean them.'

'I wish I knew the truth about you.'

At this she put her hands in her lap, turned her shoulders away from him and stared out into the garden. 'You never let me tell it.'

'I ask you. I never stop.'

'You never let me speak.'

'What? Tell me now, then,' he said. 'You can tell me now.'

'Why should I?' She shrugged. 'It was my life, not yours. Get a life of your own, you lazy cunt.' After a pause, she sighed and smoothed out her skirt. 'At least find some friends of your own.' Outside, the lawns and flower beds burned in the light; she made a gesture as if dismissing them. 'I used to love the water, Jack,' she said. 'Do you remember?'

'Who was Jack?' Shaw said, as bitterly as he could.

'Oh, don't you remember? Little Johnnie Jack! The lullaby? '"Little Johnnie Jack,"' she sang, in a frail, tuneful voice, '"with his wife and family all up his back."'

He didn't remember, Shaw said. He had never heard that song before. 'You probably sang it to someone else.' After that, they were both quiet and then she began to weep. Shaw put his arm awkwardly round her shoulders. 'I've had friends,' he wanted to say. 'Honestly I have.' He tried to tell her something about his involvement with Tim and Annie Swann, but he couldn't, even now, seem to bring it into focus for himself; and he could see she wasn't interested. Ten minutes of anything was the most she could manage. Ten minutes after he came in, she would always have forgotten who he was or what she owed him or why he was there. She would sit hands in lap and listen to the midday traffic pass east and west outside the home.

Presently she said:

'Everything smells so musty in here. Can't you get them to do something about it? It smells like earwax.'

Shaw, whose own earwax had frightened him at eight years old by reeking of Marmite, failed to smell anything. 'I brought us a film,' was all he could think of to say. '*Night Moves*, Gene Hackman as a detective whose emotional intelligence isn't up to the case. I thought we could watch that.'

She stared emptily at the DVD then dropped it in her lap.

'It's really good,' Shaw said.

'Aren't we having the photographs?'

'All you ever do is tear them up.'

'Do I? I was such a Little Janey Jack, that's all. Although,' she said, as if to a third person in the room, 'who could blame me now?'

'We both had a life,' Shaw found himself insisting.

'I hate this place.'

By noon next day he had begun to wonder what exactly had happened at Brent. He knew it was something big, but not how big; he knew it had relieved his crisis, but not to what degree. He returned there at lunchtime to find the mooring empty. All the chains and cables that had tethered Tim Swann's lighter to the land hung slack; low water revealed the filling outline of a hull in the mud.

Shaw stood on the towpath a minute or two, gazing upriver into the tangled geography of the Brent confluence then down again towards Kew Bridge floating in the water light above its own quivering white reflection. Between these two stations the midstream aits lay like derelict China clippers sweltering in tropical light. All along the reach, he now understood, islands were turning into boats; while boats gave up and, settling in on the back end of some late-winter tide, quietly turned into islands. It was the story of every life. Morning and evening, neither one thing nor the other, they seemed to drift in and out of the thin fog like the mystery floating kingdoms of cheap Celtic myth which, drawing alongside for an hour or two, tempt you across with an introductory offer, then depart the same night leaving a gap year in your life and a few Nectar points for services you don't remember rendering. A magical hat. A stone with a hole in it. A necklace that, giving off the faint smell of tidal habitats, ruderal scrub and a broad spectrum of invertebrates including several kinds of leech, turns abruptly into a handful of shells.

His favourite pissing place having also sailed, Shaw took himself up to the Terrace Bar at the Watermans Centre, then went home via the rental agency, where he gave notice on 17 Wharf Terrace. Two or three days later he had found a new room in Turnham Green.

Ob and Emma, in their late thirties, had been at the BBC forever. 'Not,' Emma said with a laugh, 'that either of us does anything very interesting there.' They'd always been aware of each other, they said, but then Emma turned up at a fancy-dress party as Van Eyck's mystic lamb, and that was that. They both wanted children, but she didn't feel quite ready. Ob was on the production side of contemporary history. He looked like a thinner version of the young Rupert Brooke, with aquiline features a little too unearthly – a little too intense – for his age. He played the piano and could listen to François Couperin all day – 'Or anything Baroque, really.' They both loved exercise and nature – wild camping and, in particular, wild swimming. Ob had done a few of the easier hard swims: 'But Em's the serious one, not interested unless it features a twelve-mile walk-in and a five-mil wetsuit.' Emma had a way of looking up at him then playfully sliding her gaze away. 'Wild anything, really,' she agreed with a laugh; at the same time, she seemed to be denying something intrinsic to Ob's view of their partnership, his deep sense of who 'Ob and Emma' might now be.

Shaw laughed too.

'Fifty per cent of my dreams are about not wanting to jump into moving water,' he admitted. 'Hard to know if it's a neurosis or a survival characteristic.'

There was a silence. Emma looked at Ob.

'We've never had a lodger before,' she said.

They were offering the room and, obviously, use of the kitchen. It was a new thing for them. It was an experiment of sorts. If Shaw hadn't already stored his stuff, and there wasn't too much of it, he could have a share of the loft space? They wouldn't charge for wi-fi. Would he like to look around?

He'd love to look around, Shaw told them.

The room was on the second floor at the back, with a view over gardens towards Chiswick Common. The gardens already had an early-autumn look about them. At night you could be comforted by the surf of traffic on Chiswick High Road. Shaw soon fitted in, got the hang of the De'Longhi PrimaDonna, learned how his hosts preferred their coffee made, the dishwasher loaded. The house was narrow but spacious enough to cope with Ob's piano; empty enough of other objects to seem tranquil. Polished wood floors conducted the light in a single long sweep from the garden towards the bay window in the old front room, lacquering a pot here, the corner of a picture frame there, on the way.

'I quite like it,' he told his mother on the phone. 'Ob and Em collect Ravilious prints, and we have serious wisteria on the back wall. Em has promised to teach me to swim.'

Em was up at five most mornings, biking over to Hampton outdoor pool to put in her basic couple of miles; she proved to be out on her own more often than Shaw expected. As time went on, he found Ob's gaze less piercing than thwarted, which, in those days, at the height of the Brexit debacle, was par for the course at the BBC. Every newly empowered demographic selects its typical physiognomy and body language, the phenotype which will do best under the new conditions. Everyone is sensitised, nervous, ready to take advantage or regret that their own face doesn't fit. For a few weeks, as he settled into his new surroundings, Shaw wandered an uncanny valley filled with bad suits, Edwardian-looking overcoats, sudden gurning smiles and a cheerful vigour which contested with rubbery, fishlike faces and curious hand movements. It was like living among aliens. He was puzzled, then grew used to it. He had his own problems. A cold front had blown in across his life, he had to admit, then passed over: in its wake he was reconnecting shyly; picking up digital work, gig-economy work, of the kind he had been used to before his crisis; rejoining the world. That was enough effort for now.

Autumn moved into winter. He drank less. He began walking again, waking early, taking the Tube from Turnham Green to Wimbledon, making his way to and fro across the common, slope to acid slope, pool to hidden pool, between the bare trees and polished roots, down through Robin Hood's Gate to Richmond Park. He photographed stags in the six o'clock mist; later, ate a bacon sandwich among the dog walkers at the Pen Ponds snack van as the sky cleared over the trees around the ballet school. He was learning the lie of the land. Generally, his thoughts did not occupy him. They passed through easily and without consequence.

On his way home one day, he cut through Old Mortlake Burial Ground. It was cold in there, coming on lunchtime, and the colours were as sharp as they would ever be that day. It was smaller than he remembered, more like a walled garden than a cemetery. December seemed to have worked its way into the relationships between graves and paths like an additional dimension, fixing them in heritage arrangements. Off to his left, the medium's house lay closed and empty: two or three estate agent's boards leaned out of its garden at angles over the pavement. In front of him, a man in late middle age, wearing an oiled cotton jacket over a dark blue Guernsey sweater and yellow corduroy trousers, sat on a bench eating a smoked-salmon sandwich. His face was smooth and pink, his blue eyes watery yet still boyish. Crouched between his feet were two little black-and-tan dachshunds on a shared leash.

Shaw hesitated in front of him and said, 'Do I know you from the seances?'

The man stared emptily and kept chewing. He smiled and addressed his dogs, who were alert and full of hope. 'We all need to eat,' he teased them. Then, transferring his attention to Shaw: 'Wouldn't you say?'

Shaw, uncertain what he was being asked, could think of no reply.

'I have my lunch like anyone else; it's shop-bought stuff but often good. I come and read a book. I eat my lunch.'

'I thought I'd met you before, that's all.'

'Today, as you can see, it's *The Water-Babies*.'

He offered Shaw a glimpse of the book, which was knocked about and had a torn cover, adding thoughtfully, but without disappointment: 'I'm enjoying it less than I hoped, like all these childhood reads.'

Once he was certain that Shaw had no response to that either, he continued: 'The vandalism this place sees is extraordinary. They work their way up from the river at night, looking for mischief.' Then, as if making some much more generalised statement: 'Really, anything unanchored is at risk. Many of these cheaper Victorian memorials were only balanced on a flat stone.' With an apologetic shrug to his dogs, he put the last of the sandwich in his mouth. 'I always scrub my hands on the napkin provided,' he said to Shaw, holding out both the napkin and the sandwich wrapper.

Shaw took them from him and went to the litter bin, stopping to examine the toppled crosses and angels on the way. It was as if, he thought, they had been pushed over by something furious but without much leverage in the world; some force for which well-founded objects, properly set in the earth, would always prove too strong. He went over and stood under a holly tree by the wall of the mental hospital. Water squeezed up from the black mud around the toes of his Converse shoes. Half-eaten rubbish lay strewn around. A red plastic watering can lay on its side among dead flowers and hanks of florist ribbon. When he next looked up he was alone in the cemetery, although the little dogs could still be heard barking. Light from the north and east was reflected briefly in one of the upper windows of the medium's cottage, as if someone had just closed it.

Arriving at Hammersmith Bridge half an hour later, shocked by the amount of space trapped between the river's banks, he wondered if he'd change his mind and walk to Kew – but crossed and went back to Turnham Green, where he found Ob home early, practising Couperin's *Les Barricades Mystérieuses* on the piano in the long, warmly lit downstairs space while Emma sat sorting through the seasonal decorations and watched everything from the corner of her eye and laughed.

Christmas afternoon he spent with his mother at the care facility. She seemed older, sitting by the window in her best skirt with her hands in her lap. The thing he wanted to show her was his new iPhone, bought on a recommendation from Emma.

'Emma's good on phones,' he explained – indeed, she was one of those people who were good on what was good. 'Here's a photo of her with Ob in the background.' He had taken it by accident while trying to get the phone to do something else. Ob looked as awkward as anyone caught halfway through reaching for a pair of scissors; Em seemed, as she always did, both perfectly natural and perfectly posed, already halfway to becoming an image of herself yet always maintaining something in reserve, something neither the camera nor the viewer would ever see. Christmas was important to Ob and Em – although because they always spent it in Em's parents' house in Shropshire? – on the banks of the River Severn? – they wouldn't be home on the day itself. But they didn't expect he would be either?

'That's the piano behind them,' Shaw told his mother. 'We were decorating it with holly.'

'I can recognise a piano when I see one,' his mother said.

She stared at the phone, tapped its screen as if drawing attention to something so obvious only Shaw could have failed to see it, and added: 'I'm glad you're showing some common sense at last.'

'They're basically just very nice.'

'You always did leave it to the last minute to do the clever thing.'

Shaw took the phone off her.

'I just live with them,' he said. 'Ob and Em are just the people I live with.'

He put his hands over hers. They felt warm. The skin felt papery and thin. He squeezed them gently, and tried to make eye contact. 'I really do feel as if I'll soon be back on track,' he said. It was a promise he had always hoped would make him safe. For a moment everything in life seemed less ephemeral and fragmentary, and he felt as if he might be past his crisis, whatever it had been, and have something to offer at last. Then his mother pulled her hands away. A shiver seemed to pass through her, like a wave of probability. She gave him her most brilliant smile.

'Let's have the photographs!' she said.

But what use was the past, Shaw thought, its vague promises and windy shingle beaches, its puzzled-looking dogs of no particular breed or talent suddenly allotted fifteen minutes of freedom on the bleak plaque of grass at the centre of a sixty-year-old housing estate? What use would it be to re-examine the fathers, blunt, amiable, stupid? Their obsessions and excuses, team scarves and holiday plans, their insistence on being there in front of you and needing you to speak or act – do the homework, learn to ride the bike, assemble the model – react and relate and be there for them? Above all, he didn't want to confront her, his only mother, at her best in the clothes of a distant decade, her arm around one or another of his dads or distant cousins or even more distant brothers and sisters, wincing away from camera after camera, her eyes narrowed against the light of one sea coast or the next. When you measured all that against Ob and Emma's way – life as an amused but careful practice – it was, he thought, just too fucked up.

This idea caused him to remember a passage from *Journeys of Our Genes*, which described, in terms not easy to follow and for reasons the text wasn't clear about, 'a single repetitive interaction, wired into human beings long before they became properly human. It may even have been passed on from a previous form of life, a repeating pattern of DNA, the dimorphism of a single gene on a single chromosome, coding for some lost state of consciousness only now resurfacing.'

Tim Swann: a father if ever you met one, to judge only by his consistent urge to explain everything outside his own head in terms of what went on inside it.

Shaw was out in the corridor again. It smelled of floor wax and care-home Christmas dinner. He was kicking a chair. When that didn't help he went to the nearest toilet and, after making certain the door was bolted, stuck three fingers of his right hand down his throat in the hope of encouraging all things curdled to come to light and stop being such a simple hindrance. Nothing did; and when he got back, his mother had not only torn up many of the photographs and wrenched the albums themselves apart, but also smashed the screen of his new phone, perhaps by standing repeatedly on it, before sitting down, folding her hands, staring up at the Böcklin print on the wall and retreating to those frozen shores of behaviour he recognised so well.

'That cost four hundred pounds,' he said.

She stared at him in wonder. 'I don't know what I'll do with you, Leo,' she said. 'I really don't.'

'I'm not Leo,' said Shaw. 'No one is called fucking Leo.'

She had her longings, why not him? He thought finally of some of the things he might want, and wondered if he'd ever get them. He picked up the iPhone, gently touched its starred and yielding screen; then he went out of the room. Everything had too much give in it.

'For God's sake,' she called after him, 'something's always the matter with you.' Then: 'You never learned to get on with things.' And finally: 'It's Christmas Day! It's Christmas Day!'

He took an Uber home, quarrelled about politics with the driver in Mortlake and, getting out under a sunset raging orange and pink, decided to walk the rest of the way to Turnham Green via Chiswick.

It was cold. Halfway across Chiswick Bridge he leaned over the parapet and looked out north and west. Wintry light slanted into the upstream reach at a surprising angle from the broken edges of the clouds, leaving the air architectural yet transparent between darkening banks. After a minute or two he heard bells, ringing he assumed for some late-afternoon service at St Mary the Virgin on the high street – although for a moment he thought the sound had come up from the water itself.

Safe at Em and Ob's he set about making some tea; tapped, while he waited for the kettle to boil, a few keys of the piano. He turned the television on, then off again. His room was warm. He had lived in it comfortably, autumn to winter. The time had stretched out. Yesterday, before she and Ob caught the train from Euston to Shrewsbury, Emma had woven a nest of old-fashioned fairy lights into the clean little Victorian fireplace. On the mantelpiece above stood their Christmas card to him – a 1920s-style linocut of a mill race and clean foam on dark water. Things come and go; they assign you a shape, like it or not. 'You should have some of your own belongings here,' Shaw remembered her advising him shortly after he moved in: 'not just our daft old rent-a-room stuff. You do have some things of your own, don't you?'

Thus prompted, Shaw had retrieved a few bits and pieces from the loft, starting with his library (now including, in addition to *Pincher Martin*, *The Water-Babies* and *Journeys of Our Genes*), which he placed, in alphabetical order by author's surname, on the shelf above the bed; and moving on to items the function of which was harder to pin down. He also set his recently uprated MacBook Air on the little table in front of the window, causing Emma to applaud:

'You see? You can even work from home!'

Now he sat drinking second-flush Assam and eating ginger biscuits while he tried to remember how he had come by an ashtray with horses on it. He didn't even smoke. There was a red plastic box two inches on a side, empty. A collection of post-cards bound together with perished rubber bands, addressed in handwriting he didn't recognise to recipients he didn't know. A small dusty ceramic brooch in the shape of a rose. What use might he have found for objects like this? He couldn't put a date to them, let alone associate them with his own history. It was as if he had collected other people's souvenirs. In pride of place was the silver fish Victoria Nyman had given him just after he moved into 17 Wharf Terrace. Shaw stared at it in growing dismay. Misproportioned, blubbery-lipped, at ease with itself, the fish stared back. Victoria's emails had continued to arrive on a weekly basis all year. Most of them he had never answered, some he hadn't even opened. Now, full of guilt, he set about trying to catch up.

'It's very Brexit up here,' she had written on her first night out of London. 'Eight pubs in a mile and deep surrounding woods.'

There followed descriptions: of the town, which kept its Christmas lights on all year round; of the town next door, which had made a lot of money from the Industrial Revolution but 'not much since'; of her house, her 'beautiful house with its beautiful staircase', where she went from room to big empty room in a trance of delight. These early good spirits were maintained for two or three months – 'I love blanket boxes!' 'Don't you think hollyhocks are ridiculously tall?' – but soon she was as restless as Shaw remembered her, out all day on her own, driving fifty miles to an antiques shop or a repurposed Victorian garden.

'It gets me out,' she explained. 'I'm meeting people. They don't say much, but I'm meeting them. You'd think I'd buy a dog.'

Amusement graded into irony, irony slipped back into a

kind of binding, self-protective fiction, quick to make space between it and the things it found. 'But for the tractor porn on the newsagent's top shelf, I could be anywhere in Brexitania.' Or: 'Why would you find apples under a holly tree? Windfall apples under a holly tree! I don't think I've quite understood the countryside.' Some of these stories he could follow; others, though they seemed simple, resisted interpretation. 'You tell yourself, "The valley is not uncanny." And it's true, isn't it? Off to the nearest town then, and buy stuff!' She began to refer to emails he hadn't received. She seemed as uncertain about herself as her situation, asking apropos of nothing, 'What will you think of me now?' It soon seemed like a massive collapse of confidence. By late November things were racing away from her. She overheard two women talking in a café, and this caused her to wonder 'if the world will end, or just take some simple, beautiful, really amazing direction'. A week or two later, a single-line message read:

'It's a nice little town, but something is happening here.'

That was all. Shaw could make nothing of it. Nevertheless he felt compelled to write back. 'It seems ages since you came down here and we were together,' he started. Then, having erased that: 'Sorry not to be in touch.'

There was too much to tell. Where could he start? 'I feel a bit as if I've abandoned you. I feel as if I owe you an explanation.' Victoria would dismiss this, he knew, with a more or less wry laugh. Evidently they had abandoned each other. But he couldn't reconnect on his own, and without her help fell back on trying to explain himself. Soon he was writing, 'I've never really known who I was,' and after that it was as if he could never stop. When he next looked up it was midnight, and he couldn't see anything in the garden. Turnham Green was quiet except for some seasonal shouting off towards the bars on Chiswick High Road; the only other thing he could hear was a sporadic whine that seemed to originate in the Mac. He was hungry.

'You were right about me. I was always in a panic.'

He couldn't remember when that subject had come up. He thought it had been early on in their relationship, in some pub. The way he saw the problem now, he told her, was this: before his crisis, he had known too exactly who he was. There was a core to him so coherent it never needed anything exterior to give it shape. He had been so certain of himself he could reject anything or anyone, even someone he liked and wanted, for the next thing that came along. 'I could always rely on that. But then I wasn't so sure.' What happens to you, he asked, the first time you lose your balance that way and wonder whose life you're looking at? 'Maybe,' he finished, 'that's what it was always about, not just for me but for everyone. We all were wondering that, for a while, but no one knew why.'

He read this over, added, 'Anyway, how is it with you?' then stared at the email box while the roulette of things hovered between delete and send.

It came to rest at send; but he received no response, that day or the next. In a way, he hadn't expected one. Christmas passed. West London felt the insistent approach of another year – turned to meet it halfway while rain blew up and down the river. December trickled into January. Winter trickled away into the beginning of spring. Shaw wrote again. 'Dear Victoria, I often wonder how you're getting along.' No answer to that either. On a third or fourth run through the emails, he found her street address. As soon as the weather improved, he thought, he would go up there to the heartlands, to the inland cities, and see how she was.